Christmas Tales

THE NIGHT BEFORE CHRISTMAS AND 21 OTHER CHRISTMAS STORIES

Fairytalez

CHRISTMAS TALES
The Night Before Christmas and 21 Other Illustrated Christmas Stories

Published by Fairytalez.com

www.fairytalez.com

©2016 Fairytalez™

Edited by Bri Ahearn

Cover design and interior art by Loreta Petkova

Contents

Foreword

C hristmas is a time that has been associated with fairy tales and folklore for hundreds of years. The Brothers Grimm published their collection, Children's and Household Tales, just four days before Christmas and it was a popular gift for young and old. The Grimms tapped into the tradition of reading tales as a winter pastime as a way to spend those snowy cold nights.

The tradition continued with years of publishers frequently sharing collections of fairy tales meant for holiday reading, and we want to celebrate that tradition with this new collection. Here you'll find stories of the sights, sounds, and experience of Christmas. We've gathered tales of Santa Claus, winter nights, Christmas trees, gift-giving, and other elements that are associated with the holiday from North America, Norway, Germany, and other parts of the world.

We're delighted to share obscure children's tales such as *The Nodding Donkey*, and from the fairy tale master Hans Christian Andersen to include classic fairy tales like *The Fir Tree* and *The Little Match Girl*. You'll find the tale of *The Elves and the Shoemaker*, as well as *Christmas Every Day*, a classic tale about the value of Christmas being just once a year. Russia gives us the tale of *Babouscka*, while Norway contained the tale of *The Cat on the Dovrefell*, a tale told while the Yule log burns. Fairytalez.com hopes this collection becomes part of your Christmas tradition, year after year, and we invite you to read all of the other fairy tales at our website - over 2,000 of them.

Bri Ahearn, Fairytalez.com

UNITED STATES

The Night Before Christmas

CLEMENT C. MOORE
ILLUSTRATIONS JESSIE WILLCOX SMITH

"T was the night before Christmas, when all through the house. Not a creature was stirring, not even a mouse; The stockings were hung by the chimney with care. In hopes that St. Nicolas soon would be there;

T he children were nestled all snug in their beds. While visions of sugar-plums danced in their heads; And mamma in her kerchief, and I in my cap. Had just settled our brains for a long winter's nap.

W hen out on the lawn there arose such a clatter. I sprang from the bed to see what was the matter. Away to the window I flew like a flash. Tore open the shutters and threw up the sash.

T he moon on the breast of the new-fallen snow. Gave the lustre of mid-day to objects below. When, what to my wondering eyes should appear, but a miniature sleigh, and eight tiny reindeer.

W ith a little old driver, so lively and quick, I knew in a moment it must be St. Nick. More rapid than eagles his coursers they came. And he whistled, and shouted, and called them by name:

"N ow, Dasher! Now Dancer! Now Prancer and Vixen! On, Comet! On, Cupid! On, Donder and Blitzen! To the top of the porch! To the top of the wall! Now dash away! Dash away! Dash away all!

A s dry leaves that before the wild hurricane fly, When they meet with an obstacle, mount to the sky. So up to the house-top the coursers they flew, with the sleigh full of Toys and St. Nicholas too.

A nd then, in a twinkling, I heard on the roof. The prancing and pawing of each little hoof. As I drew in my head, and was turning around, down the chimney St. Nicholas came with a bound.

H e was dressed all in fur, from his head to his foot. And his clothes were tarnished with ashes and soot. A bundle of Toys he had flung on his back. And he looked like a peddler just opening his pack.

H is eyes – how they twinkled! His dimples how merry! His cheeks were like roses, his nose like a cherry! His droll little mouth was drawn up like a bow. And the beard of his chin was as white as the snow.

T he stump of a pipe he held tight in his teeth. And the smoke it encircled his head like a wreath. He had a broad face and a little round belly. That shook when he laughed, like a bowlful of jelly.

H e was chubby and plump, a right jolly old elf. And I laughed when I saw him, in spite of myself. A wink of his eye and a twist of his head, soon gave me to know I had nothing to dread.

H e spoke not a word, but went straight to his work. And filled all the stockings, then turned with a jerk. And laying his finger aside of his nose, and giving a nod, up the chimney he rose.

H e sprang to his sleigh, to his team gave a whistle. And away the all flew like the dove of a thistle. But I heard him exclaim, ere he drove out of sight, "Happy Christmas to all, and to all a good-night."

Christmas Every Day

WILLIAM DEAN HOWELLS
ILLUSTRATIONS HARRIET ROOSVELT RICHARDS

T he little girl came into her papa's study, as she always did Saturday morning before breakfast, and asked for a story. He tried to beg off that morning, for he was very busy, but she would not let him. So he began:

"Well, once there was a little pig -- "

She stopped him at the word. She said she had heard little pig-stories till she was perfectly sick of them.

"Well, what kind of story shall I tell, then?"

"About Christmas. It's getting to be the season."

"Well!" Her papa roused himself. "Then I'll tell you about the little girl that wanted it Christmas every day in the year. How would you like that?"

"First-rate!" said the little girl; and she nestled into comfortable shape in his lap, ready for listening.

"Very well, then, this little pig -- Oh, what are you pounding me for?"

"Because you said little pig instead of little girl."

"I should like to know what's the difference between a little pig and a little girl that wanted it Christmas every day!"

"Papa!" said the little girl warningly. At this her papa began to tell the story.

Once there was a little girl who liked Christmas so much that she wanted it to be Christmas every day in the year, and as soon as Thanksgiving was over she began to send postcards to the old Christmas Fairy to ask if she might not have her wish. But the old Fairy never answered, and after a while the little girl found out that the Fairy wouldn't notice anything but real letters sealed outside with a monogram -- or your initial, anyway. So, then, she began to send letters, and just the day before Christmas, she got a letter from the Fairy, saying she might have it Christmas every day for a year, and then they would see about having it longer.

The little girl was excited already, preparing for the old-fashioned, once-a-year Christmas that was coming the next day. So she resolved to keep the Fairy's promise to herself and surprise everybody with it as it kept coming true, but then it slipped out of her mind altogether.

She had a splendid Christmas. She went to bed early, so as to let Santa Claus fill the stockings, and in the morning she was up the first of anybody and found hers all lumpy with packages of candy, and oranges and grapes, and rubber balls, and all kinds of small presents. Then she waited until the rest of the family was up, and she burst into the library to look at the large presents laid out on the library table -- books, and boxes of stationery, and dolls, and little stoves, and dozens of handkerchiefs, and inkstands, and skates, and photograph frames, and boxes of watercolors, and dolls' houses -- and the big Christmas tree, lighted and standing in the middle.

She had a splendid Christmas all day. She ate so much candy that she did not want any breakfast, and the whole forenoon the presents kept pouring in that had not been delivered the night before, and she went round giving the presents she had got for other people, and came home and ate turkey and cranberry for dinner, and plum pudding and nuts and raisins and oranges, and then went out and coasted, and came in with a stomachache crying, and her papa said he would see if his house was turned into that sort of fool's paradise another year, and they had a light supper, and pretty early everybody went to bed cross.

The little girl slept very heavily and very late, but she was wakened at last by the other children dancing around her bed with their stockings full of presents in their hands.

"Christmas! Christmas! Christmas!" they all shouted.

"Nonsense! It was Christmas yesterday," said the little girl, rubbing her eyes sleepily.

Her brothers and sisters just laughed. "We don't know about that. It's Christmas today, anyway. You come into the library and see."

"Christmas! Christmas! Christmas!"

Then all at once it flashed on the little girl that the Fairy was keeping her promise, and her year of Christmases was beginning. She was dreadfully sleepy, but she sprang up and darted into the library. There it was again! Books, and boxes of stationery, and dolls, and so on.

There was the Christmas tree blazing away, and the family picking out their presents, and her father looking perfectly puzzled, and her mother ready to cry. "I'm sure I don't see how I'm to dispose of all these things," said her mother, and her father said it seemed to him they had had something just like it the day before, but he supposed he must have dreamed it.

This struck the little girl as the best kind of a joke, and so she ate so much candy she didn't want any breakfast, and went round carrying presents, and had turkey and cranberry for dinner, and then went out and coasted, and came in with a stomachache, crying.

Now, the next day, it was the same thing over again, but everybody getting crosser, and at the end of a week's time so many people had lost their tempers that you could pick up lost tempers anywhere, they perfectly strewed the ground. Even when people tried to recover their tempers they usually got somebody else's, and it made the most dreadful mix.

The little girl began to get frightened, keeping the secret all to herself, she wanted to tell her mother, but she didn't dare to, and she was ashamed to ask the Fairy to take back her gift, it seemed ungrateful.

So it went on and on, and it was Christmas on St. Valentine's Day and Washington's Birthday, just the same as any day, and it didn't skip even the First of April, though everything was counterfeit that day, and that was some little relief. After a while turkeys got to be awfully scarce, selling for about a thousand dollars apiece. They got to passing off almost anything for turkeys -- even half-grown hummingbirds. And cranberries -- well they asked a diamond apiece for cranberries.

All the woods and orchards were cut down for Christmas trees. After a while they had to make Christmas trees out of rags. But there were plenty of rags, because people got so poor, buying presents for one another, that they couldn't get any new clothes, and they just wore their old ones to tatters. They got so poor that everybody had to go to the poorhouse, except the confectioners, and the storekeepers, and the book-sellers, and they all got so rich and proud that they would hardly wait upon a person when he came to buy. It was perfectly shameful!

After it had gone on about three or four months, the little girl, whenever she came into the room in the morning and saw those great ugly, lumpy stockings dangling at the fireplace, and the disgusting presents around everywhere, used to sit down and burst out crying. In six months she was perfectly exhausted, she couldn't even cry anymore.

And how it was on the Fourth of July! On the Fourth of July, the first boy in the United States woke up and found out that his firecrackers and toy pistol and two-dollar collection of fireworks were nothing but sugar and candy painted up to look like fireworks. Before ten o'clock every boy in the United States discovered that his July Fourth things had turned into Christmas things and was so mad. The Fourth of July orations all turned into Christmas carols, and when anybody tried to read the Declaration of Independence, instead of saying, "When in the course of human events it becomes necessary," he was sure to sing, "God rest you merry gentlemen." It was perfectly awful.

About the beginning of October the little girl took to sitting down on dolls wherever she found them -- she hated the sight of them so, and by Thanksgiving she just slammed her presents across the room. By that time people didn't carry presents around nicely anymore. They flung them over the fence or through the window, and, instead of taking great pains to write "For dear Papa," or "Mama " or "Brother," or "Sister," they used to write, "Take it, you horrid old thing!" and then go and bang it against the front door.

Nearly everybody had built barns to hold their presents, but pretty soon the barns overflowed, and then they used to let them lie out in the rain, or anywhere. Sometimes the police used to come and tell them to shovel their presents off the sidewalk or they would arrest them.

Before Thanksgiving came it had leaked out who had caused all these Christmases. The little girl had suffered so much that she had talked about it in her sleep, and after that hardly anybody would play with her, because if it had not been for her greediness it wouldn't have happened. And now, when it came Thanksgiving, and she wanted them to go to church, and have turkey, and show their gratitude, they said that all the turkeys had been eaten for her old Christmas dinners and if she would stop the Christmases, they would see about the gratitude.

And the very next day the little girl began sending letters to the Christmas Fairy, and then telegrams, to stop it. But it didn't do any good, and then she got to calling at the Fairy's house, but the girl that came to the door always said, "Not at home," or "Engaged," or something like that, and so it went on till it came to the old once-a-year Christmas Eve. The little girl fell asleep, and when she woke up in the morning --

"She found it was all nothing but a dream," suggested the little girl.

"No indeed!" said her papa. "It was all every bit true!"

"What did she find out, then?"'

"Why, that it wasn't Christmas at last, and wasn't ever going to be, anymore. Now it's time for breakfast."

The little girl held her papa fast around the neck.

"You shan't go if you're going to leave it so!"

"How do you want it left?"

"Christmas once a year."

"All right," said her papa, and he went on again.

Well, with no Christmas ever again, there was the greatest rejoicing all over the country. People met together everywhere and kissed and cried for joy. Carts went around and gathered up all the candy and raisins and nuts, and dumped them into the river, and it made the fish perfectly sick. And the whole United States, as far out as Alaska, was one blaze of bonfires, where the children were burning up their presents of all kinds. They had the greatest time!

The little girl went to thank the old Fairy because she had stopped its being Christmas, and she said she hoped the Fairy would keep her promise and see that Christmas never, never came again. Then the Fairy frowned, and said that now the little girl was behaving just as greedily as ever, and she'd better look out. This made the little girl think it all over carefully again, and she said she would be willing to have it Christmas about once in a thousand years, and then she said a hundred, and then she said ten, and at last she got down to one.

Then the Fairy said that was the good old way that had pleased people ever since Christmas began, and she was agreed. Then the little girl said, "What're your shoes made of?"

And the Fairy said, "Leather."

And the little girl said, "Bargain's done forever," and skipped off, and hippity-hopped the whole way home, she was so glad.

"How will that do?" asked the papa.

"First-rate!" said the little girl, but she hated to have the story stop, and was rather sober.

However, her mama put her head in at the door and asked her papa: "Are you never coming to breakfast? What have you been telling that child?"

"Oh, just a tale with a moral."

The little girl caught him around the neck again. "We know! Don't you tell what, papa! Don't you tell what!"

Then the Fairy said that was the good old way.

DENMARK

The Fir Tree

HANS CHRISTIAN ANDERSEN

ILLUSTRATIONS VILHELM PEDERSEN

F ar away in the forest, where the warm sun and the fresh air made a sweet resting place, grew a pretty little fir tree. The situation was all that could be desired; and yet the tree was not happy, it wished so much to be like its tall companions, the pines and firs which grew around it.

The sun shone, and the soft air fluttered its leaves, and the little peasant children passed by, prattling merrily; but the fir tree did not heed them. Sometimes the children would bring a large basket of raspberries or strawberries, wreathed on straws, and seat themselves near the fir tree, and say, "Is it not a pretty little tree?" which made it feel even more unhappy than before.

And yet all this while the tree grew a notch or joint taller every year, for by the number of joints in the stem of a fir tree we can discover its age.

Still, as it grew, it complained: "Oh! how I wish I were as tall as the other trees; then I would spread out my branches on every side, and my crown would overlook the wide world around. I should have the birds building their nests on my boughs, and when the wind blew, I should bow with stately dignity, like my tall companions."

So discontented was the tree, that it took no pleasure in the warm sunshine, the birds, or the rosy clouds that floated over it morning and evening.

Sometimes in winter, when the snow lay white and glittering on the ground, there was a little hare that would come springing along, and jump right over the little tree's head; then how mortified it would feel.

Two winters passed; and when the third arrived, the tree had grown so tall that the hare was obliged to run round it. Yet it remained unsatisfied and would exclaim: "Oh! to grow, to grow; if I could but keep on growing tall and old! There is nothing else worth caring for in the world."

In the autumn the woodcutters came, as usual, and cut down several of the tallest trees; and the young fir, which was now grown to a good, full height, shuddered as the noble trees fell to the earth with a crash.

A hare jumps right over the little fir tree.

After the branches were lopped off, the trunks looked so slender and bare that they could scarcely be recognized. Then they were placed, one upon another, upon wagons and drawn by horses out of the forest. Where could they be going? What would become of them? The young fir tree wished very much to know.

So in the spring, when the swallows and the storks came, it asked: "Do you know where those trees were taken? Did you meet them?"

The swallows knew nothing; but the stork, after a little reflection, nodded his head and said:

"Yes, I think I do. As I flew from Egypt, I met several new ships, and they had fine masts that smelt like fir. These must have been the trees; and I assure you they were stately; they sailed right gloriously!"

"Oh, how I wish I were tall enough to go on the sea," said the fir tree. "Tell me what is this sea, and what does it look like?"

"It would take too much time to explain—a great deal too much," said the stork, flying quickly away.

"Rejoice in thy youth," said the sunbeam; "rejoice in thy fresh growth and in the young life that is in thee."

And the wind kissed the tree, and the dew watered it with tears, but the fir tree regarded them not.

Christmas time drew near, and many young trees were cut down, some that were even smaller and younger than the fir tree, who enjoyed neither rest nor peace for longing to leave its forest home. These young trees, which were chosen for their beauty, kept their branches, and they, also, were laid on wagons and drawn by horses far away out of the forest.

"Where are they going?" asked the fir tree. "They are not taller than I am; indeed, one is not so tall. And why do they keep all their branches? Where are they going?"

"We know, we know," sang the sparrows; "we have looked in at the windows of the houses in the town, and we know what is done with them. Oh! you cannot think what honor and glory they receive. They are dressed up in the most splendid manner. We have seen them standing in the middle of a warm room, and adorned with all sorts of beautiful things—honey cakes, gilded apples, playthings, and many hundreds of wax tapers."

"And then," asked the fir tree, trembling in all its branches, "and then what happens?"

"We did not see any more," said the sparrows; "but this was enough for us."

"I wonder whether anything so brilliant will ever happen to me," thought the fir tree. "It would be better even than crossing the sea. I long for it almost with pain. Oh, when will Christmas be here? I am now as tall and well grown as those which were taken away last year. O that I were now laid on the wagon, or standing in the warm room with all that brightness and splendor around me! Something better and more beautiful is to come after, or the trees would not be so decked out. Yes, what follows will be grander and more splendid. What can it be? I am weary with longing. I scarcely know what it is that I feel."

"Rejoice in our love," said the air and the sunlight. "Enjoy thine own bright life in the fresh air."

But the tree would not rejoice, though it grew taller every day, and winter and summer its dark-green foliage might be seen in the forest, while passers-by would say, "What a beautiful tree!"

A short time before the next Christmas the discontented fir tree was the first to fall. As the ax cut sharply through the stem and divided the pith, the tree fell with a groan to the earth, conscious of pain and faintness and forgetting all its dreams of happiness in sorrow at leaving its home in the forest. It knew that it should never again see its dear old companions the trees, nor the little bushes and many-colored flowers that had grown by its side; perhaps not even the birds. Nor was the journey at all pleasant.

The tree first recovered itself while being unpacked in the courtyard of a house, with several other trees; and it heard a man say: "We only want one, and this is the prettiest. This is beautiful!"

Then came two servants in grand livery and carried the fir tree into a large and beautiful apartment. Pictures hung on the walls, and near the tall tile stove stood great china vases with lions on the lids. There were rocking-chairs, silken sofas, and large tables covered with pictures; and there were books, and playthings that had cost a hundred times a hundred dollars—at least so said the children.

Then the fir tree was placed in a large tub full of sand—but green baize hung all round it so that no one could know it was a tub—and it stood on a very handsome carpet. Oh, how the fir tree trembled! What was going to happen to him now? Some young ladies came, and the servants helped them to adorn the tree.

On one branch they hung little bags cut out of colored paper, and each bag was filled with sweetmeats. From other branches hung gilded apples and walnuts, as if they had grown there; and above and all around were hundreds of red, blue, and white tapers, which were fastened upon the branches. Dolls, exactly like real men and women, were placed under the green leaves,—the tree had never seen such things before,—and at the very top was fastened a glittering star made of gold tinsel. Oh, it was very beautiful. "This evening," they all exclaimed, "how bright it will be!"

"O that the evening were come," thought the tree, "and the tapers lighted! Then I shall know what else is going to happen. Will the trees of the forest come to see me? Will the sparrows peep in at the windows, I wonder, as they fly? Shall I grow faster here than in the forest, and shall I keep on all these ornaments during summer and winter?" But guessing was of very little use. His back ached with trying, and this pain is as bad for a slender fir tree as headache is for us.

At last the tapers were lighted, and then what a glistening blaze of splendor the tree presented! It trembled so with joy in all its branches that one of the candles fell among the green leaves and burned some of them. "Help! help!" exclaimed the young ladies; but no harm was done, for they quickly extinguished the fire.

After this the tree tried not to tremble at all, though the fire frightened him, he was so anxious not to hurt any of the beautiful ornaments, even while their brilliancy dazzled him.

And now the folding doors were thrown open, and a troop of children rushed in as if they intended to upset the tree, and were followed more slowly by their elders. For a moment the little ones stood silent with astonishment, and then they shouted for joy till the room rang; and they danced merrily round the tree while one present after another was taken from it.

"What are they doing? What will happen next?" thought the tree. At last the candles burned down to the branches and were put out. Then the children received permission to plunder the tree.

Oh, how they rushed upon it! There was such a riot that the branches cracked, and had it not been fastened with the glistening star to the ceiling, it must have been thrown down.

Then the children danced about with their pretty toys, and no one noticed the tree except the children's maid, who came and peeped among the branches to see if an apple or a fig had been forgotten.

"A story, a story," cried the children, pulling a little fat man towards the tree.

"Now we shall be in the green shade," said the man as he seated himself under it, "and the tree will have the pleasure of hearing, also; but I shall only relate one story. What shall it be? Ivede-Avede or Humpty Dumpty, who fell downstairs, but soon got up again, and at last married a princess?"

"Ivede-Avede," cried some; "Humpty Dumpty," cried others; and there was a famous uproar. But the fir tree remained quite still and thought to himself: "Shall I have anything to do with all this? Ought I to make a noise, too?" but he had already amused them as much as they wished and they paid no attention to him.

Then the old man told them the story of Humpty Dumpty—how he fell downstairs, and was raised up again, and married a princess.

And the children clapped their hands and cried, "Tell another, tell another," for they wanted to hear the story of Ivede-Avede; but this time they had only "Humpty Dumpty."

After this the fir tree became quite silent and thoughtful. Never had the birds in the forest told such tales as that of Humpty Dumpty, who fell downstairs, and yet married a princess.

"Ah, yes! so it happens in the world," thought the fir tree. He believed it all, because it was related by such a pleasant man. "Ah, well!" he thought, "who knows? Perhaps I may fall down, too, and marry a princess;" and he looked forward joyfully to the next evening, expecting to be again decked out with lights and playthings, gold and fruit.

"Tmorrow I will not tremble," thought he; "I will enjoy all my splendor, and I shall hear the story of Humpty Dumpty again, and perhaps of Ivede-Avede." And the tree remained quiet and thoughtful all night.

In the morning the servants and the housemaid came in. "Now," thought the fir tree, "all my splendor is going to begin again." But they dragged him out of the room and upstairs to the garret and threw him on the floor in a dark corner where no daylight shone, and there they left him. "What does this mean?" thought the tree. "What am I to do here? I can hear nothing in a place like this;" and he leaned against the wall and thought and thought.

And he had time enough to think, for days and nights passed and no one came near him; and when at last somebody did come, it was only to push away some large boxes in a corner. So the tree was completely hidden from sight, as if it had never existed.

"It is winter now," thought the tree; "the ground is hard and covered with snow, so that people cannot plant me. I shall be sheltered here, I dare say, until spring comes. How thoughtful and kind everybody is to me! Still, I wish this place were not so dark and so dreadfully lonely, with not even a little hare to look at. How pleasant it was out in the forest while the snow lay on the ground, when the hare would run by, yes, and jump over me, too, although I did not like it then. Oh! it is terribly lonely here."

"Squeak, squeak," said a little mouse, creeping cautiously towards the tree; then came another, and they both sniffed at the fir tree and crept in and out between the branches.

"Oh, it is very cold," said the little mouse. "If it were not we should be very comfortable here, shouldn't we, old fir tree?"

"I am not old," said the fir tree. "There are many who are older than I am."

"Where do you come from?" asked the mice, who were full of curiosity; "and what do you know? Have you seen the most beautiful places in the world, and can you tell us all about them? And have you been in the storeroom, where cheeses lie on the shelf and hams hang from the ceiling? One can run about on tallow candles there; one can go in thin and come out fat."

"I know nothing of that," said the fir tree, "but I know the wood, where the sun shines and the birds sing." And then the tree told the little mice all about its youth. They had never heard such an account in their lives; and after they had listened to it attentively, they said: "What a number of things you have seen! You must have been very happy."

"Happy!" exclaimed the fir tree; and then, as he reflected on what he had been telling them, he said, "Ah, yes! after all, those were happy days." But when he went on and related all about Christmas Eve, and how he had been dressed up with cakes and lights, the mice said, "How happy you must have been, you old fir tree."

"I am not old at all," replied the tree; "I only came from the forest this winter. I am now checked in my growth."

"What splendid stories you can tell," said the little mice. And the next night four other mice came with them to hear what the tree had to tell. The more he talked the more he remembered, and then he thought to himself: "Yes, those were happy days; but they may come again. Humpty Dumpty fell downstairs, and yet he married the princess. Perhaps I may marry a princess, too." And the fir tree thought of the pretty little birch tree that grew in the forest; a real princess, a beautiful princess, she was to him.

"Who is Humpty Dumpty?" asked the little mice. And then the tree related the whole story; he could remember every single word. And the little mice were so delighted with it that they were ready to jump to the top of the tree. The next night a great many more mice made their appearance, and on Sunday two rats came with them; but the rats said it was not a pretty story at all, and the little mice were very sorry, for it made them also think less of it.

"Do you know only that one story?" asked the rats.

"Only that one," replied the fir tree. "I heard it on the happiest evening in my life; but I did not know I was so happy at the time."

"We think it is a very miserable story," said the rats. "Don't you know any story about bacon or tallow in the storeroom?"

"No," replied the tree.

"Many thanks to you, then," replied the rats, and they went their ways.

The little mice also kept away after this, and the tree sighed and said: "It was very pleasant when the merry little mice sat round me and listened while I talked. Now that is all past, too. However, I shall consider myself happy when some one comes to take me out of this place."

But would this ever happen? Yes; one morning people came to clear up the garret; the boxes were packed away, and the tree was pulled out of the corner and thrown roughly on the floor; then the servants dragged it out upon the staircase, where the daylight shone.

"Now life is beginning again," said the tree, rejoicing in the sunshine and fresh air. Then it was carried downstairs and taken into the courtyard so quickly that it forgot to think of itself and could only look about, there was so much to be seen.

The court was close to a garden, where everything looked blooming. Fresh and fragrant roses hung over the little palings. The linden trees were in blossom, while swallows flew here and there, crying, "Twit, twit, twit, my mate is coming"; but it was not the fir tree they meant.

"Now I shall live," cried the tree joyfully, spreading out its branches; but alas! they were all withered and yellow, and it lay in a corner among weeds and nettles. The star of gold paper still stuck in the top of the tree and glittered in the sunshine.

Two of the merry children who had danced round the tree at Christmas and had been so happy were playing in the same courtyard. The youngest saw the gilded star and ran and pulled it off the tree. "Look what is sticking to the ugly old fir tree," said the child, treading on the branches till they crackled under his boots.

And the tree saw all the fresh, bright flowers in the garden and then looked at itself and wished it had remained in the dark corner of the garret. It thought of its fresh youth in the forest, of the merry Christmas evening, and of the little mice who had listened to the story of Humpty Dumpty.

"Past! past!" said the poor tree. "Oh, had I but enjoyed myself while I could have done so! but now it is too late."

Then a lad came and chopped the tree into small pieces, till a large bundle lay in a heap on the ground. The pieces were placed in a fire, and they quickly blazed up brightly, while the tree sighed so deeply that each sigh was like a little pistol shot. Then the children who were at play came and seated themselves in front of the fire, and looked at it and cried, "Pop, pop."

But at each "pop," which was a deep sigh, the tree was thinking of a summer day in the forest or of some winter night there when the stars shone brightly, and of Christmas evening, and of Humpty Dumpty,—the only story it had ever heard or knew how to relate,—till at last it was consumed.

The boys still played in the garden, and the youngest wore on his breast the golden star with which the tree had been adorned during the happiest evening of its existence. Now all was past; the tree's life was past and the story also past—for all stories must come to an end at some time or other.

The Symbol and the Saint

Eugene Field
Illustrations Florence Storer

Once upon a time a young man made ready for a voyage. His name was Norss; broad were his shoulders, his cheeks were ruddy, his hair was fair and long, his body betokened strength, and good-nature shone from his blue eyes and lurked about the corners of his mouth.

"Where are you going?" asked his neighbor Jans, the forge-master.

"I am going sailing for a wife," said Norss.

"For a wife, indeed!" cried Jans. "And why go you to seek her in foreign lands? Are not our maidens good enough and fair enough, that you must need search for a wife elsewhere? For shame, Norss! for shame!"

31

But Norss said: "A spirit came to me in my dreams last night and said, 'Launch the boat and set sail tomorrow. Have no fear; for I will guide you to the bride that awaits you.' Then, standing there, all white and beautiful, the spirit held forth a symbol — such as I had never before seen — in the figure of a cross, and the spirit said: 'By this symbol shall she be known to you.'"

"If this be so, you must need go," said Jans. "But are you well victualled? Come to my cabin, and let me give you venison and bear's meat."

Norss shook his head. "The spirit will provide," said he. "I have no fear, and I shall take no care, trusting in the spirit."

So Norss pushed his boat down the beach into the sea, and leaped into the boat, and unfurled the sail to the wind. Jans stood wondering on the beach, and watched the boat speed out of sight.

On, on, many days on sailed Norss — so many leagues that he thought he must have compassed the earth. In all this time he knew no hunger nor thirst; it was as the spirit had told him in his dream — no cares nor no dangers beset him. By day the dolphins and the other creatures of the sea gambolled about his boat; by night a beauteous Star seemed to direct his course; and when he slept and dreamed, he saw ever the spirit clad in white, and holding forth to him the symbol in the similitude of a cross.

At last he came to a strange country — a country so very different from his own that he could scarcely trust his senses. Instead of the rugged mountains of the North, he saw a gentle landscape of velvety green; the trees were not pines and firs, but cypresses, cedars, and palms; instead of the cold, crisp air of his native land, he scented the perfumed zephyrs of the Orient; and the wind that filled the sail of his boat and smote his tanned cheeks was heavy and hot with the odor of cinnamon and spices. The waters were calm and blue — very different from the white and angry waves of Norss's native fiord.

As if guided by an unseen hand, the boat pointed straight for the beach of this strangely beautiful land; and ere its prow cleaved the shallower waters, Norss saw a maiden standing on the shore, shading her eyes with her right hand, and gazing intently at him. She was the most beautiful maiden he had ever looked upon. As Norss was fair, so was this maiden dark; her black hair fell loosely about her shoulders in charming contrast with the white raiment in which her slender, graceful form was clad. Around her neck she wore a golden chain, and therefrom was suspended a small symbol, which Norss did not immediately recognize.

"Hast thou come sailing out of the North into the East?" asked the maiden.

"Yes," said Norss.

"And thou art Norss?" she asked.

"I am Norss; and I come seeking my bride," he answered.

"I am she," said the maiden. "My name is Faia. An angel came to me in my dreams last night, and the angel said: "Stand upon the beach today, and Norss shall come out of the North to bear thee home a bride.' So, coming here, I found thee sailing to our shore."

Remembering then the spirit's words, Norss said: "What symbol have you, Faia, that I may know how truly you have spoken?"

"No symbol have I but this," said Faia, holding out the symbol that was attached to the golden chain about her neck. Norss looked upon it, and lo! it was the symbol of his dreams, — a tiny wooden cross.

Then Norss clasped Faia in his arms and kissed her, and entering into the boat they sailed away into the North. In all their voyage neither care nor danger beset them; for as it had been told to them in their dreams, so it came to pass. By day the dolphins and the other creatures of the sea gambolled about them; by night the winds and the waves sang them to sleep; and, strangely enough, the Star which before had led Norss into the East, now shone bright and beautiful in the Northern sky!

When Norss and his bride reached their home, Jans, the forge-master, and the other neighbors made great joy, and all said that Faia was more beautiful than any other maiden in the land. So merry was Jans that he built a huge fire in his forge, and the flames thereof filled the whole Northern sky with rays of light that danced up, up, up to the Star, singing glad songs the while. So Norss and Faia were wed, and they went to live in the cabin in the fir grove.

To these two was born in good time a son, whom they named Claus. On the night that he was born, wondrous things came to pass. To the cabin in the fir grove came all the quaint, weird spirits, — the fairies, the elves, the trolls, the pixies, the fadas, the crions, the goblins, the kobolds, the moss-people, the gnomes, the dwarfs, the water-sprites, the courils, the bogles, the brownies, the nixies, the trows, the stille-volk, — all came to the cabin in the fir grove, and capered about and sang the strange, beautiful songs of the Mist-Land. And the flames of old Jans's forge leaped up higher than ever into the Northern sky, carrying the joyous tidings to the Star, and full of music was that happy night.

Even in infancy Claus did marvellous things. With his baby hands he wrought into pretty figures the willows that were given him to play with. As he grew older, he fashioned, with the knife old Jans had made for him, many curious toys, — carts, horses, dogs, lambs, houses, trees, cats, and birds, all of wood and very like to nature. His mother taught him how to make dolls too, — dolls of every kind, condition, temper, and color; proud dolls, homely dolls, boy dolls, lady dolls, wax dolls, rubber dolls, paper dolls, worsted dolls, ragdolls, — dolls of every description and without end. So Claus became at once quite as popular with the little girls as with the little boys of his native village; for he was so generous that he gave away all these pretty things as fast as he made them.

Claus seemed to know by instinct every language. As he grew older he would ramble off into the woods and talk with the trees, the rocks, and the beasts of the greenwood; or he would sit on the cliffs overlooking the fiord, and listen to the stories that the waves of the sea loved to tell him; then, too, he knew the haunts of the elves and the stille-volk, and many a pretty tale he learned from these little people.

When night came, old Jans told him the quaint legends of the North, and his mother sang to him the lullabies she had heard when a little child herself in the far-distant East. And every night his mother held out to him the symbol in the similitude of the cross, and bade him kiss it before he went to sleep.

So Claus grew to manhood, increasing each day in knowledge and in wisdom. His works increased too; and his liberality dispensed everywhere the beauteous things which his fancy conceived and his skill executed. Jans, being now a very old man, and having no son of his own, gave to Claus his forge and workshop, and taught him those secret arts which he in youth had learned from cunning masters. Right joyous now was Glaus; and many, many times the Northern sky glowed with the flames that danced singing from the forge while Claus moulded his pretty toys. Every color of the rainbow were these flames; for they reflected the bright colors of the beauteous things strewn round that wonderful workshop. Just as of old he had dispensed to all children alike the homelier toys of his youth, so now he gave to all children alike these more beautiful and more curious gifts. So little children everywhere loved Claus, because he gave them pretty toys, and their parents loved him because he made their little ones so happy.

But now Norss and Faia were come to old age. After long years of love and happiness, they knew that death could not be far distant. And one day Faia said to Norss: "Neither you nor I, dear love, fear death; but if we could choose, would we not choose to live always in this our son Claus, who has been so sweet a joy to us?"

"Ay, ay," said Norss; "but how is that possible?"

"We shall see," said Faia.

That night Norss dreamed that a spirit came to him, and that the spirit said to him: "Norss, thou shalt surely live forever in thy son Claus, if thou wilt but acknowledge the symbol."

Then when the morning was come Norss told his dream to Faia, his wife; and Faia said: "The same dream had I, — an angel appearing to me and speaking these very words."

"But what of the symbol?" cried Norss.

For he was so generous that he gave away all these pretty things as fast as he made them.

"I have it here, about my neck," said Faia.

So saying, Faia drew from her bosom the symbol of wood, — a tiny cross suspended about her neck by the golden chain. And as she stood there holding the symbol out to Norss, he — he thought of the time when first he saw her on the far-distant Orient shore, standing beneath the Star in all her maidenly glory, shading her beauteous eyes with one hand, and with the other clasping the cross, — the holy talisman of her faith.

"Faia, Faia!" cried Norss, "it is the same, — the same you wore when I fetched you a bride from the East!"

"It is the same," said Faia, "yet see how my kisses and my prayers have worn it away; for many, many times in these years, dear Norss, have I pressed it to my lips and breathed your name upon it. See now — see what a beauteous light its shadow makes upon your aged face!"

The sunbeams, indeed, streaming through the window at that moment, cast the shadow of the symbol on old Norss's brow. Norss felt a glorious warmth suffuse him, his heart leaped with joy, and he stretched out his arms and fell about Faia's neck, and kissed the symbol and acknowledged it. Then likewise did Faia; and suddenly the place was filled with a wondrous brightness and with strange music, and never thereafter were Norss and Faia beholden of men.

Until late that night Claus toiled at his forge; for it was a busy season with him, and he had many, many curious and beauteous things to make for the little children in the country round about. The colored flames leaped singing from his forge, so that the Northern sky seemed to be lighted by a thousand rainbows; but above all this voiceful glory beamed the Star, bright, beautiful, serene. Coming late to the cabin in the fir grove, Claus wondered that no sign of his father or of his mother was to be seen. "Father — mother!" he cried, but he received no answer. Just then the Star cast its golden gleam through the latticed window, and this strange, holy light fell and rested upon the symbol of the cross that lay upon the floor. Seeing it, Claus stooped and picked it up, and kissing it reverently, he cried: "Dear talisman, be thou my inspiration evermore; and wheresoever thy blessed influence is felt, there also let my works be known henceforth forever!"

No sooner had he said these words than Claus felt the gift of immortality bestowed upon him; and in that moment, too, there came to him a knowledge that his parents' prayer had been answered, and that Norss and Faia would live in him through all time.

And lo! to that place and in that hour came all the people of Mist-Land and of Dream-Land to declare allegiance to him: yes, the elves, the fairies, the pixies, — all came to Claus, prepared to do his bidding. Joyously they capered about him, and merrily they sang.

"Now haste ye all," cried Claus, — "haste ye all to your homes and bring to my workshop the best ye have. Search, little hill-people, deep in the bowels of the earth for finest gold and choicest jewels; fetch me, O mermaids, from the bottom of the sea the treasures hidden there, — the shells of rainbow tints, the smooth, bright pebbles, and the strange ocean flowers; go, pixies, and other water-sprites, to your secret lakes, and bring me pearls! Speed! speed you all! for many pretty things have we to make for the little ones of earth we love! "

But to the kobolds and the brownies Claus said: "Fly to every house on earth where the cross is known; loiter unseen in the corners, and watch and hear the children through the day. Keep a strict account of good and bad, and every night bring back to me the names of good and bad that I may know them."

The kobolds and the brownies laughed gleefully, and sped away on noiseless wings; and so, too, did the other fairies and elves. There came also to Claus the beasts of the forest and the birds of the air, and bade him be their master. And up danced the Four Winds, and they said: "May we not serve you, too?"

The Snow King came stealing along in his feathery chariot. "Oho!" he cried, "I shall speed over all the world and tell them you are coming. In town and country, on the mountain-tops and in the valleys, —wheresoever the cross is raised, — there will I herald your approach, and thither will I strew you a pathway of feathery white. Oho! oho!" So, singing softly, the Snow King stole upon his way.

But of all the beasts that begged to do him service, Claus liked the reindeer best. "You shall go with me in my travels; for henceforth I shall bear my treasures not only to the children of the North, but to the children in every land whither the Star points me and where the cross is lifted up!" So said Claus to the reindeer, and the reindeer neighed joyously and stamped their hoofs impatiently, as though they longed to start immediately.

Oh, many, many times has Claus whirled away from his far Northern home in his sledge drawn by the reindeer, and thousands upon thousands of beautiful gifts — all of his own making — has he borne to the children of every land; for he loves them all alike, and they all alike love him, I trow. So truly do they love him that they call him Santa Claus, and I am sure that he must be a saint; for he has lived these many hundred years, and we, who know that he was born of Faith and Love, believe that he will live forever.

GERMANY

The Elves and the Shoemaker

BROTHERS GRIMM

ILLUSTRATIONS WALTER CRANE

A shoemaker, by no fault of his own, had become so poor that at last he had nothing left but leather for one pair of shoes. So in the evening, he cut out the shoes which he wished to begin to make the next morning, and as he had a good conscience, he lay down quietly in his bed, commended himself to God, and fell asleep. In the morning, after he had said his prayers, and was just going to sit down to work, the two shoes stood quite finished on his table. He was astounded, and did not know what to say to it. He took the shoes in his hands to observe them closer, and they were so neatly made that there was not one bad stitch in them, just as if they were intended as a masterpiece.

Soon after, too, a buyer came in, and as the shoes pleased him so well, he paid more for them than was customary, and, with the money, the shoemaker was able to purchase leather for two pairs of shoes. He cut them out at night, and next morning was about to set to work with fresh courage; but he had no need to do so, for, when he got up, they were already made, and buyers also were not wanting, who gave him money enough to buy leather for four pairs of shoes. The following morning, too, he found the four pairs made; and so it went on constantly, what he cut out in the evening was finished by the morning, so that he soon had his honest independence again, and at last became a wealthy man. Now it befell that one evening not long before Christmas, when the man had been cutting out, he said to his wife, before going to bed, "What think you if we were to stay up tonight to see who it is that lends us this helping hand?"

The woman liked the idea, and lighted a candle, and then they hid themselves in a corner of the room, behind some clothes which were hanging up there, and watched. When it was midnight, two pretty little naked men came, sat down by the shoemaker's table, took all the work which was cut out before them and began to stitch, and sew, and hammer so skillfully and so quickly with their little fingers that the shoemaker could not turn away his eyes for astonishment. They did not stop until all was done, and stood finished on the table, and then they ran quickly away.

Next morning the woman said, "The little men have made us rich, and we really must show that we are grateful for it. They run about so, and have nothing on, and must be cold. I'll tell thee what I'll do: I will make them little shirts, and coats, and vests, and trousers, and knit both of them a pair of stockings, and do thou, too, make them two little pairs of shoes." The man said, "I shall be very glad to do it;" and one night, when everything was ready, they laid their presents all together on the table instead of the cut-out work, and then concealed themselves to see how the little men would behave. At midnight they came bounding in, and wanted to get to work at once, but as they did not find any leather cut out, but only the pretty little articles of clothing, they were at first astonished, and then they showed intense delight. They dressed themselves with the greatest rapidity, putting the pretty clothes on, and singing,

"Now we are boys so fine to see,
  Why should we longer cobblers be?"

Then they danced and skipped and leapt over chairs and benches. At last they danced out of doors. From that time forth they came no more, but as long as the shoemaker lived all went well with him, and all his undertakings prospered.

The Night After Christmas

UNKNOWN AUTHOR

ILLUSTRATIONS W.B. CONKEY COMPANY

'T was the night after Christmas, and all through the house. Not a creature was stirring – excepting a mouse. The stockings were flung in a haste over the chair, for hopes that St. Nicholas were no longer there.

The children were restlessly tossing in bed. For the pie and the candy were heavy as lead. While mamma in her kerchief, and I in my gown, had just made up our mind that we would not lie down.

W hen out on the lawn there arose such a clatter, I sprang from my chair to see what was the matter. Away to the window I went with a dash, flung open the shutters, and threw up the sash.

T he moon on the breast of the new-fallen snow. Gave the lustre of noon-day to objects below. When what to my long anxious eyes should appear, but a horse and a sleigh, both old-fashioned and queer.

W ith a little old driver, so solemn and slow. I knew at a glance it must be Dr. Brough. I drew in my head, and was turning around, when upstairs came the Doctor, with scarcely a sound.

H e wore a thick overcoat, made long ago. And the beard on his chin was white with the snow. He spoke a few words, and went straight to his work. He felt all the pulses, then turned with a jerk.

A nd laying his finger aside of his nose. With a nod of his head to the chimney he goes. "A spoonful of oil, ma'am, if you have it handy; No nuts and no raisins, no pies and no candy.

T hese tender young stomachs cannot well digest. All the sweets that they get; the toys and books are the best. But I know my advice will not find many friends. For the custom of Christmas the other way tends.

T he fathers and mothers, and Santa Claus ,too, are exceedingly blind. Well a good-night to you!" And I heard him exclaim, as he drove out of sight: "These feastings and candies make Doctor's bills right!"

The Osbornes' Christmas

Lucy Maude Montgomery

Illustrations The Century Co. 1899

C ousin Myra had come to spend Christmas at "The Firs," and all the junior Osbornes were ready to stand on their heads with delight. Darby—whose real name was Charles—did it, because he was only eight, and at eight you have no dignity to keep up. The others, being older, couldn't.

But the fact of Christmas itself awoke no great enthusiasm in the hearts of the junior Osbornes. Frank voiced their opinion of it the day after Cousin Myra had arrived. He was sitting on the table with his hands in his pockets and a cynical sneer on his face. At least, Frank flattered himself that it was cynical. He knew that Uncle Edgar was said to wear a cynical sneer, and Frank admired Uncle

Edgar very much and imitated him in every possible way. But to you and me it would have looked just as it did to Cousin Myra—a very discontented and unbecoming scowl.

"I'm awfully glad to see you, Cousin Myra," explained Frank carefully, "and your being here may make some things worth while. But Christmas is just a bore—a regular bore."

That was what Uncle Edgar called things that didn't interest him, so that Frank felt pretty sure of his word. Nevertheless, he wondered uncomfortably what made Cousin Myra smile so queerly.

"Why, how dreadful!" she said brightly. "I thought all boys and girls looked upon Christmas as the very best time in the year."

"We don't," said Frank gloomily. "It's just the same old thing year in and year out. We know just exactly what is going to happen. We even know pretty well what presents we are going to get. And Christmas Day itself is always the same. We'll get up in the morning, and our stockings will be full of things, and half of them we don't want. Then there's dinner. It's always so poky. And all the uncles and aunts come to dinner—just the same old crowd, every year, and they say just the same things. Aunt Desda always says, 'Why, Frankie, how you have grown!' She knows I hate to be called Frankie. And after dinner they'll sit round and talk the rest of the day, and that's all. Yes, I call Christmas a nuisance."

"There isn't a single bit of fun in it," said Ida discontentedly.

"Not a bit!" said the twins, both together, as they always said things.

"There's lots of candy," said Darby stoutly. He rather liked Christmas, although he was ashamed to say so before Frank.

Cousin Myra smothered another of those queer smiles.

"You've had too much Christmas, you Osbornes," she said seriously. "It has palled on your taste, as all good things will if you overdo them. Did you ever try giving Christmas to somebody else?"

The Osbornes looked at Cousin Myra doubtfully. They didn't understand.

"We always send presents to all our cousins," said Frank hesitatingly. "That's a bore, too. They've all got so many things already it's no end of bother to think of something new."

"That isn't what I mean," said Cousin Myra. "How much Christmas do you suppose those little Rolands down there in the hollow have? Or Sammy Abbott with his lame back? Or French Joe's family over the hill? If you have too much Christmas, why don't you give some to them?"

The Osbornes looked at each other. This was a new idea.

"How could we do it?" asked Ida.

Whereupon they had a consultation. Cousin Myra explained her plan, and the Osbornes grew enthusiastic over it. Even Frank forgot that he was supposed to be wearing a cynical sneer.

"I move we do it, Osbornes," said he.

"If Father and Mother are willing," said Ida.

"Won't it be jolly!" exclaimed the twins.

"Well, rather," said Darby scornfully. He did not mean to be scornful. He had heard Frank saying the same words in the same tone, and thought it signified approval.

Cousin Myra had a talk with Father and Mother Osborne that night, and found them heartily in sympathy with her plans.

For the next week the Osbornes were agog with excitement and interest. At first Cousin Myra made the suggestions, but their enthusiasm soon outstripped her, and they thought out things for themselves. Never did a week pass so quickly. And the Osbornes had never had such fun, either.

Christmas morning there was not a single present given or received at "The Firs" except those which Cousin Myra and Mr. and Mrs. Osborne gave to each other. The junior Osbornes had asked that the money which their parents had planned to spend in presents for them be given to them the previous week; and given it was, without a word.

The uncles and aunts arrived in due time, but not with them was the junior Osbornes' concern. They were the guests of Mr. and Mrs. Osborne. The junior Osbornes were having a Christmas dinner party of their own. In the small dining room a table was spread and loaded with good things. Ida and the twins cooked that dinner all by themselves. To be sure, Cousin Myra had helped some, and Frank and Darby had stoned all the raisins and helped pull the home-made candy; and all together they had decorated the small dining room royally with Christmas greens.

Then their guests came. First, all the little Rolands from the Hollow arrived—seven in all, with very red, shining faces and not a word to say for themselves, so shy were they. Then came a troop from French Joe's—four black-eyed lads, who never knew what shyness meant. Frank drove down to the village in the cutter and brought lame Sammy back with him, and soon after the last guest arrived— little Tillie Mather, who was Miss Rankin's "orphan 'sylum girl" from over the road. Everybody knew that Miss Rankin never kept Christmas. She did not believe in it, she said, but she did not prevent Tillie from going to the Osbornes' dinner party.

Just at first the guests were a little stiff and unsocial; but they soon got acquainted, and so jolly was Cousin Myra—who had her dinner with the children in preference to the grown-ups—and so friendly the junior Osbornes, that all stiffness vanished. What a merry dinner it was! What peals of laughter went up, reaching to the big dining room across the hall, where the grown-ups sat in rather solemn state. And how those guests did eat and frankly enjoy the good things before them! How nicely they all behaved, even to the French Joes! Myra had secretly been a little dubious about those four mischievous-looking lads, but their manners were quite flawless. Mrs. French Joe had been drilling them for three days.

After the merry dinner was over, the junior Osbornes brought in a Christmas tree, loaded with presents. They had bought them with the money that Mr. and Mrs. Osborne had meant for their own presents, and a splendid assortment they were. All the French-Joe boys got a pair of skates apiece, and Sammy a set of beautiful books and Tillie were made supremely happy with a big wax doll. Every little Roland got just what his or her small heart had been longing for. Besides, there were nuts and candies galore.

Then Frank hitched up his pony again, but this time into a great pung sleigh, and the junior Osbornes took their guests for a sleigh-drive, chaperoned by Cousin Myra. It was just dusk when they got back, having driven the Rolands and the French Joes and Sammy and Tillie to their respective homes.

"This has been the jolliest Christmas I ever spent," said Frank, emphatically.

"I thought we were just going to give the others a good time, but it was they who gave it to us," said Ida.

"Weren't the French Joes jolly?" giggled the twins. "Such cute speeches as they would make!"

"Me and Teddy Roland are going to be chums after this," announced Darby. "He's an inch taller than me, but I'm wider."

That night Frank and Ida and Cousin Myra had a little talk after the smaller Osbornes had been haled off to bed.

"We're not going to stop with Christmas, Cousin Myra," said Frank, at the end of it. "We're just going to keep on through the year. We've never had such a delightful old Christmas before."

"You've learned the secret of happiness," said Cousin Myra gently.

And the Osbornes understood what she meant.

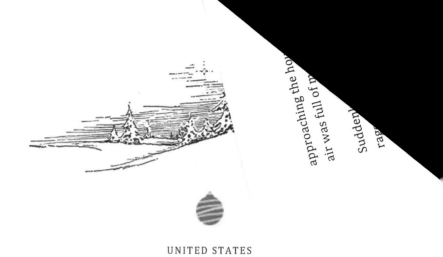

approaching the ho
air was full of
Sudden
rag

UNITED STATES

The Legend of the Christmas Tree

LUCY WHEELOCK

ILLUSTRATIONS FLORENCE STORER

T wo little children were sitting by the fire one cold winter's night. All at once they heard a timid knock at the door, and one ran to open it.

There, outside in the cold and the darkness, stood a child with no shoes upon his feet and clad in thin, ragged garments. He was shivering with cold, and he asked to come in and warm himself.

"Yes, come," cried both the children; "you shall have our place by the fire. Come in!"

They drew the little stranger to their warm seat and shared their supper with him, and gave him their bed, while they slept on a hard bench.

In the night they were awakened by strains of sweet music and, looking out, they saw a band of children in shining garments

se. They were playing on golden harps, and the
elody.

y the Stranger Child stood before them; no longer cold and
ed, but clad in silvery light.

His soft voice said: "I was cold and you took Me in. I was hungry, and you fed Me. I was tired, and you gave Me your bed. I am the Christ Child, wandering through the world to bring peace and happiness to all good children. As you have given to Me, so may this tree every year give rich fruit to you."

So saying, He broke a branch from the fir tree that grew near the door, and He planted it in the ground and disappeared. But thebranch grew into a great tree, and every year it bore wonderful golden fruit for the kind children.

The Little Match Girl

HANS CHRISTIAN ANDERSEN
ILLUSTRATIONS EDNA F. HART & RIE CRAMER

I t was dreadfully cold; it was snowing fast, and was almost dark, as evening came on — the last evening of the year. In the cold and the darkness, there went along the street a poor little girl, bareheaded and with naked feet. When she left home she had slippers on, it is true; but they were much too large for her feet — slippers that her mother had used till then, and the poor little girl lost them in running across the street when two carriages were passing terribly fast. When she looked for them, one was not to be found, and a boy seized the other and ran away with it, saying he would use it for a cradle some day, when he had children of his own.

So on the little girl went with her bare feet, that were red and blue with cold. In an old apron that she wore were bundles of matches, and she carried a bundle also in her hand. No one had bought so much as a bunch all the long day, and no one had given her even a penny.

Poor little girl! Shivering with cold and hunger she crept along, a perfect picture of misery.

The snowflakes fell on her long flaxen hair, which hung in pretty curls about her throat; but she thought not of her beauty nor of the cold. Lights gleamed in every window, and there came to her the savory smell of roast goose, for it was New Year's Eve. And it was this of which she thought.

In a corner formed by two houses, one of which projected beyond the other, she sat cowering down. She had drawn under her her little feet, but still she grew colder and colder; yet she dared not go home, for she had sold no matches and could not bring a penny of money. Her father would certainly beat her; and, besides, it was cold enough at home, for they had only the house-roof above them, and though the largest holes had been stopped with straw and rags, there were left many through which the cold wind could whistle.

And now her little hands were nearly frozen with cold. Alas! a single match might do her good if she might only draw it from the bundle, rub it against the wall, and warm her fingers by it. So at last she drew one out. Whisht! How it blazed and burned! It gave out a warm, bright flame like a little candle, as she held her hands over it. A wonderful little light it was. It really seemed to the little girl as if she sat before a great iron stove with polished brass feet and brass shovel and tongs. So blessedly it burned that the little maiden stretched out her feet to warm them also. How comfortable she was! But lo! the flame went out, the stove vanished, and nothing remained but the little burned match in her hand.

She rubbed another match against the wall. It burned brightly, and where the light fell upon the wall it became transparent like a veil, so that she could see through it into the room. A snow-white cloth was spread upon the table, on which was a beautiful china dinner-service, while a roast goose, stuffed with apples and prunes, steamed famously and sent forth a most savory smell. And what was more delightful still, and wonderful, the goose jumped from the dish, with knife and fork still in its breast, and waddled along the floor straight to the little girl.

But the match went out then, and nothing was left to her but the thick, damp wall.

She lighted another match. And now she was under a most beautiful Christmas tree, larger and far more prettily trimmed than the one she had seen through the glass doors at the rich merchant's. Hundreds of wax tapers were burning on the green branches, and gay figures, such as she had seen in shop windows, looked down upon her. The child stretched out her hands to them; then the match went out.

Still the lights of the Christmas tree rose higher and higher. She saw them now as stars in heaven, and one of them fell, forming a long trail of fire.

"Now some one is dying," murmured the child softly; for her grandmother, the only person who had loved her, and who was now dead, had told her that whenever a star falls a soul mounts up to God.

She struck yet another match against the wall, and again it was light; and in the brightness there appeared before her the dear old grandmother, bright and radiant, yet sweet and mild, and happy as she had never looked on earth.

"Oh, grandmother," cried the child, "take me with you. I know you will go away when the match burns out. You, too, will vanish, like the warm stove, the splendid New Year's feast, the beautiful

Christmas tree." And lest her grandmother should disappear, she rubbed the whole bundle of matches against the wall.

And the matches burned with such a brilliant light that it became brighter than noonday. Her grandmother had never looked so grand and beautiful. She took the little girl in her arms, and both flew together, joyously and gloriously, mounting higher and higher, far above the earth; and for them there was neither hunger, nor cold, nor care — they were with God.

But in the corner, at the dawn of day, sat the poor girl, leaning against the wall, with red cheeks and smiling mouth — frozen to death on the last evening of the old year. Stiff and cold she sat, with the matches, one bundle of which was burned.

"She wanted to warm herself, poor little thing," people said. No one imagined what sweet visions she had had, or how gloriously she had gone with her grandmother to enter upon the joys of a new year.

GERMANY

The Nutcracker

E.T.A. Hoffman
Illustrations Ludwig Willem Reymert Wenckebach

Chapter One: Christmas Eve

On Christmas Eve, the children of Doctor Stahlbaum were not allowed into the family room, let alone the adjoining living room. Evening had come, and Fritz and Marie Stahlbaum sat huddled in a corner. As was usual on Christmas Eve, no-one had brought in a light, and so they sat in an eerie darkness.

Fritz was whispering to his younger sister Marie (who had just turned seven) how early that morning, he had heard rattlings and poundings from the forbidden chambers, and how he had just seen a small, dark man slipping a large box under his arm across the corridor, and how he knew it was none other than Godfather Drosselmeier.

Marie's eyes lit up, and she clapped her hands and cried, "Oh, what do you think Godfather Drosselmeier has made for us?"

Now, Judge Drosselmeier was not the least bit handsome. He was small and thin with a face full of wrinkles, and where his right eye ought to have been he wore a black eyepatch. He had no hair at all on his head, and so he wore a cleverly-made white wig of glass threads. In general, Godfather Drosselmeier was a clever sort of man who knew a great deal about watches and clocks and even made some himself. When one of the Stahlbaum family clocks was sick and couldn't sing, Godfather Drosselmeier would come and take off his glass wig and yellow coat and put on a blue apron. He would then stab all sorts of sharp instruments into the clock. Marie felt sympathy pains, but the clocks weren't at all hurt. In fact, the clocks purred and sang as joyfully as ever, which made the whole family happy again.

Drosselmeier always had something in his pockets for the children when he came to visit. Sometimes it was a funny little man who rolled his eyes and bowed, sometimes it was a box from which a small bird hopped, and sometimes it was something else. But every Christmas, the judge would go to extra effort to create something spectacular – so spectacular that the children's parents would put it away for safekeeping afterward.

"What do you think Godfather Drosselmeier has made for us?" Marie anxiously asked.

Fritz said it probably wouldn't be any different this time. He expected a fortress where soldiers marched and drilled about. Other soldiers would come to overtake it, but brave soldiers inside the fortress would fire booming cannons to keep the intruders away.

"No, no," Marie interrupted, "Godfather Drosselmeier told me of a beautiful garden with a big lake, with beautiful swans swimming around wearing gold necklaces and singing pretty songs. Then a little girl comes to the lake and calls the swans, and feeds them marzipan."

"Swans don't eat marzipan," Fritz said scornfully. "And Godfather Drosselmeier can't make a whole garden. Besides, they always take what he gives us away. I prefer what Papa and Mama give us; we can keep those and do what we want with them."

The children continued to guess and wonder. Marie pointed out that her large doll, Madame Trudie, was more awkward than ever these days. She fell on the floor time and again, which put nasty marks on her face and was getting her dress filthy. She'd tried scolding her, but to no avail. Also, there had been the way Mama had smiled when she saw how happy Marie was with the little parasol for Gretchen. Fritz pointed out that his father was quite aware that his stables were missing a chestnut horse and that he was short of an entire cavalry.

The children were certain their parents had bought them many wonderful presents, and that through the blessings of the Christ Child (who looked down upon them with kind, loving eyes), Christmas presents were much better than any other presents. Their older sister Louise added that the Christ Child, who brought them gifts through the hands of their loving parents, knew much better what they would like than they, so rather than wishing and hoping they should remain patient and quiet. This gave Marie pause for thought, but Fritz muttered, "I'd still like a chestnut horse and some hussars."

Night had fallen, and Fritz and Marie huddled together in silence. It suddenly seemed there was a rushing of wings and a distant, but beautiful music. A bright light touched the wall, and the children knew that the Christ Child had flown away on shimmering clouds to other happy children. At that moment, a silvery bell rang and the doors flew open.

"Ah-ah!" The children froze as they stepped on the threshold, but Papa and Mama lead them inside by the hand.

"Come in and see what the Christ Child has brought you."

Chapter Two: The Gifts

I ask you, the reader, to remember your most wonderful Christmas. Remember the beautiful, colorful presents and the lavishly decorated Christmas tree? You should be able to imagine how the children felt. With sparkling eyes, the children were completely silenced for awhile. Then Marie gave a deep sigh, and said "Oh, how beautiful... oh, how nice."

Fritz made a few exuberant leaps into the air. They must have been very good that year, because they had never been given so many wonderful and magnificent presents before. The big fir tree in the center of the room was covered in golden apples, silver apples, buds, and blossoms. Besides that, there were sugared almonds, colorful candies, and many other delicacies. Each and every branch was adorned, and best of all, hundreds of lights sparkled from within its branches like tiny stars. Its warm and inviting glow beckoned the children to pluck its fruits.

Around the tree were such colorful and lovely gifts to defy description. Marie saw the prettiest dolls and all sorts of neat little items and tools for them. What especially caught her eye was a dress hanging from a rack so it could be seen from all sides. It was made of silk and adorned with colorful ribbons, and after admiring it for a moment, Marie exclaimed "It's so beautiful! Oh, I love it! Surely I'll be allowed to wear it!"

Fritz had already galloped three or four circles around the tree on his toy horse, which he had found bridled next to the table. After dismounting he said it was a wild beast, but that was all right – he'd tame it sure enough. Then he inspected his new squadron of hussars, who were dressed handsomely in red and gold. They carried tiny silver weapons and rode on horses so white that they almost looked like they were made of pure silver.

When the children quieted down they turned to the picture books, which were filled with beautifully-drawn pictures of flowers, children at play, and colorful people. They were so life-like that one could almost believe they might really move or speak.

They had scarcely begun to delve into the books when the silvery bell rang again, and they knew Drosselmeier's gift was ready. They ran to the table, where a silken screen Drosselmeier had been behind all along was lifted up. Sitting upon the table was a green lawn decorated with flowers, and upon that sat a beautiful miniature palace with many golden towers, delicate little mirrors, and windows to see the elegant rooms inside. A bell rang, and the palace's doors opened. Inside, ladies with long dresses and gentlemen with plumed hats walked about the halls. There were so many candles burning in the silver chandeliers in the central hall that the whole room seemed to be on fire. A gentleman in an emerald cloak would presently poke out of a window, wave, and return into the palace again. Likewise, by the door of the castle, a miniature Drosselmeier – no bigger than Papa's thumb – came out to wave at the children before returning inside.

Fritz had been watching the whole scene with his hands on his hips. Presently he said, "Godfather Drosselmeier, let me go into the castle!"

The judge gave him a disparaging look, and for good reason. Fritz was quite foolish to even suggest such a thing, for he was far too big to fit inside the tiny castle – its golden towers weren't even as tall as he was.

After watching the lords, ladies, children, the emerald-cloaked man, and the miniature Drosselmeier moving through their routines for awhile, Fritz said impatiently, "Godfather Drosselmeier, come out of the other door."

"That cannot be done, Fritzling," the judge responded.

"Then let the man in green come out and walk with the others."

"That cannot be done, either."

"Let the children come down. I want to see them up close."

"It cannot be done," the judge said flatly. "Once it has been put together, it cannot be changed."

"So," Fritz said dramatically, "then nothing can be changed? If that's how it is, then all your pretty little people don't mean much to me. I think my hussars are better, because they can go forward or backward on my command, and they're not locked up in any house."

And so Fritz sprang to the Christmas table, where he let out his squadrons mounted on silvery horses to trot, turn, charge, and fire to his heart's content.

Marie had also quietly slipped away, because she too had begun to find the walking and dancing dolls dull. But unlike Fritz, she was too polite to show it.

"A machine like this isn't meant for simple children," the judge said angrily to their parents. "I'm going to pack it up."

But their mother came over and asked to see the inside of the castle and the intricate clockwork that made the dolls move. So the judge took everything apart and put it back together again, which cheered him right up. He gave the children some beautiful brown men and women with gold faces. They smelled as sweet and pleasant as gingerbread, and both Fritz and Marie enjoyed them very much.

At their mother's request, their sister Louise had put on the new dress she had received, and she looked very beautiful in it. But when Marie was asked to wear hers as well, she said she'd rather simply look at it, which she was gladly permitted to do.

He stood there quietly and modestly, as if waiting his turn.

Chapter Three: The Favorite

M arie had lingered near the Christmas table when the others had left because she had seen something nobody else seemed to have noticed. After Fritz had disengaged his hussars from parading about the tree, a splendid little man became visible. He stood there quietly and modestly, as if waiting his turn.

His build left much to be desired: aside from the fact that his stocky and somewhat long upper body didn't quite fit his small and spindly legs, his head was much too large. However, his fine clothing suggested that he was a man of taste and education: he wore a beautiful hussar's jacket of vivid violet with lots of white trimming and buttons with matching trousers. He wore the most beautiful pair of boots that a student, or even an officer, had ever worn. They were so tight on his legs that they seemed to be painted on.

He stood there quietly and modestly, as if waiting his turn.

Somewhat amusingly, a narrow and clumsy cloak was attached to his back that seemed to be made of wood. He also wore what looked like a miner's hat on his head. However, Marie remembered that Drosselmeier wore an awful morning coat and an equally dreadful hat, but nevertheless was a kind and loving godfather.

It also occurred to Marie that if Drosselmeier were to dress as elegantly as the tiny man, he would not look nearly as handsome.

She had quite fallen in love with the tiny man at first sight, and the more she looked at him, the more she could appreciate his good-natured face. His light green eyes, though protruding, were kind and friendly. The craftsman who had given him his combed white beard had done a fine job, for it made his sweet red smile stand out even more.

"Oh!" Marie exclaimed at last. "Papa, who does the charming little man at the tree belong to?"

"That," her father said, "that, dear, will work hard for all of you to crack many a tough nut, and he belongs as much to Louise as to you and Fritz."

He gently removed the little man from the table and lifted up his wooden cloak. His mouth opened wide and wider, revealing two rows of sharp, white teeth. At her father's behest, Marie put a nut into the little man's mouth and – crack! – the nut's shells fell away, and the sweet meat inside fell into her hand.

Her father then explained that the Nutcracker – for that is what the tiny man was – had descended from a long line of Nutcrackers. The children shouted with joy, and Dr. Stahlbaum said, "Marie, since you're so fond of the Nutcracker, you can look after him. But remember, Louise and Fritz have as much right to use him as you."

Marie immediately took the Nutcracker into her arms and gave him nuts to crack, though she always chose the smallest so he wouldn't have to open his mouth very wide, as she felt it wasn't very attractive. Louise came over to use the Nutcracker, and their new friend cracked nuts for her, too. His friendly smile made it seem that he was happy to serve them.

Fritz presently grew tired from his drilling and riding, and when he heard his sisters cracking nuts he went over to investigate. He laughed heartily at the funny-looking little man.

Now Fritz wanted to eat nuts, and the Nutcracker was passed from hand to hand between the three of them. Fritz shoved the biggest and toughest nuts into his mouth. Suddenly, there was a dreadful cracking sound that wasn't from the shell of a nut – and three teeth fell out of the Nutcracker's mouth, and his jaw hung loose and wobbly.

"Oh! My poor dear Nutcracker!" Marie wailed, and took him from Fritz's hands.

"He's a naive, stupid amateur," Fritz declared. "He probably doesn't even understand his own craft. Just give him to me, Marie, and he'll crack nuts for me, even if he loses the rest of his teeth – or even his good-for-nothing jaw."

"No, no!" Marie had begun to cry. "You can't have my dear Nutcracker. Look at how sadly he looks at me and shows me his wounded mouth! You're a cold-hearted person! You've beaten your horses and you even had a soldier shot!"

"It had to be done. You don't understand these things," Fritz said. "The Nutcracker is mine, too, so give him to me."

Marie began to cry harder and wrapped the injured Nutcracker in her little handkerchief. Then their parents came in with Godfather Drosselmeier, who to Marie's dismay took Fritz's side.

However, her father said, "I have specifically placed the Nutcracker into Marie's care, which I can see he clearly needs right now, so no-one may take him from her. Also, I'm very surprised at Fritz – as a good soldier, he should know that an injured man is never sent out to fight."

Fritz looked very ashamed of himself, and without another word concerning nuts and nutcrackers crept off to the other side of the table, where he posted some of his hussars as look-outs and sent the rest to bed for the night.

Marie found Nutcracker's lost teeth and tied a pretty white ribbon from her dress around his injured jaw as a bandage. The poor fellow looked pale and frightened, so she held him more carefully than before, as if he were a small child, and looked at the beautiful pictures in the new picture-books, which were now among the other presents.

Marie became quite angry – which was was quite unlike her – when Godfather Drosselmeier laughed and continually asked how she could humor such an ugly little man so.

The Nutcracker's odd similarity to Drosselmeier came back to Marie's mind, and she said very seriously, "I'm not sure, dear Godfather, if you were dressed like my dear nutcracker and had such nice shiny boots, whether you would look as nice as he does."

Marie had no idea why her parents suddenly laughed so loud, or why Drosselmeier's nose turned so red, or why his laugh seemed so weak. There was probably some reason for it.

He stood there quietly and modestly, as if waiting his turn.

Chapter Four: Wonders

As you enter the Stahlbaum family living room from the front door, to your left is a beautiful glass-fronted cabinet in which the children keep all of the wonderful things they receive every year. Louise was still very small when their father hired a skilled carpenter to build the cabinet, and he used such brilliant panes of glass and set them so skillfully that anything you put inside looked brighter and prettier than when you held it in your hands.

In the highest shelf (too high for Fritz and Marie to reach) were Godfather Drosselmeier's works of art. On the shelf below were the picture-books, and on the two shelves below that Fritz and Marie could put whatever they wanted, though it always happened that Marie put her dolls on the bottom shelf and Fritz quartered his soldiers on the shelf above it.

And so tonight Fritz put his hussars in the second shelf, and Marie moved Madame Trudie out of the way to make room for her new doll in the beautifully-furnished room and invited herself in for sweets.

As I've said, the room was very beautifully-furnished, and that's the truth. I don't know whether you, my attentive reader, have such a nice miniature flower-print sofa, charming little chairs, an adorable tea-table – and best of all, a bed with a bright and shiny frame for your most beautiful dolls to rest on. Everything stood in the cabinet's corner, where the walls were papered with colorful little pictures, and you can well imagine that the new doll Marie had received (whose name was Madame Clarette, as Marie had learned that evening) was quite content with her quarters.

It was now very late – almost midnight, and Godfather Drosselmeier had long since gone home. But the children did not want to leave the cabinet, so their mother had to remind them that it was time for bed.

"You're right," Fritz said finally. "The poor fellows-" (referring to his hussars) "-want a little peace and quiet, and they don't dare nod off while I'm still around!" And so Fritz scampered off.

But Marie said, "Just a little while longer, just a minute. Leave me here, Mama. I have some things to take care of, and once I finish I'll go straight to bed."

Marie was a trustworthy child, so her mother knew she could leave her alone with the toys without worry. Still, she was concerned that Marie might be so distracted by her new doll and the other new toys that she might forget to put out the lights before leaving, so Mrs. Stahlbaum extinguished all of the lights except for the one that hung from the middle of the ceiling, which cast a gentle, graceful light into the room.

"Come to bed soon, dear, or you won't be able to get up on time!" she called as she left for her bedroom. Once Marie was alone, she hurried to do what had been on her mind, something that she wasn't sure why she hadn't been able to mention to her mother earlier. She carried the injured Nutcracker to the table and gently set him there, where she unwrapped her makeshift bandages to see the wound. The Nutcracker was very pale, but he smiled a kind, sad smile that wrenched her heart.

"Oh, Nutcracker," she said softly, "I know Fritz hurt you badly, but he didn't mean any harm. It's just that his wild soldier's life has made him a little hard-hearted, but otherwise he's a very good boy. I promise I'll take very good care of you until you're healthy and happy and can use your teeth and stand with your shoulders straight. Godfather Drosselmeier will fix you up, he knows all about-"

Marie could not finish what she had started saying because when she had said the name "Drosselmeier," Nutcracker's face had turned up in disgust and his eyes shot green sparks. But just as she became frightened, Nutcracker looked at her with his kind, sad smile again. Marie realized that the awful face she had seen was only a trick of the light caused by the flickering lamp above.

"I'm not a silly girl who gets scared so easily, who thinks that a wooden doll could make faces!" Marie told herself. "But I love Nutcracker because he's so funny and kind, which is why he must be looked after – which is proper."

So Marie took her friend the Nutcracker into her arms and took him to the glass-fronted cabinet, where she knelt down in front of it. "I request, Miss Clarette, that you give up your bed to the injured Nutcracker, and manage with the sofa as well as you can. Remember, you're quite healthy and full of energy, because otherwise you wouldn't have such round red cheeks – and anyway, very few dolls – even the most beautiful – have such a comfortable sofa."

Madame Clarette looked very grand and morose in her Christmas finery, but she didn't make a peep.

"What else can I do..." Marie wondered. She took the bed out of the cabinet and gently laid Nutcracker upon it, still wrapped in a beautiful waist-sash from his sore shoulders to above his nose.

"He can't stay with naughty Clarette," she said, and lifted the bed along with the Nutcracker up to the second shelf, where she placed it next to the picturesque village where Fritz had stationed his hussars. She locked the cabinet and was making her to make her way to her bedroom when – pay attention now! – a quiet whispering and rustling sound came from behind the stove, the chairs, and the walls. The clock whirred over them, but it didn't strike. Marie looked up at the clock, and the large gold-painted owl that sat on the top had lowered its wings so that the whole clock was covered, and its ugly cat-like head and beak jutted forward. What's more, the owl seemed to be speaking with audible words:

Tick-tock, Stahlbaum clocks, only whir and purr
Mouse-king is so sharp of ear (whir whir, purr purr)
Only sing the old song (whir whir, purr purr)
Ding dong, ding dong.
I promise you, he won't last long

Marie was now terrified and was just about to run away when she saw that Godfather Drosselmeier, not the owl, was sitting on top of the clock. What she had taken for wings were really his yellow coat tails.

Marie gathered up what little courage she had left and cried up tearfully, "Godfather Drosselmeier! Godfather Drosselmeier! What are you doing up there? Come down and stop scaring me, you bad Godfather Drosselmeier!"

But suddenly there was a great commotion all around – first a shrill giggling and squeaking, then a pitter-patter like a thousand tiny feet behind the walls, and then a thousand tiny lights peeping out from the cracks in the floorboards. No - not lights! They were small, twinkling eyes! From every crack and crevice, mice had begun to squidge and squeeze their furry gray bodies into the room. Soon there were packs of mice running back and forth everywhere, until they all stood in rank and file just as Fritz would position his soldiers before a battle.

Marie thought they looked quite cute (unlike some children, she was not at all afraid of mice), and her fear had all but passed when a squeal so shrill and sharp pierced the air that it made ice-cold shivers run through her back! And oh, what she saw!

Now dear readers, I know that you're just as clever and courageous as young Commander Fritz Stahlbaum, but I honestly think if you had seen what stood before Marie's eyes, you would have run away, jumped into your bed, and pulled up the covers high above your ears.

But poor Marie couldn't run to the safety of her bedroom, because – listen! - just in front of her feet, a plume of sand, lime, and brick shards spouted into the air as if by some underground force, and seven mouse heads with seven shining crowns rose hissing and squeaking from the ground. Then up came a mouse's body, at whose neck all seven heads were attached. The mouse army gave three cheers in unison upon the arrival of this horrendous beast.

The mouse army had been sitting until now, but now they hopped to their feet and set themselves into motion. They hopped right toward the cabinet - and toward Marie, who stood near it. She was so terrified that her heart beat so violently she thought it might jump out of her chest and she would die. Then her blood seemed to stand completely still in her veins.

Nearly fainting, she stepped backward - and with a crash and a tinkle, shards of glass fell from the cabinet doorpane, which she had accidentally pushed her elbow into. She felt a very sharp pain in her left arm, but her chest untightened and she no longer heard the squeaks and squeals of the mice. Everything had become completely quiet, and although she didn't look she believed that the noise of the breaking glass had frightened them into scampering back into their holes.

But wait! What was that? Just behind Marie, in the cabinet, a small, delicate voice began: "Awake! Awake! Onto battle! This very night! Awake! Awake!"

And then there was a beautiful and musical tinkling of bells. "Oh, that's my miniature carillon!" Marie exclaimed happily. She jumped quickly to the side and looked inside the cabinet. There was a strange glow coming from within, and several dolls were running helter-skelter with their small arms waving about. Suddenly, Nutcracker rose up, threw off his blanket, and jumped with both feet out of the bed, and loudly shouted:

Crack crack crack!
Stupid mousepack!
Squeaking, squealing!
Gnawing, clawing!
Crack crack crack!
Stupid mousepack!

And Nutcracker drew his little sword, brandished it in the air, and shouted, "my dear vassals, friends, and brothers, will you assist me in this difficult fight?"

Three scaramouches, a Pantaloon, four chimney sweeps, two zither players, and a drummer immediately shouted, "Yes, my lord! We will loyally follow you through death, victory, and battle!"

Inspired by the Nutcracker's speech, they made the dangerous leap down from the second shelf to the floor.

They were not at all hurt because, not only were they dressed in soft wool and silk, there wasn't much inside them other than cotton and sawdust. So they plopped down like little sacks of wool.

Nutcracker, on the other hand, would have almost certainly broken himself to pieces. He he two feet to fall to the ground, and his body was as brittle as linden wood. Indeed, he would have likely broken his arms and legs had not Madame Clarette sprang from the sofa and thrust herself out from the bottom shelf to catch the

Nutcracker (who had descended brandishing his sword) in her arms.

"Oh, good dear Clarette!" Marie cried. "I've misjudged you so badly. I'm sure you were happy to give the Nutcracker your bed!"

But Madame Clarette spoke now, embracing the young hero in her silken chest. "Please, my lord, as injured and sick as you are, do not go into the battle. See how your courageous vassals are ready to fight and how certain they are of victory. Scaramouche, Pantaloon, chimney sweep, zither player, and drummer are already down, and you can see that the standard bearers on my shelf are moving. Please, my lord, either rest in my arms or watch your victory from the brim of my feathered hat."

Thus Clarette spoke, but Nutcracker refused to be still and kicked his legs until she had no choice to put him down.

Nutcracker politely bowed on one knee and said, "my lady, I will always remember your grace and compassion in combat and strife."

Then Clarette bent down so she could take Nutcracker by the arm. She gently lifted him up, quickly took off her sequined cincher, and tried to put it about his shoulders as a cape. But he took two steps back, put his hand on his breast, and said solemnly, "please do not waste your favors on me, my lady, because..." he paused, then tore off the ribbon that Marie had put about his shoulders and pressed it to his lips. He let it fall, and it hung from him like a field bandage.

Brandishing his sword, he jumped as nimbly as a bird over the ledge of the bottom shelf and down to the floor.

You have probably noticed, observant reader, that the Nutcracker had felt Marie's love and kindness before he was properly alive, which is why he preferred Marie's simple white ribbon over Clarette's, even though it was quite shiny and looked very pretty.

And what now?

As Nutcracker jumped down, the squeaks and squeals began again. What a noise! Under the big Christmas table, the deadly hordes of mice waited, and over all of them the monstrous mouse with seven heads loomed.

What will happen next?

Chapter Five: The Battle

"Strike the battle march, loyal vassal drummer!" Nutcracker shouted. The drummer beat his drum so furiously that the glass in the cabinet shook and reverberated the sound. A rattle and clatter came from within the cabinet, and Marie saw that the lids of the boxes where Fritz's army was quartered had popped open. The soldiers were jumping out of their boxes and forming regiments on the bottom shelf.

Nutcracker was running back and forth shouting words to inspire his troops. "I see that dog of a trumpeter isn't moving himself!" he cried furiously. Then he quickly turned to Pantaloon, who had become quite pale and whose long chin trembled. To Pantaloon he said, "General, I know how courageous and experienced you are. We need a quick eye and a quicker mind, so I'm trusting the cavalry and artillery to you. You don't need a horse – your legs are so long you can gallop quite well on them. Now, do your job."

Pantaloon immediately put his long, spindly fingers into his mouth and trumpeted so loud that it may as well have been a hundred trumpets. From within the cabinet, there came a nickering and stamping. Marie looked inside and saw Fritz's dragoons and cuirassiers, and especially his new hussars dropping down to the floor. With flags flying and music playing, regiment after regiment marched marched across the floor and lined themselves up into neat, wide rows.

With clanks and clinks, Fritz's cannons were brought to the front. Boom! Boom! Boom! they went. They fired tiny balls of sugar – no bigger than peas – that exploded and covered the mice in powdered sugar upon impact. Although it didn't really hurt, it was very demoralizing.

Meanwhile, an artillery battery up on Mama's footstool was doing a considerable amount of damage – they were firing volleys of peppernuts, which took down many of the mice.

Yet the mice continued to advance, even overtaking some of the cannons. And there was now so much noise, smoke, and dust that Marie could barely make out what was going on. But one thing she could tell for sure was that both sides were fighting as hard as they could. Sometimes it seemed that the toys would win, and other times it looked like the mice would take the victory.

Yet the numbers of mice were increasing rather than decreasing, and the small silver pills they shot with great skill had already begun to strike the glass-fronted cabinet. Madame Clarette and Madame Trudie anxiously paced inside and wrung their hands.

"Am I to die in the flower of my youth? I, the most beautiful of dolls?" Clarette asked.

"Was I so well-preserved, just to die here in my own home?" Trudie asked.

Then they fell into each other's arms and cried so loudly that they could be heard above the commotion outside.

And what a commotion it was! You can hardly begin to imagine the noise! Cannons boomed and clanked, tiny muskets fired, the Mouse King and his mice squeaked, and the Nutcracker shouted orders from amidst the cannons.

Pantaloon, to his credit, had lead some brilliant cavalry charges, but the mouse artillery had pelted Fritz's hussars with foul-smelling balls that left stains on their red jackets. Because of this, they lost the will to advance.

Pantaloon ordered them to turn left. Caught up in the excitement of giving orders, he himself also turned left – and so did his cuirassiers and dragoons. And so they all marched left and went home.

This left the battery on the footstool unprotected, and it wasn't long before a swarm of very ugly mice came and knocked the whole thing over – stool, guns, and gunners alike.

Nutcracker looked very worried and ordered the right wing to retreat. Those of you who have lead any battles yourself will know that retreating is no different than running away, and I'm quite sure that you feel just as sorry as I do that things turned out so badly for the army of Marie's beloved Nutcracker.

But let us turn from this now and look at the left wing of Nutcracker's army, where everything is still going well and there is hope for the soldiers and their general.

During the worst of the battle, cavalry mice waiting quietly under the bureau threw themselves upon the left wing of the Nutcracker's army with horrible squeaks and squeals – but what resistance they found!

Slowly, because of the difficult terrain (that is, the edge of the cabinet), the standard-bearers under the command of two Chinese emperors had moved over and formed a square. These brave, colorful, and splendid troops consisted of gardeners, Tyroleans, Tunguses, barbars, harlequins, lions, tigers, monkeys, apes, all of whom fought with composure, courage, and determination.

With Spartan bravery, this elite battalion would have snatched the victory from the hands of the enemy had not a bold captain of the mouse cavalry daringly bitten off the head of one of the Chinese emperors, who in turn killed two Tunguses and a monkey as he fell. This formed a gap that the enemy could penetrate, and soon the whole battalion had been gnawed through.

But the enemy gained little advantage from this unfortunate turn of events, because every mouse who viciously bit into the middle of his valiant opponent got a printed piece of paper lodged in his throat and he immediately choked to death.

Despite this small gain, things were looking bad for the Nutcracker's army. Once they had begun to fall back, they found themselves falling back further and further and losing more people until all that remained was a small group backed against the cabinet.

"Bring up the reserves!" Nutcracker ordered.

"Pantaloon, Scaramouche, Drummer, where are you?" He was hoping for fresh troops from the glass-fronted cabinet.

Some brown men and women with golden faces, hats, and helmets appeared, but they were so awkward with their swords that they were no help at all. The only thing they managed to knock down was General Nutcracker's hat. The enemy chasseurs had soon bitten off their legs, and when they fell they crushed and killed several more of the Nutcracker's men.

The enemy drew closer still, and there was no escape. Nutcracker would have jumped up to the cabinet's ledge, but his legs were too short. Madame Clarette and Madame Trudie could not help him, for they both laid in a faint. Hussars and dragoons sprang past him into the cabinet. In desperation he called out, "a horse! A horse! My kingdom for a horse!"

But that that moment, two enemy marksmen took hold of Nutcracker's wooden cloak and held him fast. Squeaking in triumph from seven throats, the Mouse King sprang forward to take his kill.

Marie could no longer keep what little composure she had, and without really knowing why she removed her left shoe and threw it as hard as she could into the thickest patch of mice she could see – right at their king. At that moment, everything faded from Marie's vision. She felt a stabbing pain in her arm, and fell fainting to the floor.

Chapter Six: The Illness

M arie awoke from a deathlike sleep to find herself in her own bed. The sun was shining through the window, making the frost on the panes sparkle and shimmer.

Sitting nearby was a stranger – no, Dr. Wendelstern, the surgeon. "She's awake now," he said in a soft voice.

Her mother came over and looked at Marie with frightened, searching eyes.

"Oh Mama, dear, are all the mice gone? Is good Nutcracker safe?"

"Don't talk about nonsense like that, Marie. What do mice have to do with the Nutcracker? You've been a very naughty child and worried us very much. That's what happens when a child is willful and doesn't do as her parents tell her. You played with your dolls until you became sleepy, and it may be that a mouse – which I find unlikely – jumped out and frightened you, and you fell back and pushed your arm through the glass. Dr. Wendelstern, who removed the glass from your arm, says if you'd cut an artery you might have been left with a stiff arm – or bled to death. Thank God I woke up after midnight and noticed you weren't in your bed. I went into the living room and found you passed out in front of the toy cabinet, bleeding heavily. I almost fainted from shock myself, and then I saw Fritz's soldiers, a lot of other dolls, and broken banners, gingerbread men, and not far away, your left shoe."

"Oh, Mama, Mama!" Marie interrupted, "don't you see – that's what was left of the battle between the dolls and the mice. The mice wanted to take the Nutcracker and I got scared, so I threw my shoe at them – and after that, I don't know what happened."

Dr. Wendelstern glanced at Mrs. Stahlbaum, then said to Marie very gently: "There's no need to worry, my dear child. The mice are all gone and Nutcracker is safe in the toy cabinet."

Then the physician (that is, Marie's father) came in and spoke with Dr. Wendelstern for a considerable length of time. He took Marie's pulse, and she heard mention of wound fever. She had to stay in bed and take some medicine for a few days; though aside from the pain in her arm she didn't really feel ill or uncomfortable.

She now knew that Nutcracker had escaped the battle safe and sound. Occasionally, she would hear as if in a dream the Nutcracker's voice, distinct yet weak. "Marie, dear lady, I already owe you so much, but there is more you could do for me!"

Marie tried to think of what it could possibly be, but she could think of nothing.

She could not play with her toys because of the pain in her arm, and the illustrations in the picture books swam before her eyes until she had to give up on them. And so time seemed to draw on forever. She could hardly wait for evening, because then her mother would come and read her all sorts of beautiful stories.

One evening, her mother had just finished the story of Prince Fakardin when the door opened and Godfather Drosselmeier stepped into the room. "Now I must see for myself how the sick and injured Marie is doing," he said.

As soon as Marie saw his yellow coat, the image of the Nutcracker losing the battle against the mice came back into her mind. Automatically she said: "Oh, Godfather Drosselmeier, you were so ugly! I saw you up there on the clock, covering it with your wings so it couldn't strike and scare away the mice. I even heard you call the Mouse King! Why didn't you help the Nutcracker or me, you ugly Godfather Drosselmeier? It's your fault that I'm hurt and sick and stuck in bed, isn't it?"

Marie's mother, shocked, asked, "what is wrong with you, Marie?"

However, Godfather Drosselmeier made an odd face and said in a rasping, monotonous voice:

The pendulum had to purr and pick
It could not strike, nor could it tick
But now the bells sound loud and strong
Dong and ding, ding and dong
Doll girl, don't be afraid
The king of mice has gone away
The owl returns now swift and quick
Pick and peck, peck and pick
Bells ring, dong and ding
Clocks whirr, purr and purr
Pendulums must also purr
Clink and clank, whirr and purr

Marie stared wide-eyed at Godfather Drosselmeier. The judge looked somehow uglier than usual, and his right arm was moving back and forth as if he were manipulating a marionette. Marie would have been very frightened had it not been for her mother's presence, and for the fact that Fritz (who had quietly crept in) suddenly burst out in loud laughter.

"Oh, Godfather Drosselmeier, you're too funny today," Fritz said. "You're just like the jumping jack I threw behind the stove awhile back."

But their mother had a serious expression on her face and said, "Dear Mr. Drosselmeier, what odd entertainment. What is it all about?"

"Heavens!" the judge responded with laughter. "Don't you know about my watchmaker's ditty? I always sing it to patients like Marie." He quickly sat close beside Marie's bed and said, "Don't be angry at me for not putting out all fourteen of the Mouse King's eyes, but I've got something for you that I think will make you really happy." With those words, he reached into his pocket and swiftly pulled out the Nutcracker. His missing teeth had all been set firmly back in and his wobbly jaw was set straight again.

Marie shouted with joy, and her mother said, "See how well Godfather Drosselmeier thinks of Nutcracker?"

"You still have to admit, Marie," Drosselmeier interrupted, "he's quite ugly. I'll tell you how such ugliness came into his family, if you want to listen. Or maybe you already know the story of Princess Pirlipat, the witch Mouserinks, and the clockmaker?"

"Wait a minute," Fritz said suddenly, "you've fixed the Nutcracker's teeth and jaw, but he's got no sword – why's he missing a sword?"

"Oh!" Drosselmeier responded indignantly, "you have to complain about everything, boy! Why should I find him a sword? I've fixed his body; it's up to him to get a sword if he wants one."

"That's true," Fritz said. "If he's any good, he'll know where to find his weapons."

The judge turned again to Marie. "So, Marie, do tell me – do you know the story of Princess Pirlipat?"

"Oh, no," Marie said. "Do tell, dear godfather – do tell!"

"I hope, dear Mr. Drosselmeier, that your story won't be as horrible as the ones you usually tell," her mother said.

"Not at all, dear lady," Drosselmeier replied. "On the contrary, the story which I have the honor of telling is a fairytale."

"Tell us the story, dear godfather!" the children begged, and so he began.

Chapter Seven: Tale of the Hard Nut

Pirlipat's mother was the wife of the king and therefore the queen, and that made Pirlipat a princess from the very moment she was born. The king was beside himself with joy at the sight of his beautiful little daughter. He whooped and hollered and swiveled around on one leg and cried out again and again: "Oh, joyous day! Have you ever seen anything more beautiful than my Pirlipat?" And the ministers, generals, and staff likewise spun on one leg and cried, "No! Never!"

Anyone who had seen the little princess could not deny that she was probably the most beautiful little girl in the whole world. Her face was like the finest lily-white and rose-red silk ever woven, her lively little eyes were like two sparkling azure stones, and her curly hair was like threads of pure gold. In addition, Princess Pirlipat had come into the world with two rows of pearly-white teeth, which she used for the very first time when she bit the finger of the chancellor who tried to get a better look at her face. The chancellor cried out "oh, jiminy!" Or maybe it was "that hurt!" Opinions to this day are divided on the matter.

But Pirlipat had most certainly bitten the chancellor's finger, and the delighted kingdom knew at once that their princess was spirited, sharp, and clever.

All were cheerful and merry – all except the queen, who looked anxious and fearful for reasons no-one knew. In addition to the two guards standing outside the door of the princess's room, the queen had ordered that six female attendants sit closely around her cradle every night. What seemed completely mad and utterly incomprehensible to everyone, however, was that each attendant had to hold a tomcat on her lap and stroke him so that he never stopped purring.

It's impossible for you dear children to guess why Pirlipat's mother gave these orders, but I know, and I shall tell you.

It had happened some time ago in the royal court that many splendid kings and excellent princes were gathered. It was a marvelous affair – there were jousts, comedies, and dancing. In order to show that he wasn't at all lacking in gold or silver, the king took a sizable sum out of the royal treasury to do something really spectacular.

Having heard from the head chef that the court astronomer had privily told him that now was the proper time for slaughtering the livestock, the king ordered the preparation of a lavish sausage feast. Then he threw himself into his carriage and invited all of the kings and princes to have a "spoonful of soup" so he could enjoy their surprise when they saw what he really had planned for them.

Then he approached his queen and said very kindly, "you do know, sweetie, how I like sausages."

The queen knew what he meant – that she, as she had done in times past, should take up the useful job of sausage-making. The chief treasurer immediately had the golden sausage boiler and silver casserole dishes sent to the kitchen, a roaring fire of sandalwood was set ablaze, and the queen put on her damask apron. It wasn't long before the delicious smell of sausage soup wafted out of the boiler and into the council of state.

The king was seized with such delight that he could not contain himself. "Pardon me, gentlemen!" he shouted, and leapt away to the kitchen where he hugged the queen and stirred the soup with his golden scepter. Feeling much better, he returned to the council.

The crucial moment had come in which the fat had to be cut into cubes and roasted on silver grills. The ladies-in-waiting left the kitchen because the queen wished to perform this task alone out of love and devotion to her royal spouse.

As soon as the fat began to sizzle, a tiny little voice called out: "Give me some of that fat, sister! I'm also a queen, and I deserve to feast, too! Give me some fat!"

The queen knew that it was Lady Mouserinks. Lady Mouserinks had lived for years in the palace and claimed to be related to the royal family and even queen of of a realm called Mouseland. She also claimed to have a large court under the stove.

The queen was a good and charitable woman, so although she didn't recognize Mouserinks as a queen or a sister she was willing to let her enjoy the feast as well. "Come out and you may have some of my fat," she said.

Lady Mouserinks jumped out, hopped up to the stove, and grabbed piece after piece of fat from the queen in her delicate little paws. But then came her cousins, aunts, uncles, and her seven sons, and the latter were such unruly brats that they ran all over the fat and the terrified queen could do nothing to stop them. Fortunately, the head lady-in-waiting came in and chased away the unwanted guests before all of the fat could be gobbled up. The court mathematician was called in, and he calculated how best to distribute what was left of the fat among the sausages.

Trumpets and drums sounded. The kings and princes arrived – some on white horses, some in crystal coaches, and all in their best clothes. The king greeted them cordially, then sat down at the end of the table in kingly dignity with his crown on his head and his scepter in his hand.

During the liver sausage course, the king gradually grew paler and he raised his eyes toward the heavens. A sigh escaped his chest, as if some enormous pain was digging at his insides.

During the blood sausage course, he fell back into his chair sobbing and moaning, with both hands over his face. Hearing the king's wailing and howling, everyone jumped up from the table. The court physician tried in vain to take the unfortunate king's pulse. A deep, nameless misery seemed to be tearing him up.

Finally, after much persuasion and attempts to use the strongest remedies available (feather quills and such), the king stammered in a barely audible voice, "too little fat."

The queen threw herself at his feet in despair and cried, "oh, my poor unfortunate royal husband – oh, what pain you've had to endure – you see the guilty one here at your feet. Punish – punish her hard – Lady Mouserinks and her cousins and uncles and aunts and seven sons have eaten the fat..."

With that, the queen fell back in a faint.

The king jumped up and demanded, "Chief lady-in-waiting, how did this happen?"

The chief lady-in-waiting told him all she knew, and the king decided to take revenge on the Lady Mouserinks and her family. The privy council was summoned, and it was decided that Lady Mouserinks would stand trial and all her property would be confiscated. But the king was worried that Lady Mouserinks and her family would go on eating his fat in the meantime, so the task of solving the problem was given over to the clockmaker and wizard.

The clockmaker, whose name is the same as mine – Christian Elias Drosselmeier – promised to rid the palace of Lady Mouserinks and her family forever. He created many small and very intricate little machines into which a piece of fat was placed and set near the home of Lady Mouserinks.

Lady Mouserinks was too clever to fall for it herself, but despite her warnings all of her cousins, aunts, uncles, and even her seven sons went after the fat. Just as their greedy little paws reached for the fat, a grate slammed shut trapping the lot of them. Then they were promptly taken to the kitchen and executed in disgrace.

Fearing for her life, Lady Mouserinks left the castle with what family she had left. Grief, despair, and rage filled her chest.

All of the royal court cheered – all except the queen, who was worried. She knew what sort of woman Lady Mouserinks was, and that she would not let the deaths of her sons and other family members go unavenged. Indeed, Lady Mouserinks appeared one day when the queen was preparing another one of the king's favorite dishes and said, "My family is dead – take care, my queen, that the Mouse Queen does not bite your little princess to pieces! Take care!"

Then Lady Mouserinks disappeared from sight. The queen was so startled that she dropped the food she was preparing into the fire. For the second time Lady Mouserinks had spoiled one of the king's favorite dishes, which made him very angry.

Well, that's enough for tonight – I'll tell the rest later."

As much as Marie, who had her own thoughts about the story, asked her godfather to tell the rest of it, he refused. He jumped up saying, "too much at once is unhealthy. I'll finish it tomorrow."

Just as the judge was about to leave through the door, Fritz asked, "but tell me, Godfather Drosselmeier – is it really true that you invented the mousetrap?"

"How can you ask such a silly question?" their mother asked him.

But the judge smiled strangely and said quietly to Fritz, "am I not a clever enough clockmaker that I could invent a mousetrap?"

Chapter Eight: Continuation of the Tale of the Hard Nut

"Now you well know," the judge told the children the next evening, "why the queen was keeping their beautiful princess so carefully guarded. How could she help but worry that Lady Mouserinks would return and make good on her threat to bite the princess to death? Drosselmeier's contraptions were of no use against the clever and shrewd Lady Mouserinks, and the court astronomer, who was also the royal family's private astrologer, had said that Mr. Purr and his family would be able to keep Lady Mouserinks away from the cradle. Therefore it happened that every attendant was ordered to hold a tomcat on her lap and stroke his back to make his job a little less tedious.

One night at midnight, one of the attendants woke from a deep sleep. The room was as silent as death; there was not a purr to be heard. One could have heard the woodworms nibbling at the timbers.

Then she saw a large, ugly mouse standing on its hind feet near the princess's face. With a frightened cry that woke everyone else, the attendant jumped to her feet. Lady Mouserinks (for it was none other) ran into a corner. The cats ran after her, but they were too late – she disappeared into a crack in the floor. Just then, Pirlipat woke up from the noise and began crying pitifully.

"Thank Heavens, she's alive!" they said.

But what horror awaited them! Instead of an angelic little face and a perfect little body, a hideous and huge head was attached to a shrunken and shriveled body. Her sparkling little azure eyes had become staring green eyes that almost looked as if they'd pop out of her head, and her sweet little mouth now stretched from ear to ear.

The queen shut herself away in mourning, and the walls of the king's study had to be padded because he would very often bang his head against the walls and cry most pitifully, "Oh, what an unhappy monarch am I!"

One might think that he might have realized that it may have been better to go on eating his sausages without fat and leave Lady Mouserinks and her family in peace under the stove, but he didn't. Instead, he put all the blame on the court clockmaker and wizard, Christian Elias Drosselmeier of Nuremberg, and issued him an order: restore the princess to her former self within four weeks or find a cure that was certain to work, or suffer the disgraceful death of beheading.

Drosselmeier was in no small state of terror, but he trusted in his craft and in luck and set to the first thing that seemed useful to him. He carefully took the little princess apart without harming her and examined her internal structure, but all he could discover was that the larger the princess grew, the worse her condition would become. He put the princess back together again and sat down by her cradle in despair, which he was not allowed to leave.

·PRINSES· PIRLIPAT·

It was into the fourth week – Wednesday, in fact – when the king looked at Drosselmeier with eyes flashing in rage and cried, "Christian Elias Drosselmeier, cure the princess – or die!"

Drosselmeier began to cry bitterly, but Princess Pirlipat happily cracked nuts. For the first time, Drosselmeier took note of the princess's unusual appetite for nuts, which she cracked with the very teeth she had been born with. In fact, the princess had cried for hours after her transformation until a nut chanced to roll by. She promptly snatched it up, cracked it open, ate the core, and immediately quieted down. Since then, all attendants were advised to bring nuts whenever they came in.

"Oh, holy and unfathomable instinct of nature, present in all things!" Christian Elias Drosselmeier cried, "you now show me the door to the answer to this mystery; I will knock, and it will open!"

He immediately requested to speak with the court astronomer, and was lead by guards to him. Both men tearfully embraced each other, for they were close friends. Then they went together into a secret room where they consulted many books concerning instincts, sympathies, antipathies, and other such mysteries.

When night fell, the astronomer looked to the stars, and with the help of Drosselmeier (who was also quite familiar with astrology) took the princess's horoscope. It was no easy task, for the lines of the stars were so crossed and tangled. But at last, it became clear that in order to break the curse and restore the princess's beauty, all she would have to do is eat the sweet core of the nut Crackatook.

Now, the nut Crackatook had such a hard shell that you could run the wheel of a cannon over it without breaking it. This nut had to be given to a young man who had neither yet shaven nor worn boots, and he would have to bite it open before the princess and give the core to her with his eyes closed. What's more, he could not open his eyes until he had taken seven steps backward without tripping or stumbling.

Drosselmeier and the astronomer worked for three days and three nights. That Saturday, the king had sat down for his midday meal when Drosselmeier (who was scheduled to be executed the following Sunday) joyously rushed into the room and announced that he had found the means to restore the princess's lost beauty. The king gave Drosselmeier a fierce bear hug and promised him a diamond sword, four medals, and two new Sunday suits.

"After lunch, I expect you'll get to work on this," the king added amiably. "And I trust, excellent wizard, that you'll make sure that this young man with the nut Crackatook in hand hasn't had any wine to drink so he doesn't trip when he goes walking seven steps backward like a crab. Afterward, he can drink all he wants."

Drosselmeier was dismayed at this and with trembling and fear informed the king that they neither begun to search for the nut or the boy to crack it, and it was uncertain whether nut or nutcracker would ever be found.

The king waved his scepter high above his head in a rage and roared, "then the beheading shall proceed as scheduled!"

Fortunately for Drosselmeier, the food had tasted particularly good that day and the king was in a better mood than usual. This made him more open when the queen, who was touched by Drosselmeier's distress, asked that he reconsider. Drosselmeier gathered his courage and explained that he had indeed found out how to cure the princess, and had therefore rightfully won his life back. The king decided that Drosselmeier was stalling with silly excuses, but after taking a tonic for his stomach he announced that both the clockmaker and astronomer should set off on foot and not return until they had the nut Crackatook in their possession. The queen suggested that they could find the man to do the cracking by regularly placing advertisements in local and foreign newspapers.

And here the judge broke off again, and promised to tell the rest of the story the next evening.

NEURENBERG

Chapter Nine: The End of The Tale of The Hard Nut

On the third evening, the lights had barely been lit in the Stahlbaum house when the judge returned to finish his story:

Drosselmeier and the astronomer searched for fifteen years without coming across the nut Crackatook. I could spent four weeks telling you children all about the places they went and the strange things they saw, but I'll just say that Drosselmeier, in his deep sorrow and disappointment, began to feel a longing for his beloved home city of Nuremberg. A particularly nasty attack hit him when he was smoking his pipe with his friend the astronomer in the middle of some great forest in Asia. And suddenly he cried:

"Oh, beautiful beautiful Nuremberg, my beautiful hometown Nuremberg, whom I have not seen for so long, though I've traveled to London, Paris, and Petrovaradin, they cannot fill my heart and I must always ask of you. Oh, beautiful city of Nuremberg, with your lovely houses and their windows!"

Drosselmeier's cries were so sorrowful that the astronomer felt deep compassion for him, and he began to cry and wail as well. In fact, his cries were so loud that they could be heard through a sizable portion of Asia.

Then he wiped his eyes and said, "Esteemed colleague, instead of sitting here pining away over Nuremberg, why don't we go to Nuremberg? After all, it doesn't matter where we search for that accursed nut."

"True," Drosselmeier said. He brightened up a little. They both knocked the ashes out of their pipes and straightaway headed from the middle of Asia to Nuremberg. No sooner than they had arrived, Drosselmeier went to see his cousin, the dollmaker, painter, and gilder Christoph Zecharias Drosselmeier, whom he had not seen in many years. The clockmaker told him all about Princess Pirlipat, the Lady Mouserinks, and the nut Crackatook. The dollmaker clapped his hands in amazement and said, "what a marvelous story!"

Drosselmeier further related his adventures, of how he had spent two years with the King of Dates, how the Prince of Almonds had disdainfully rejected him, how his search at the Society of Natural Science in Squirrelton had yielded nothing, and how he had failed everywhere to find even a trace of the nut Crackatook.

Through the story, Christoff Zecharias frequently snapped his fingers and turned around on one foot. Finally he exclaimed, "well, that'd be the devil, wouldn't it!" and threw his hat and wig into the air. He gave the clockmaker a hug and said, "Cousin – cousin, all your troubles are over because unless all the world has conspired to deceive me, I own the nut Crackatook!"

He immediately brought out a box from which a pulled a gilded nut of moderate size. "Behold," he said. "Many years ago, a nut seller with a bag of nuts came into town around Christmastime. He got

into a fight with a local nut seller who didn't think he had any right selling nuts here right outside my shop and had to set his bag down. Then a heavily-loaded cart drove over it and broke all of the nuts except one. The stranger offered it to me, with the oddest smile, for a twenty from 1720. Strangely enough, that's just the coin I found when I checked my pocket. So I bought it and gilded it without really knowing why I paid so much for it or why I'd wanted it so badly."

Any doubt that the nut wasn't really Crackatook was soon lifted when the astronomer scraped off the gold gilding and found the word "Crackatook" engraved in Chinese characters. The joy of the travelers was immense and his cousin was the happiest man under the sun when Drosselmeier told him that his fortune was made, for he would soon receive a handsome pension and plenty of gold for gilding.

Both wizard and astronomer had just put on their nightcaps and were ready to go to bed when the latter said, "My esteemed colleague, good fortune never comes but in packs – not only have we found the nut Crackatook, but also the young man to break it and present the princess with the core of beauty! No, I cannot sleep now," he said excitedly, "I must draw up this young man's horoscope this very night!" With that, he tore off his nightcap and began at once to observe the stars.

Christoph Zechariah's son was a handsome boy who had never shaved and had never worn boots. In his early childhood he had been a jumping-jack for a few Christmases, but there was no trace of that now as his father had taught him how to be a proper gentleman. During the Christmas season (which was now) he wore a red coat trimmed in gold, a sword, a hat carried under his arm, and an excellent wig. Thus he stood splendidly in his father's shop and gallantly cracked nuts for young girls – and for this reason they had nicknamed him "Nutcracker."

The next morning the astronomer gave the wizard a hug and said, "here he is! We have him! Now, there are two things we must not ignore. First, you must make your splendid nephew a sturdy wooden tail that attaches under the jawbone so that his jaw can be firmly shut therewith, and then we must not reveal that we have the young man who will crack the nut when we arrive at the palace, but instead he must wait for some time to reveal himself for I have read in the horoscope that after a few young men have broken their teeth on Crackatook, the king will promise the kingdom and the hand of the princess in marriage to whoever can crack the nut open and restore the princess's beauty."

The dollmaker was pleased to have his son marry the princess and become prince and later king, so he gave him up to the travelers. The little wooden tail Drosselmeier attached to his hopeful young nephew's head worked so well that he was able to crack the hardest of peach pits.

Drosselmeier and the astronomer reported to the palace that they had found the nut Crackatook, and the palace immediately issued requests for young men who might break the nut. Many arrived to try their own sturdy teeth on the nut and restore the princess, including a few princes.

Our two travelers were considerably startled when they saw the princess. Her shriveled body with its tiny hands and feet could hardly carry her enormous head. The ugliness of her face was enhanced by a cotton-white beard that had sprouted around her mouth and on her chin.

Everything happened exactly as the astronomer predicted: young men with shoes on their feet and peach fuzz on their faces bit down on the nut Crackatook and only got a few broken teeth and a sore jaw for their troubles without helping the princess in the slightest. Every young man who had injured himself thus would be carried away half-fainting by specially-appointed dentists. Many could be heard sighing, "that was a hard nut!"

The king, now fearing that his daughter might never be restored, promised the kingdom and the princess to whomever could crack the nut. At that moment young Drosselmeier stepped out and asked if he could try to crack the nut.

None of the other young men had caught the princess's eye the way young Drosselmeier had. She put her little hands over her heart and sighed, "oh, let it be this one who breaks the nut and becomes my husband!"

After paying his respects to the king, queen, and princess (the latter especially politely), he took the nut from the Grand Master of Ceremonies. He put it in his mouth and tugged at the tail Drosselmeier had made for him, and – crack crack! – the shell broke into many pieces.

The young man removed the fibers from the core of the nut, closed his eyes, gave it to the princess, and began his seven steps backward. The princess swallowed the core and – oh, wonders! – an angelically beautiful young lady stood before them with a face of lily white and rose red, eyes like azure, and hair like curled strands of gold. Trumpets and drums mingled with the cheers of the people. The king and his court danced on one leg as they had the day of the princess's birth, and the queen had to be revived with strong-smelling perfumes because she had fainted from happiness.

The commotion did not at all ruffle young Drosselmeier, who was just taking his seventh and last step. But then who should pop out of a crack in the floor but Lady Mouserinks, ugly, squeaking, and squealing – and right under the young man's heel. This caused him to stumble so that he almost fell. Oh, calamity! The boy was instantly as hideous as Princess Pirlipat had been a few moments ago. His shriveled body could hardly hold up his ugly head with its protruding green eyes and hideously wide smile. Instead of the little tail the clockmaker had made for him, a small wooden cloak hung from his shoulders that controlled his jaw. The clockmaker and astronomer were beside themselves with horror.

Then they saw Lady Mouserinks roll onto the floor. Her malice had not gone unavenged, for the pointed heel of young Drosselmeier's shoe had hit her sharply and fatally in the neck. The fear of death had seized her, for she squeaked and squealed piteously:

"Oh, Crackatook, hard nut, now I must die

Hee hee, pee pee
Nutcracker, young man, you too will die
My seven-crowned son will avenge my death
And take from you your living breath
Oh life, so vibrant and red, I – squeak!

With that, the mouse queen died and was promptly carried to the royal furnace for disposal.

In the heat of the moment everyone had forgotten the young Drosselmeier, but the princess reminded the king of his promise and he immediately ordered that the young man be brought before them. But upon seeing how hideous the unfortunate boy had become, the princess held her hands over her face and cried, "take him away! Take that horrible nutcracker away!"

The chamberlain seized him by the shoulders and threw him out the door. The king was furious that someone had tried to give him a nutcracker for a son-in-law and blamed everything on the clockmaker and astronomer, whom he banished forever. None of these developments had been in the horoscope taken at Nuremberg, but the astronomer was not deterred from reading the stars again, which now revealed that young Drosselmeier would become a prince and a king despite his ugliness. Furthermore, he could lift the curse put upon him if he could defeat the seven-headed mouse born to Lady Mouserinks after the death her seven sons and find a lady who would love him despite his looks. You may have seen young Drosselmeier in his father's shop in Nuremberg around Christmastime, and now you know that he is not just a nutcracker, but also a prince. And now you know the tale of the hard nut, why people say 'that was a hard nut to crack!', and how the nutcracker became so ugly."

Thus the judge ended his story. Marie thought that Princess Pirlipat was a cruel, ungrateful brat, and Fritz said that if the Nutcracker was worth anything he'd quickly defeat the Mouse King and get restored to his former self again.

Chapter Ten: Uncle and Nephew

I f any of my dear readers have ever cut themselves on glass, then they know how badly it hurts and how dreadfully slowly it heals. Marie had to spend almost a whole week in bed because she became dizzy whenever she tried to get up. But at last she recovered and could run and play as merrily as before.

The glass cabinet had been repaired as good as new and was again filled with trees, flowers, houses, and beautiful dolls. Marie was thrilled to see her beloved Nutcracker standing on the second shelf smiling with all of his teeth intact.

As she looked at her favorite toy, she remembered the story Drosselmeier had told of the history of the Nutcracker and his quarrel with Lady Mouserinks and her son. She realized that her Nutcracker could be none other than the pleasant – but unfortunately cursed – young Drosselmeier from Nuremberg. The clockmaker from the court of Pirlipat's father could be none other than Judge Drosselmeier, which Marie had never once doubted. "But why... why didn't your uncle help you?"

It became clear to Marie that the battle she had seen was in fact a battle for the Nutcracker's kingdom and crown. Were not the dolls his subjects, and had he not fulfilled the astronomer's prediction by becoming their leader? As the clever Marie pondered over this, the more she thought of the Nutcracker and the dolls as living people, and she half-expected them to start moving about. But they remained stiff and motionless in the cabinet. But Marie, certain beyond any doubt that they really were alive, decided it was because of Lady Mouserinks's curse.

"But," she said to Nutcracker, "even if you can't move or speak, dear Mr. Drosselmeier, I know that you can understand me – I know it very well. You can count on me to help you, if you need it. At the very least I'll ask your uncle if he can help."

Nutcracker didn't move or stir, but Marie thought she heard a faint sigh and a gentle voice through the cabinet, just barely audible:

Little Marie,
Guardian sweet,
I'm yours to keep
Little Marie

A shiver ran down Marie's spine, but she was comforted nonetheless.

Dusk fell, and her father stepped into the room with Godfather Drosselmeier. Before long Louise had arranged the tea table and the family sat down and had a merry conversation. Marie quietly moved her little easy chair near Drosselmeier's feet and sat down. When everyone had quieted down she looked up at the judge with her big blue eyes and said, "Godfather Drosselmeier, I realize that the Nutcracker is your nephew, the young Drosselmeier from Nuremberg, and that he has become prince – no, king – as the astronomer had predicted, but you already know this – and that he is at battle with the son of Lady Mouserinks. Why don't you help him?" Marie once again told everyone about the battle and how it went. Everyone except for Fritz and Drosselmeier began laughing.

"Where does the girl get such ridiculous ideas into her head?" Dr. Stahlbaum asked.

"She's always had a vivid imagination," her mother said. "These are just dreams brought about by her fever."

"It's not true, any of it," Fritz said. "My hussars aren't such cowards. If they were, I'd personally discipline them."

But Godfather Drosselmeier put Marie on his lap and with an odd smile said very quietly, "Dear Marie, you were born a princess like Pirlipat, for you rule a bright and beautiful land. But you will have to suffer much if you are to look after Nutcracker, for the Mouse King will pursue him in every land and across any border. I cannot help him – only you can do that. Be faithful and strong."

Neither Marie nor anyone else knew what to say after that. The doctor took Drosselmeier's pulse and said, "You have, my esteemed friend, a severe head cold. I'll write you out a prescription."

But Mrs. Stahlbaum shook her head slowly and said quietly, "I think I know what he's saying, but I can't quite explain it." ,

Chapter Eleventh: The Victory

It wasn't long after that incident that Marie was wakened one moonlit night by a strange rumbling that seemed to come from the corner of the room. It was as if small stones were being thrown about with squeaks and squeals mixed in.

"The mice – the mice have come back!" Marie cried in surprise. She wanted to wake her mother, but found herself unable to make a sound or move a muscle. She could only watch as the Mouse King squeezed himself out through a hole in the wall. His fourteen eyes and seven crowns glistened as he bounded through the room and made a huge leap up to the top of Marie's nightstand.

"Hee hee hee, I must have your sugar balls and marzipan, or I will bite your Nutcracker through!" he squeaked, and gnashed his teeth hideously. Then he jumped off the table and disappeared through the hole in the wall.

Marie was so frightened by his horrific appearance that the next morning she was very pale and could barely say a word. A hundred times she wanted to tell her mother, Louise, or at least Fritz what had happened, but she thought, "will they believe me, or will they laugh at me?"

But one thing was certain, and that was that she would have to give up her sugar balls and marzipan. She put each and every piece in front of the toy cabinet that night. The next morning her mother said, "I don't know how all these mice got into our living room – look, Marie! They've eaten all your candy!"

Indeed they had. The marzipan wasn't to the Mouse King's taste, but he nibbled it with his sharp teeth so that it had to be thrown out.

Marie wasn't concerned with the candy, however. She was quite happy inside for she believed that Nutcracker was safe.

But that night she heard a dreadful squeaking and squealing right by her ear. The Mouse King was there again and looked even more horrible than before. His eyes gleamed and he hissed more threateningly from between his gnashing teeth, "I must have more. Give me your sugar dolls, or I'll bite your Nutcracker through!"

And he jumped away again.

Marie was very sad. The next morning she went to the cabinet and looked mournfully at her sugar dolls. Her pain was not unreasonable – her sugar dolls were beautifully shaped and molded into figures even you might find difficult to believe. A shepherd and shepherdess looked after grazing flocks of milky-white lambs while their merry little dog scampered about, two mailmen walked with letters in their hand, and four handsome couples – men in dapper suits and women in beautiful dresses – rocked in a Russian swing. Behind that there were dancers, then Pachter Feldkümmel and Joan of Arc, whom Marie didn't particularly care about. But in the corner stood a red-cheeked child, Marie's favorite. Tears welled from her eyes. "Oh!" she exclaimed, turning to the Nutcracker, "Dear Mr. Drosselmeier, I'll do everything I can to save you, but it's very hard!"

She looked at the Nutcracker, who looked so helpless that she couldn't help but imagine the Mouse King with all seven mouths open to devour the unfortunate young man. At that, she was ready to sacrifice everything. She took all of her sugar dolls and set them by the base of the cabinet as she had with the sugar balls and marzipan the night before. She kissed the shepherd, the shepherdess, the lambs, and her favorite, the red-cheeked child, which she put in the very back. Pachter Feldkümmel and Joan of Arc were put in front.

"Now that's too bad," Marie's mother said the next morning. "A very big and nasty mouse must live in the toy cabinet, because poor Marie's sugar dolls are all gnawed and chewed up."

Marie could not keep herself from crying, but she soon smiled again when she thought to herself, "what does it matter? Nutcracker is safe."

That evening, after Marie's mother told the judge about the damage caused by the mouse in the cabinet, Dr. Stahlbaum said, "it's a shame we can't exterminate that infernal mouse that's destroying Marie's candy."

"Hey," Fritz interrupted enthusiastically, "the baker downstairs has got a big gray cat I'd like to bring up. He'll take care of things and bite off that mouse's head, even if it's Lady Mouserinks or the Mouse King himself!"

Their mother laughed. "And jump around on tables and couches, knock down the glasses and cups, and cause a thousand other damages."

"Oh, no, he wouldn't," Fritz protested. "He's a clever cat. I wish I could walk as gracefully on the roof as he does."

"Please, no tomcats tonight," said Louise, who could not tolerate cats.

"Actually, Fritz has a point," Dr. Stahlbaum said. "But could we set up a trap? Or do we have none?"

"Godfather Drosselmeier can make one. He invented them," Fritz said.

Everyone laughed, and after Mrs. Stahlbaum informed everyone that there were no mousetraps in the house the judge announced that he had several, and within an hour he had gone to his home and brought back a splendid mousetrap.

The tale of the hard nut was very much alive inside Fritz and Marie's heads. When Marie saw Dora the cook (whom she knew quite well) browning the fat, all of the stories came rushing back to her head. She began to tremble and she blurted "oh my queen, beware of Mouserinks and her family!"

At that, Fritz drew his sword and said, "if any of them showed up here, I'd take them out!"

Later, as Fritz watched Drosselmeier bait the mousetrap and set it into the cabinet, he said, "careful, Godfather Drosselmeier, that the Mouse King doesn't play some trick on you."

That night, Marie felt something like ice-cold feet crawling up her arm and something rough and disgusting brush against her cheek. There was a horrible squealing in her ear – the Mouse King sat on her shoulder. He drooled blood-red, gnashed his teeth even more ferociously than before, and hissed into Marie's ear:

Don't go to the house

Don't go to the feast
Can't let yourself get caught
Like a wretched little beast
Give me all your picture books
Give me your Christmas dress
Or I'll nibble Nutcracker all to bits
And you'll never have any peace
Squeak!

Marie was miserable and visibly distressed. She was haggard and pale, and when her mother – who though that Marie was still upset over her candy and terrified of the mouse – noticed this she said, "I'm afraid that nasty mouse hasn't been caught yet." Then she added, "but we'll get it, don't worry. If the trap doesn't work, we'll have Fritz bring up the baker's cat."

As soon as Marie was alone in the living room, she stood in front of the glass cabinet and sobbing, said, "oh, Mr. Drosselmeier, what more can an unfortunate girl like me do for you? The Mouse King wants my picture books and the dress the Christ Child gave me – and when he's bitten through those he'll just demand more. I'm afraid when I run out of things to give him he'll want to bite me up instead. What am I supposed to do now?"

As Marie complained to the Nutcracker, she noticed a large spot of blood on his neck.

Since learning that the Nutcracker was really Drosselmeier's nephew, she no longer carried him about in her arm nor kissed him as she had before, and in fact she found herself becoming quite shy in front of him. However, she removed him from the toy cabinet and wiped away the blood with her handkerchief. Suddenly, she felt him growing warm in her hand – and even moving. She quickly set him back down, and he spoke with apparent difficulty, "my dear Miss Stahlbaum, to whom I owe everything, do not sacrifice your picture books or your Christmas dress for me. I just need a sword – if I had a sword, I could-"

And suddenly he stopped, and his melancholic eyes became still and lifeless once more.

Marie was no longer frightened or worried. In fact, she jumped with joy because she now knew how to save the Nutcracker without sacrificing any more of her treasured possessions. But where to find a sword? She decided to ask Fritz, and that evening after their parents had departed from the living room, told him the complete story of what had happened in front of the toy cabinet that fateful night, and what she had to do to save Nutcracker now.

Fritz had never thought over anything as hard than what he should do with his hussars after he heard from Marie how badly they'd performed in battle. He asked her very seriously whether it was really true, and after Marie assured him that it was he hurried to the glass-fronted cabinet and gave them a stern speech. Then he cut the insignias off their caps and forbade them from playing the Hussar's March for a year. Then he turned to Marie and said, "I can help Nutcracker with a sword. I just retired an old colonel of the cuirassiers with a pension yesterday, and he's got a bright and shiny sword he won't be needing anymore."

The aforementioned colonel was making use of his pension in the back corner of the third shelf. Fritz brought him out, removed his silver sword, and hung it from the Nutcracker's belt.

That night, Marie was so anxious she was unable to sleep. She could hear clattering and banging coming from the living room, and suddenly, "squeak!"

"The Mouse King – the Mouse King!" Marie cried, and jumped out of her bed in fright. For awhile it was completely quiet, then there was a knock at the door and a small voice said, "Excellent Mistress Stahlbaum, be of glad heart – for I have good news!"

Marie recognized the voice of young Mr. Drosselmeier. She threw on her dressing gown and opened quickly opened the door.

Nutcracker stood outside the door with a bloody sword in one hand and a candle in the other. He knelt down on one knee and said, "you, and you alone, my lady, have given me the courage of a knight to fight the insolent scoundrel who dared treat you so disrespectfully. The treacherous Mouse King now lies mortally wounded and wallowing in his own blood. Please accept, my lady, these tokens of my victory from your devoted knight." Nutcracker removed the seven crowns he had strung over his left arm and presented them to Marie, who accepted them gladly.

Nutcracker rose to his feet and said, "my excellent lady, with my enemy defeated I can now show you the most wonderful things, if you will kindly follow me for a short while. Please come with me – please come, excellent lady!"

Chapter Twelve: The Kingdom of the Dolls

I believe every one of you children would have instantly followed the honest and good-natured Nutcracker, who never had an evil thought in his head. Marie was glad to follow him all the more because of her gratitude to him, and because she was convinced he would keep his word. So she said, "I'll go with you, Mr. Drosselmeier, but it can't be too far or take too long because I haven't had enough sleep yet."

"Then we'll take the shortcut, though it is a bit harder."

He walked ahead and Marie followed him until they reached the big old wardrobe in the hall. To Marie's surprise, its doors – which were normally locked – hung open. She could see her father's fox-fur traveling coat hanging in the front.

Nutcracker nimbly climbed up the coat by grabbing onto its trimmings until he reached the large tassels that hung from its back. He pulled on one of them, and a little cedar ladder descended from the coat sleeve. "Please climb up, my dear lady."

Marie – who had somehow become as small as the Nutcracker in the meantime – did. When she drew close to where the collar ought to have been, she could see a blinding light through it. When she pulled herself up and her eyes adjusted, she could see that she was standing in a wonderfully fragrant meadow that sparkled like millions of shimmering gems.

"We are in Candy Meadow now," Nutcracker said. "But we'll soon pass through that gate."

Marie looked up and saw the beautiful gate, which was just ahead of them. It seemed to be made of white, brown, and rosy-colored speckled marble, but when she got closer she could see that it was really made of almonds and raisins baked in sugar. Nutcracker informed her that for this reason it was known as the Almond-and-Raisin Gate, though the common folk had rather disparagingly nicknamed it the "Student's Snack Gate."

A gallery made from barley sugar had been built out from the gate where six monkeys in little red jackets played Turkish marching music. Their music was so beautiful that Marie almost didn't notice that the marbled path that lead through the meadows was really made of beautifully-crafted nougat.

Soon they approached a grove with an opening on each end, and the loveliest smells drifted out from it. Although it was rather dark inside, gold and silver fruits hanging from the trees sparkled brightly. The branches and trunks were adorned with bouquets and ribbons like a joyous bride and groom and their wedding guests. When orange-scented zephyrs drifted through, the tinsel tinkled and clinked to make cheery music and twinkling little lights bounced about.

"Oh, it's so beautiful here," Marie said in delight.

"We are in Christmas Forest, excellent lady," Nutcracker said.

"I'd love to stay here awhile – it's so beautiful!"

Nutcracker clapped his little hands and immediately a few shepherds, shepherdesses, hunters, and huntresses appeared. They were all so white you'd have thought they were made of pure sugar. They had been about all along, but Marie had not noticed them while she'd been walking. They brought Marie an adorable little golden chair with a cushion of white licorice and invited her to sit down on it. No sooner than she had done so the shepherds and shepherdesses danced a magnificent ballet and the hunters blew their horns. When they finished, they all disappeared into the bushes again.

"Pardon me, excellent Lady Stahlbaum," Nutcracker said, "and forgive me that the dance turned out so badly, but the people are part of our wire ballet; they can't do anything differently; it's always and forever the same. And the hunters and their sleepy, dull blowing – that has its reasons, too. The candy hangs a bit high over their noses in the Christmas tree! Even so, why don't we move on?"

"I thought it was very pretty; I liked it quite well!" Marie said as she stood up and followed the Nutcracker.

Soon they came to a murmuring, whispering creek that seemed to be the source of the wonderful smells that filled the woods.

"This is Orange Creek," Nutcracker explained when she asked. "But aside from the lovely fragrance, it's not nearly as impressive as Lemonade River. They both pour into Almond Milk Lake."

Before long, Marie heard a louder rippling noise and saw the wide Lemonade River flowing in amber-colored waves between bushes as bright and green as emeralds and peridots. A cool, fresh scent that strengthened the heart and chest rose from the water. Not far away a dark yellow stream that smelled uncommonly sweet plodded along, and all kinds of pretty little children sat fishing at its banks. They pulled up small, round fish that they ate immediately. As she drew near, she noticed that the fish looked like hazelnuts.

In the distance a lovely little village sat near the river. The houses, church, parson's home, and barns were all dark brown, though the roofs were covered in gold. Many of the walls were painted with bright colors, as though they had been pasted with candied orange peels and almonds.

"That's Gingerbreadholm," Nutcracker said. "It's on the Honey River. The people there are nice to look at, but they're in terrible moods because they suffer from toothaches. So we'll pass them by."

Then Marie saw a small and beautiful town full of colorful and translucent houses. Nutcracker headed straight up to it.

Marie heard a ruckus and clamor and saw what had to be thousands of little people unloading carts that had been packed as full as they could in the marketplace. Upon closer inspection, their goods seemed to be multicolored paper and bars of chocolate.

"This is Bonbonville," the Nutcracker said. "Shipments from Paperland and from the Chocolate King have just arrived. The poor town has been threatened by the mosquito admiral, so they're covering their houses with donations from Paperland and building walls with the bars the Chocolate King sent them. But what we really want to see, excellent lady, are not these small country towns and cities. Let us hurry to the capital – the capital!"

Full of curiosity, Marie hurried after Nutcracker. Before long the air was filled with the scent of roses, and everything around them seemed to have a gentle rosy glow. She saw that the glow came from light reflecting from a body of rosy water that splashed with silvery-pink waves just ahead of them, and as they drew nearer she could see that it was really a large lake.

Silvery-white swans with golden collars swam about the lake singing the most beautiful songs in chorus while fish that shimmered like diamonds jumped up and down as if in dance.

"Oh!" Marie exclaimed. "That's the lake Godfather Drosselmeier promised to make me, and I'm the girl who will pet the swans!"

Nutcracker smiled a mocking smile she'd never seen before. "Uncle could never do anything like that; even you would be more likely to make a lake, dear Miss Stahlbum. But let's not worry about that right now, and sail across Rose Lake to the capital."

Chapter Thirteen: The Capital

N utcracker clapped his little hands again and the silvery-pink waves of Rose Lake came faster and higher. Marie could see what looked like a chariot made from a giant seashell covered with glittering gems in the distance. As it drew closer she could see that it was pulled by two golden dolphins. When it reached the shore, twelve little Moors with hats and tunics woven from glistening hummingbird feathers jumped off and took Marie, then Nutcracker onto the little sea-chariot and immediately took off again.

The golden dolphins raised their heads out of the water and blew crystalline sprays through their blowholes and sang in in silvery voices:

Who is this who crosses Rose Lake?
A fairy! A bumblebee!

Bim bim little fishes
Sim sim swans
Tweet tweet golden birds
Little fairy, come along
Come along the fragrant rosy waves

But the little Moors who were at the back of the sea-chariot didn't seem to like the dolphin's song very much at all. They shook their palm-leaf parasols so hard that the fronds they were made from rustled loudly. They stamped their feet in a strange rhythm and sang:

Click-a-clack
Clack-a-clop
The Moorish dance mustn't stop
Swim on, fishes, swim on swans
Roll along, shell-boat, roll along on
Click-a-clack
Clack-a-clop
Cloppa-clicka-clop!

"The Moors are amusing enough," Nutcracker said, sounding a little embarrassed, "but they're going to make the whole lake rebellious."

In fact, it wasn't long before a ruckus of voices from the air and the sea could be heard, but Marie wasn't paying attention. Instead, she was looking at the face of a lovely and charming girl in the rose-colored waters who was smiling up at her.

"Oh, look, Mr. Drosselmeier! Look down there! It's Princess Pirlipat and she's smiling at me! Please look, Mr. Drosselmeier!"

Nutcracker sighed sadly and said, "oh, excellent Lady Stahlbaum, that is not Princess Pirlipat, but your own face smiling up at you."

Marie sat up very quickly, closed her eyes, and felt very ashamed. At that same moment the Moors lifted her out of the sea-chariot and carried her to land. She was in a small thicket that was almost more beautiful than Christmas Forest. Everything shone and sparkled, and the fruits that hung from the trees were of the most unusual colors and smelled marvelous.

"We're in Marmalade Grove," Nutcracker said, "but there is the capital!"

And what Marie saw now! I will describe to you children the beauty and splendor of the city which opened into a wide meadow of flowers before Marie's eyes. The walls and towers were resplendent in beautiful colors, and their shape and design was like nothing else seen on Earth. Instead of roofs, the houses were topped with finely-wrought crowns and the towers were adorned with garlands of the most delicate multicolored foliage.

As they passed through the gate (which appeared to be made of macaroons and and candied fruits) silver soldiers saluted with with their rifles and a man in a brocade gown threw his arms around the Nutcracker's neck. "Welcome, excellent prince! Welcome to Confectionery City!"

Marie was not a little surprised when she saw young Drosselmeier recognized as a prince by the distinguished-looking man. Then she noticed the confused and noisy din of the city with its merry and joyous shouting, laughing, playing, and singing, and such was the noise that she was distracted from all other thoughts.

"Nutcracker, what's all this noise about?" she asked.

"Excellent Lady Stahlbaum, this isn't anything special.

Confectionery City is a densely populated and merry city; it's always like this. Please come farther inside."

They had hardly taken but a few steps when they came to a huge
marketplace. It was a glorious sight – all of the houses were made
from sugar filigree, rows of pillars and arches were stacked high,
and in the center of it all was an obelisk made of cake. On each side
of the latter were four marvelous fountains that bubbled with

lemonade, orangeade, and other delicious sweet drinks, and the basin was full of cream so thick you could have eaten it with a spoon.

But prettier than all of this were the people gathered together by the thousands. They laughed, joked, and sang – in short, they were the source of the noise Marie had noticed earlier. There were finely-dressed gentlemen and ladies of all sorts: Armenians, Greeks, Jews, Tyroleans, officers, soldiers, preachers, shepherds, clowns, and as many other kinds of people as there are in the world.

At one corner there was an even greater din and the people were scattering in all directions, for the Grand Mogul who had been carried in on a palanquin accompanied by ninety three grandees of the realm and seven hundred slaves had unexpectedly run into the annual parade conducted by the fishermen's guild, which comprised of five hundred members. Unfortunately, a Turkish general suddenly had the idea to ride into the marketplace with three thousand Janissaries, and by an extra stroke of bad luck the Procession of the Interrupted Sacrifice came by singing and playing "Let Us Thank The Almighty Sun!" right up to the cake obelisk.

When all four of these parties met, there was a great pushing, shoving, and squeaking. There was suddenly a great wailing, as a fisherman had knocked a Brahmin's head off and the mogul had nearly been run over by a clown. The noise grew louder and it looked like a riot was going to break out when the man in the brocade robe climbed to the top of the cake obelisk, rang a bell three times, and cried out, "Candyman! Candyman! Candyman!"

Suddenly the din died down, and everyone was busy getting back to their business as best as they could. The processions involved got back on their tracks, the mogul was picked up and dusted off, and the Brahmin's head was put back on his shoulders. The merry din resumed itself and everything went back to normal.

"Who is this 'Candyman' they're talking about, Drosselmeier sir?" Marie asked.

"Excellent Lady Stahlbaum, the Candyman is an unknown but terrifying power which is believed to control the destiny of these people, and is the eventual doom of them all. They are so terrified of it that the mere mention of its name can quell the greatest turmoil, as the Lord Mayor has just demonstrated. When its name is mentioned no-one thinks any more of Earthly matters such as pokes in the ribs or knocks to the head, but stops and asks, 'what is the nature of man, and what is his fate?'"

Marie could not contain a cry of astonishment when she stood before a castle with a hundred towers shining with a rosy-red glow. Now and then rich bouquets of violets, narcissuses, tulips, and matthiolas were hung from the walls. Their dark and vivid colors contrasted against the pinkish-white plaster behind them.

The great expanse of the central dome and the pyramidal roofs of the towers were studded with thousands of twinking stars of gold and and silver.

"Now we're at Marzipan Castle," Nutcracker said.

Marie was completely lost in the sight of the magical castle, and it didn't escape her notice that one of the towers was completely missing its roof, which little men on scaffoldings of cinnamon sticks were working hard to build.

Before she could ask about it, Nutcracker said, "not too long ago this beautiful castle was threatened by devastation, if not utter ruin. The giant Sweettooth came along and bit off the roof of that tower and had even started in on the great dome, but the people offered him a whole district and part of Marmalade Grove instead, which he ate up and continued on his way."

At that moment a soft and pleasant music began to play and the gate opened. Twelve little pageboys walked out holding lighted clove sticks like torches. Each of their heads was a single pearl and their bodies were made of ruby and emerald. They were followed by four ladies almost as tall as Marie's Clarette, and their clothes were so beautiful and brilliantly-colored that she knew at once they were princesses. They tenderly embraced Nutcracker and shouted joyously, "my lord – my prince – my brother!"

Nutcracker seemed very moved by this display of affection and wiped tears from his eyes. He took Marie by the hand and said emotionally, "this is Lady Marie Stahlbaum, the daughter of a very respectable doctor, and the one who saved my life. Had she not thrown her shoe at the right time and later found me a sword, I would be in the grave, bitten to death by the Mouse King. Tell me, does Pirlipat, who was born a princess, compare to Marie's beauty, goodness, and virtue? No, I say! No!"

All of the ladies shouted "no!" and tearfully embraced Marie crying, "oh, noble savior of our brother, noble Lady Stahlbaum!"

The ladies escorted Nutcracker and Marie into the interior of the castle, into a room where the walls were made of pure sparkling crystals of every color. But Marie was most taken by the dear little chairs, tables, dressers, desks, and other furniture standing around made of cedar and Brazil wood and strewn with golden flowers. The princesses had Marie and Nutcracker sit down and immediately announced that they themselves would prepare them a meal.

The princesses fetched bowls and pots of the finest Japanese porcelain, as well as spoons, forks, knives, and graters and other kitchen utensils plated with gold and silver.

❈HET·MARSEPIJNSLOT❈

The brought in the finest fruits and sweets, such as Marie had never seen before, and began to squeeze the fruits, crush the spices, and grate the sugared almonds with their delicate snow-white hands. They were so efficent in their work that Marie could see what expert chefs they all were and that she could expect a splendid meal. It was all so exciting to watch that she secretly wished she could help them.

As if reading her mind, the most beautiful of Nutcracker's sisters handed Marie a golden mortar and said, "sweet friend and rescuer of my brother, please crush this sugar candy."

Marie cheerfully crushed the candy in the mortar, which made a pleasant, almost musical sound. Nutcracker began to tell at length how he had fared badly against the Mouse King's army and how the cowardice of half the troops had lead to their defeat, how the Mouse King had wanted to bite him to pieces, how Marie had been forced to sacrifice many of his subjects in her service, and so on.

As Marie listened to him tell the tale, the sound of the mortar seemed to grow more distant and indistinct, and a silver mist seemed to rise out of the floor and surround the princesses, the Nutcracker, and even herself. She heard strange singing, buzzing, and humming noises in the distance that seemed to draw closer, and felt herself rising as if on waves higher, higher, higher, and higher...

Chapter Fourteen: Conclusion

Poof! Marie felt herself falling from an immense height. What a jolt!

Suddenly she opened her eyes and found herself laying in her little bed, and it was broad daylight. Her mother stood over her and said, "how can you sleep so long? Breakfast is ready!"

You have probably realized, honored listeners, that Marie, exhausted from her adventures, had fallen asleep at last in the hall of Marzipan Castle and the Moors, pages, or even the princesses themselves had carried her home and put her to bed. "Oh, Mama – Mama! Young Drosselmeier took me and showed me the most beautiful things last night!" Then Marie told her mother everything she saw, just as I have told you, and her mother looked at her in amazement.

"You've had a long, beautiful dream, dear Marie, but now you must put it from your mind."

But Marie insisted that it wasn't a dream and that it had really happened. So her mother took her to the glass-fronted cabinet and showed her the Nutcracker, sitting on the second shelf as usual. "How, silly girl, can you believe that a wooden doll can be alive and move?" she asked.

"But Mama, I know very well that Nutcracker is young Mr. Drosselmeier from Nuremberg, Godfather Drosselmeier's nephew."

Both of her parents broke out into peals of laughter.

"Oh!" Marie exclaimed, nearly in tears, "now you're laughing at my nutcracker, Papa! And he spoke so well of you! When we arrived at Marzipan Castle and he introduced me to the princesses – his sisters – he called you a respectable doctor!"

But they only laughed harder, and Louise and Fritz started to laugh too. Marie quickly went to her bedroom and retrieved the seven crowns of the Mouse King, which she presented to her mother. "Look, Mama, these are the crowns of the Mouse King, which Nutcracker gave me last night as a token of his victory."

Her mother marveled over the tiny crowns, which were made of an unknown but brilliant metal and seemed impossible for human hands to have forged. Even her father was completely fascinated by them, and they both asked in ernest where she had gotten them. She could only repeat what she had said before, and when her father scolded her harshly and even called her a little liar, she began to cry violently and said to herself, "oh, poor me, poor me – what am I to say?"

At that moment the door opened and the judge stepped through and shouted, "what's happening? Why is my godchild Marie crying? What's going on?"

The doctor informed him of all that had happened while he showed him the little crowns. However, the judge had hardly listened to a word of it when he laughed and said, "what a silly fuss! These are the crowns I wore for years on my watch chain. I gave them to Marie for her second birthday. Have you forgotten?"

Neither one of them could remember such a thing. When Marie saw that they were no longer angry, she ran up to Godfather Drosselmeier and said, "you know everything, Godfather Drosselmeier. Tell them that Nutcracker is your nephew, young Drosselmeier from Nuremberg!"

But Godfather Drosselmeier frowned and muttered, "ridiculous foolish nonsense."

Then the doctor took Marie aside and said very seriously, "listen, Marie, forget all these tall tales and foolishness. If you ever insist that the nutcracker is Drosselmeier's nephew again, I will throw not only the Nutcracker, but all of your dolls – Madam Clarette included – out the window."

Of course Marie could no longer speak of it, but her mind was filled with it nonetheless. You can well imagine that if you'd seen anything so marvelous yourself, you wouldn't be able to forget it, either.

Even Fritz would ignore Marie if she ever began to tell him of the fantastic realm that had delighted her so. It's even rumored he would occasionally muttered "silly goose!" between his teeth, but given his usual good demeanor I find this doubtful. This much is certain, however – he no longer believed what Marie had told him earlier and made a formal apology to his hussars with a public parade, replaced their lost field insignias with taller, fancier goose feathers, and allowed them to play the Hussar's March once more. However, you and I know just how pathetic those hussars were when those nasty little balls left stains on their red jackets!

Although Marie couldn't talk about her adventure, the images of that marvelous fairyland and its lovely sounds played over and over in her mind. Instead of playing with her toys, Marie would often sit still and silent as she remembered it all. The others would scold her and call her a 'little dreamer.'

144

It happened one day that as the judge was repairing one of the family clocks, Marie sat next to the glass-fronted cabinet remembering her adventures. She looked up at the Nutcracker and suddenly found herself saying, "dear Mr. Drosselmeier, if you really were alive, I wouldn't be like Princess Pirlipat and hate you because you stopped being handsome for my sake!"

At that moment the judge cried, "foolish nonsense!"

But there was suddenly a bang so loud that Marie fainted from her chair. When she awoke, her mother was looking over her. "How can a big girl like you fall off your chair?" she asked. "Anyway, the judge's nephew from Nuremberg has just arrived, so behave yourself."

Marie looked up. The judge had put on his spun-glass wig and yellow coat and was smiling happily. He held the hand of a small, yet handsome young man with a face as white as milk and red as blood. He wore a beautiful red coat trimmed with gold, shoes and stockings of white silk, a powdered wig, and a splendid braid down his back. In one hand he carried a most delightful bouquet of flowers and under his other arm he carried his hat, which was woven from silk. The small sword at his side was encrusted with flashing jewels.

The young man was polite and well-mannered. He gave Marie all sorts of toys and replaced the marzipan and sugar dolls the Mouse King had chewed up. To Fritz he gave a beautiful sabre.

At the table he cracked nuts for everyone; even the hardest could not resist him. With his right hand he put the nut in his mouth and with his left hand he gave a tug on his pigtail, and – crack! – the shell broke into pieces.

Marie had blushed a fiery red when she first saw the young man, and after dinner she blushed even redder when he invited her to come into the living room to the glass-fronted cabinet.

"Just behave when you play, children," the judge said. "Now that all the clocks are telling the right time I've nothing against it."

Hardly were they alone when young Drosselmeier knelt down on one knee and spoke thus: "my most excellent lady Stahlbaum, you see at your feet the happy Drosselemeier, whose life you saved right here. When you said that you would not hate me like the cruel Princess Pirlipat for whose sake I became ugly, I immediately ceased to be a hideous nutcracker and received my former and not-unpleasant form again. Oh noble young lady, please make me happy by giving me your worthy hand and sharing my kingdom and crown. If you do, you shall reign with me in Marzipan Castle, for there I am king!"

Marie took him up by the hand and said, "dear Mr. Drosselmeier, you are a gentle and good man, and also since you rule a country with such wonderful people I accept you as my bridegroom."

With that, they were engaged. In a year (so they say) he came to take her to his kingdom in a golden carriage drawn by silver horses. When they were married in due time, there were twenty-two thousands of the most brilliant dancers dressed in pearls and diamonds to entertain at the wedding, and to this day Marie should still be the queen of a country in which shimmering Christmas forests and glazed marzipan castles – in short, the most marvelous things you can imagine – can be seen if you only look.

Story of a Nodding Donkey

LAURA LEE HOPE

ILLUSTRATIONS HARRY L. SMITH

Chapter One: The Santa Claus Shop

The Nodding Donkey dated his birth from the day he received the beautiful coat of varnish in the workshop of Santa Claus at the North Pole. Before that he was just some pieces of wood, glued together. His head was not glued on, however, but was fastened in such a manner that with the least motion the Donkey could nod it up and down, and also sidewise.

It is not every wooden donkey who is able to nod his head in as many ways as could the Donkey about whom I am going to tell you. This Nodding Donkey was an especially fine toy, and, as has been said, his first birthday was that on which he received such a bright, shiny coat of varnish.

"Here, Santa Claus, look at this, if you please!" called one of the jolly workmen in the shop of St. Nicholas. "Is this toy finished, now?" and he held up the Nodding Donkey.

Santa Claus, who was watching another man put some blue eyes in a golden-haired doll, came over to the bench where sat the man who had made the Nodding Donkey out of some bits of wood, glue, and real hair for his mane and tail.

"Hum! Yes! So you have finished the Nodding Donkey, have you?" asked Santa Claus, as he stroked his long, white beard.

"I'll call him finished if you say he is all right," answered the man, smiling as he put the least tiny dab more of varnish on the Donkey's back. "Shall I set him on the shelf to dry, so you may soon take him down to Earth for some lucky boy or girl?"

"Yes, he is finished. Set him on the shelf with the other toys," answered dear old St. Nicholas, and then, having given a last look at the Donkey, the workman placed him on a shelf, next to a wonderful Plush Bear, of whom I shall tell you more in another book.

"Well, I'm glad he's finished," said Santa Claus' worker, as he took up his tools to start making a Striped Tiger, with a red tongue. "That Nodding Donkey took me quite a while to finish. I hope nothing happens to him until his coat of varnish is hard and dry. My, but he certainly shines!"

And the Nodding Donkey did shine most wonderfully! Not far away, on the same shelf on which he stood, was a doll's bureau with a looking glass on top. In this looking glass the Nodding Donkey caught sight of himself.

The Nodding Donkey's First Appearance.

"Not so bad!" he thought. "In fact, I'm quite stylish. I'm almost as gay as some of the clowns." And his head bobbed slowly up and down, for it was fastened so that the least jar or jiggle would move it.

"I must be very careful," said the Nodding Donkey to himself. "I must not move about too much nor let any of the other toys rub against me until I am quite dry. If they did they would blur or scratch my shiny varnish coat, and that would be too bad. But after I am dry I'll have some fun. Just wait until to-night! Then there will be some great times in this workshop of Santa Claus!"

The reason the Nodding Donkey said this, was because at night, when Santa Claus and his merry helpers had gone, the toys were allowed to do as they pleased. They could make believe come to life, and move about, having all sorts of adventures.

But, presto! the moment daylight came, or any one looked at them, the toys became as straight and stiff and motionless as any toys that are in your playroom. For all you know some of your toys may move about and pretend to come to life when you are asleep. But it is of no use for you to stay awake, watching to see if they will, for as long as any eyes are peeping, or ears are listening, the toys will never do anything of themselves.

The Nodding Donkey knew that when Santa Claus and the workers were gone he and the other toys could do as they pleased, and he could hardly wait for that time to come.

"But while I am waiting I will stay here on the shelf and get hard and dry," said the Nodding Donkey to himself.

Once more he looked in the glass on the doll's bureau, and he was well pleased with himself, was the Nodding Donkey.

Such a busy place was the workshop of Santa Claus at the North Pole, where the Nodding Donkey was drying in his coat of varnish!

The place was like a great big greenhouse, all made of glass, only the glass was sheets of crystal-clear ice. Santa Claus needed plenty of light in his workshop, for in the dark it is not easy to put red cheeks and blue eyes on dolls, or paint toy soldiers and wind up the springs of the toys that move.

The workshop of Santa Claus, then, was like a big greenhouse, only no flowers grew in it because it is very cold at the North Pole. All about was snow and ice, but Santa Claus did not mind the cold, nor did his workmen, for they were dressed in fur, like the polar bears and the seals.

On each side of the big shop, with its icy glass roof, were work benches. At these benches sat the funny little men who made the toys.

Some were stuffing sawdust into dolls, others were putting the lids on the boxes where the Jacks lived, and still others were trying the Jumping Jacks to see that they jerked their legs and arms properly.

Up and down, between the rows of benches, walked Santa Claus himself. Now and then some workman would call:

"Please look here, Santa Claus! Shall I make this Tin Soldier with a sword or a gun?"

And St. Nicholas would answer: "That Soldier needs a sword. He is going to be a Captain."

Then another little man would call, from the other side of the shop: "Here is a Calico Clown who doesn't squeak when I press on his stomach. Something must be wrong with him, Santa Claus."

Then Santa Claus would put on his glasses, stroke his long, white beard and look at the Calico Clown.

"Humph! I should say he wouldn't squeak!" the old gentleman would remark. "You have his squeaker in upside down! That would never do for some little boy or girl to find on Christmas morning! Take the squeaker out and put it in right."

"How careless of me!" the little workman would exclaim. And then Santa Claus and the other workmen would laugh, for this workshop was the jolliest place in the world, and the man would fix the Calico Clown right.

"I'm glad I was born in this place," said the Nodding Donkey to himself, as his head swayed to and fro. "This is really the first day of my life. I wish night would come, so I could move about and talk to the other toys. I wonder how long I shall have to wait?"

Not far from the doll's bureau, which held the looking glass, was a toy house, and in it was a toy clock. The Donkey looked in through the window of the toy house and saw the toy clock. The hands pointed to four o'clock.

"The men stop work at five," thought the Donkey. "After that it will be dark and I can move about—that is if my varnish is dry."

Santa Claus was walking up and down between the rows of work benches. The dear old gentleman was pulling his beard and smiling.

"Come, my merry men!" he called in his jolly voice, "you must work a little faster. It is nearly five, when it will be time to stop for the day, and it is so near Christmas that I fear we shall never get enough toys made. So hurry all you can!"

"We will, Santa Claus," the men answered. And the one who had made the Nodding Donkey asked: "When are you going to take a load of toys down to Earth?"

"The first thing in the morning," was the answer. "Many of the stores have written me, asking me to hurry some toys to them. I shall hitch up my reindeer to the sleigh and take a big bag of toys down to Earth tomorrow. So get ready for me as many as you can.

"Yes," went on Santa Claus, and he looked right at the Nodding Donkey, "I must take a big bag of toys to Earth tomorrow, as soon as it is daylight. So hurry, my merry men!"

And the workmen hurried as fast as they could.

Ting! suddenly struck the big clock in the workshop. And ting! went the little toy clock in the toy house.

"Time to stop for supper!" called Santa Claus, and all the little men laid aside the toys on which they were working. Then such a bustle and hustle there was to get out of the shop; for the day had come to an end.

Night settled down over North Pole Land. It was dark, but in the house where Santa Claus lived with his men some Japanese lanterns, hung from icicles, gave them light to see to eat their supper.

In the toy shop it was just dimly light, for one lantern had been left burning there, in case Santa Claus might want to go in after hours to see if everything was all right.

And by the light of this one lamp the Nodding Donkey saw a curious sight. Over on his left the Plush Bear raised one paw and scratched his nose. On the Donkey's right the China Cat opened her china mouth and softly said:

"Mew!"

And then, on the next shelf, a Rolling Elephant, who could wheel about, spoke through his trunk, and said:

"The time has come for us to have some fun, my friends!"

"Right you are!" mewed the China Cat.

"And we have a new toy with us," said the Plush Bear. "Would you like to play with us?" he asked the Nodding Donkey.

The Nodding Donkey moved his head up and down to say "yes," for he was afraid of speaking aloud, lest he might wrinkle his new varnish.

"All right, now for some jolly times!" said the Rolling Elephant, and he began to climb down from the shelf, using his trunk as well as his legs.

"Ouch! Look out there! You're stretching my neck!" suddenly cried a Spotted Wooden Giraffe, and the Nodding Donkey, looking up, saw that the Elephant had wound his trunk around the long neck of the Giraffe.

"Oh, I'm going to fall! Catch me, somebody!" cried the Spotted Giraffe."Oh, if I fall off the shelf I'll be broken to bits! Will no one save me?"

Chapter Two: A Wonderful Voyage

"**G**oodness me! this is a lot of excitement for one who has just come to life and had his first coat of varnish!" thought the Nodding Donkey as he saw what seemed to be a sad accident about to happen. "I wonder if I could do anything to help save the Spotted Giraffe? I must try to do all I can. It will be the first time I have ever moved all by myself."

"Stand aside, if you please! I'll save the Spotted Giraffe!" suddenly called a voice, and from a shelf just underneath the one from which the Rolling Elephant had pulled the long-necked creature there stepped a Jolly Fisherman. This toy fisherman had a large net for catching crabs or lobsters, and he held it out for the Spotted Giraffe to fall into.

Down the Giraffe fell, but he landed in the net of the Jolly Fisherman, just as a circus performer falls into a net from a high trapeze, and he was not harmed.

"Dear! I'm glad you caught me," said the Giraffe, after he had managed to climb out of the net to the top of a work table which ran under all the shelves.

"Yes, I got there just in time," replied the Jolly Fisherman, as he slung his net over his shoulder again.

"And I'm very sorry I pulled you from the shelf," said the Rolling Elephant. "I didn't mean to do it, Mr. Giraffe."

"Well, as long as no harm is done, we'll forget all about it and have some fun," put in the Plush Bear. "This doesn't happen every night," the Bear went on, speaking to the Nodding Donkey. "You must not get the idea that it is dangerous here."

"Oh, no, I think it's a very nice place," the Nodding Donkey answered. "It's my first day here, you see."

"Oh, yes, it's easy to see that," said the China Cat. "You are so new and shiny any one would know you were just made. Well, now what shall we do? Who has a game to suggest or a riddle to ask?" and, as she spoke, she put out her paw and began to roll a red rubber ball on the shelf near her. For, though she was very stiff in the daytime, being made of china like a dinner plate, the Cat could easily move about at night if no human eyes watched her.

"Let's play a guessing game," suggested the Rolling Elephant, who, by this time had managed to get down to the table without upsetting any more of the toys. "If we play tag or hide and go seek, I'm so big and clumsy I may knock over something and break it."

"That's so—you might," growled the Plush Bear, but, though he spoke in a growling voice he was not at all cross. It was just his way of talking. "Well, what sort of a guessing game do you want to play, Mr. Elephant?"

"I'll think of something, and you must all see if you can guess what it is."

"That's too hard a game," objected the China Cat. "There are so many things you might think of."

"Well, I'll give you a little help," returned the Rolling Elephant. "I'm thinking of something that goes up and down and also sideways."

For a moment none of the toys spoke. Then, all of a sudden, the Plush Bear cried:

"You're thinking of the Nodding Donkey! His head goes up and down and also sideways."

"That's right!" admitted the Rolling Elephant. "I didn't imagine you'd guess so soon. Now it's your turn to think of something."

"Let's have the Nodding Donkey give the next question," suggested the China Cat. "It's his birthday, you know, and we ought to help him remember it."

"Go ahead! Give us something to guess, Nodding Donkey!" growled the Plush Bear.

"Let me think," said the new toy, slowly. "Ah, I have it! What am I thinking of that is like a snowball and has two eyes?"

"A snowman!" guessed a wax doll.

"No," said the Nodding Donkey, laughing.

"A Polar Bear," suggested the Rolling Elephant.

"No," said the Donkey again.

Then the toys thought very hard.

"Is it a rubber doll?" asked a Jack in the Box. "No, it couldn't be that," he went on, "for a rubber doll isn't as white as a snowball. I give up!"

"But I don't!" suddenly cried a Tin Soldier. "You were thinking of our White China Cat, weren't you?" he asked.

"Yes," answered the Nodding Donkey, "I was. You have guessed it!"

"Now it's the Tin Soldier's turn to give us something to guess," said the Elephant. "Oh, we're having lots of fun!"

And so the toys were. All through the night they played about in the North Pole workshop of Santa Claus. When it was nearly morning the Nodding Donkey spoke to the Plush Bear, asking:

"Where is this Earth place, that Santa Claus said he was going to take some of us?"

"Oh, my! don't ask me," said the Plush Bear. "I've never been down to Earth, though I know packs and packs of toys have been taken there. But it must be a real jolly sort of place, for every time Santa Claus goes there he comes back laughing and seems very happy. Then he loads up some more toys to take there."

"I think I should like to go," murmured the Nodding Donkey. "How does one go—in one of the toy trains of cars I see on the shelves?"

"Oh, my, no!" laughed the Plush Bear. "Santa Claus takes the toys to Earth in his sleigh, drawn by reindeer."

"Oh, how wonderful!" brayed the Donkey. "I wonder if I shall soon take that wonderful voyage. I hope I may!"

"Hush!" suddenly called the Rolling Elephant. "Santa Claus and the workmen are coming in and they must not see us at our make-believe play. Quick! To your shelves, all of you!"

Such a scramble as there was on the part of the toys! Some helped the others to climb up, and just as the last of them, including the Nodding Donkey, were safely in place, the door of the shop opened and in came Santa Claus and his men.

Then such a bustling about as there was! And from outside the shop could be heard the jingle of bells.

"Those must be the reindeer," thought the Nodding Donkey. "Oh, what a jollytime I shall have if I ride in the sleigh with Santa Claus!"

Never was there such a busy time in the shop of Santa Claus! Jolly St. Nicholas himself hurried here and there, helping his men pick up different toys which were put in a big bag. One of the men stopped in front of the Nodding Donkey.

"Shall I put this chap in, Santa Claus?" the man inquired.

"Is the varnish dry?" asked St. Nicholas.

"Yes," answered the little man, testing it lightly with his finger.

"Then put him in," said Santa Claus. "I'll take the Nodding Donkey to Earth with me."

"Oh, joy! Now I shall have some adventures! Now I shall see what the Earth is like!" thought the Nodding Donkey.

A moment later he was picked up, wrapped in soft paper, and thrust into a bag.

"Oh, how very dark it is here," said the Donkey in a whisper.

"Hush!" whispered a Jumping Jack near him. "Don't talk! Santa Claus might hear you. He has very sharp ears. You'll be all right. It is no darker than night."

More toys, all carefully wrapped, came tumbling into the bag, and the merry jingle of bells grew louder. Then the voice of Santa Claus could be heard shouting:

"Hi there, Dasher! Stand still, Prancer! Whoa, Blitzen! What's the matter, Comet? Are you anxious to get to Earth again? Well, we'll soon start. Steady there, Cupid! Whoa!"

"He's talking to his reindeer," whispered the Jumping Jack.

Suddenly the toys in the big sack felt themselves being picked up. Santa Claus had slung them over his back to carry out to the sleigh. A moment later the Nodding Donkey felt a breath of cold air strike him, but he did not mind, as he had on a warm coat of varnish.

Up and down, and from side to side the toys in the bag felt themselves being jostled, until they were set down in the big sleigh.

"All aboard!" called Santa Claus, as he took his seat and gathered up the reins. "Come, Dasher! On, Prancer! Hi, Donner and Blitzen! Down to Earth you go with the Christmas toys!"

There was another jolly jingle of bells, and the toys felt themselves being whisked away over the snow. There was a little hole in the bag near the Nodding Donkey, and also a hole in the paper in which he was wrapped. He could look out, and on every side he saw big piles of snow. Snow was also falling from the clouds.

On and on rushed the sleigh of Santa Claus, drawn by the eight reindeer. Over the clouds and drifts of snow, and through the white flakes they rushed, the sleigh-bells playing a merry tune.

"Oh, this is a wonderful voyage!" thought the Nodding Donkey. "I wonder when I shall reach the Earth?"

Suddenly there was a hard shock. The sleigh stopped as Santa Claus shouted, and then, all at once, the Nodding Donkey felt himself shooting out of the hole in the bag. Into a deep snowdrift he fell, and there he stuck, head down and feet up in the air!

Chapter Three: The Jolly Store

"**D**ear me," thought the Nodding Donkey to himself, as he felt the cold, chilly snow all about him, "this is most dreadful! I hope Santa Claus has not become angry with me and sent me back to the North Pole. I did so much want to go down to Earth and be in a big store for Christmas. I hope I'm not back at the North Pole."

The Nodding Donkey said this aloud, and, as he spoke, he wobbled his head from side to side and tried to turn over so he could stand on his feet.

"Here! Don't do that!" suddenly whispered a voice in one of the Donkey's large ears. "Don't you know it isn't allowed for you to move when any one is looking at you?"

"I didn't know any one was looking at me," the Nodding Donkey answered. "I thought Santa Claus had tossed me back to the North Pole."

"Hush! No! Nothing like that has happened," the voice went on, and, by turning his loose head to one side, the Nodding Donkey saw that a large Jumping Jack was whispering to him.

"There has been an accident," went on the Jumping Jack. "The sleigh of Santa Claus banged into a hard, frozen snow cloud, and we were thrown out into a snowdrift. I am not hurt, and I hope you are not. But we must not talk or move much more, for I see Santa Claus coming this way, and even he is not allowed to see us pretend to be alive, so that we move and talk. He is coming to pick us up, I guess."

And then both toys had to keep quiet, for Santa Claus came stalking along in his big leather boots. St. Nicholas was wiping some snowflakes out of his eyes, his breath made clouds of steam in the frosty air and his cheeks were as red as the reddest apple you ever saw.

"Oh, ho! Here are some of my toys!" cried the jolly old gentleman as he saw the Nodding Donkey and the Jumping Jack. "I was afraid I had lost you. We nearly had a bad accident," he went on, speaking to himself, but loudly enough for the Nodding Donkey to hear. "My reindeer got off the road and ran into a snow cloud and the sleigh was upset."

"It's just as the Jumping Jack told me," thought the Nodding Donkey.

"Steady there, Comet! Keep quiet, Prancer!" called St. Nicholas to his animals, who, stamping their legs, made the bells jingle. "We shall soon be on our way again. Nothing is broken."

Santa Claus picked up the Donkey and the Jumping Jack and carried them back to the sleigh. There the two toys could see their friends, some lying on the seat of the sleigh and others resting in the big bag, through the hole of which the Nodding Donkey had slipped out, falling into the snow.

"Ha! I must fix that hole in the bag," cried Santa Claus, as he noticed it.

St. Nicholas tied some string around the hole in the sack, and then, having again wrapped the tissue paper around the Donkey, the Jumping Jack, and the other toys that had fallen out, the red-cheeked old gentleman put them in the bag and fastened it shut.

"Now we're off again!" cried Santa Claus, as he took his seat in the sleigh. "Trot along, Comet! Fly away, Prancer! Lively there, Donner and Blitzen! We must get down to Earth with these toys, and then back again to North Pole Land for another load! Trot along, my speedy reindeer!"

The reindeer shook their heads, which made the bells jingle more merrily than before, they stamped their feet on the hard, frozen road that led from the North Pole to Earth, and then away they darted. Santa Claus drove them carefully, steering away from snow clouds, and soon the motion was so swift and smooth that the Nodding Donkey went to sleep, and so did most of the other toys in the big sack.

And what a funny dream the Nodding Donkey had! He imagined that he was tumbling around a feather bed and that a Blue Dog was chasing him with a yellow feather duster.

"Don't tickle me with that feather duster!" he thought he cried.

"I won't if you'll sing a song through your ears," said the Blue Dog.

"I can't sing through my ears," wailed the Nodding Donkey, and then of a sudden he seemed to roll over and the dog and the feather bed came down on top of him. Then he seemed to give a sneeze and that blew the dog away and sent the feathers of the bed out into one big snowstorm!

It was dark when the Nodding Donkey awoke. He did not hear the jingle of the bells, nor could he feel the sleigh being drawn along by the reindeer. He could see nothing, either, for it was very black and dark. But he heard some voices talking, and one he knew was that of Santa Claus.

"Now I have brought you a whole sleighful of toys," said St. Nicholas.

"Yes, and I am glad to get them," another voice answered. "The stores are almost empty and it is near Christmas time. I shall send a lot of the toys to the stores the first thing in the morning."

Santa Claus had arrived, in the night, at a large warehouse, where boxes, bales and bags of toys were kept until they could be sent around to the different stores. The Nodding Donkey, the Jumping Jack and the others felt themselves being lifted out of the bag and placed on the floor or on shelves. But they could see nothing, for Santa Claus always comes to Earth in the darkness, so no one sees him. And it was the Earth that the toys had now reached.

"Dear me, this isn't much fun!" complained the Nodding Donkey, as he stood on a shelf in the darkness. Faint and far off he could hear the bells of Santa Claus' reindeer jingling as jolly St. Nicholas drove back to North Pole Land. "I thought the Earth was such a wonderful place," went on the Nodding Donkey. "But I don't like it here at all."

"Hush!" begged the Jumping Jack. "It is night. You have seen nothing yet. Wait until morning."

And, after a while, streaks of light began to come in through the windows of the warehouse where the toys had been left. The sun was rising. From a window near him the Nodding Donkey caught a glimpse of snow outside, but the land was very different from the North Pole where he had been made.

The Nodding Donkey was turning his head to speak to the Jumping Jack, and he was going to take a look and see what other toys were near him, when, all of a sudden, three or four men came into the room. They had hammers, nails and boards in their hands.

"Hurry now!" cried one of the men. "We must box up a lot of these toys and send them to the different stores. It will be Christmas before we know it."

Suddenly one of the men caught hold of the Nodding Donkey, and also of a large doll that had been on the same shelf.

"I'll pack these in a box," said the man. "I just need them to fill one corner. Then I'll ship them off."

The Nodding Donkey wished his friend the Jumping Jack might go in the same box with him, but it was not to be. The Donkey gave one last look at his companion of the snowdrift, and a moment later he was being wrapped in tissue paper again, and was packed down in a corner of a large box. The doll was treated the same way.

Then the board cover was put on the box, and nailed shut with a loud hammering noise.

"Dear me, in the dark again!" said the Nodding Donkey. "I don't seem to be having a good time at all."

"Never mind! It will not last long," said the Doll, who was made of cloth, so it did not matter how much she was squeezed. "We will soon be in the light again."

The toys in the box could hear loud talking going on in the warehouse where they had been left by Santa Claus. They could also hear men moving about and the bang and rattle of boxes, like theirs, as the cases were nailed up and taken away.

Finally the Nodding Donkey, the doll, and other toys who were packed together, felt their box being tilted up on one end. By this time the Nodding Donkey was getting used to being stood on his head, or turned over on his back, and he did not mind it.

"Hurry up! Load this box on a truck and take it to the Mugg store!" cried a voice.

"The Mugg store! I wonder where that is!" thought the Nodding Donkey.

And then he felt the box in which he lay being lifted up and carried along. There were bumps, thumps, turnings and twistings, and then the Nodding Donkey felt himself gliding along.

But he soon noticed that this ride was not as smooth as had been the one from North Pole Land to the Earth. Instead of riding in a sleigh drawn by reindeer, the Nodding Donkey was riding on an automobile truck, and as it went out in the street it bumped and rattled along.

There was so much noise and confusion, and it was so warm and cosy in the box where he was packed, that, before he knew it, the Nodding Donkey had fallen asleep. And, as he slept, the Nodding Donkey dreamed.

He dreamed that he was back in the workshop of Santa Claus at the North Pole and on a shelf with other toys. Suddenly a Wooden Soldier began beating on the Donkey's back with the end of a gun.

"Rub-a-dub-dub!" drummed the Soldier, and the Donkey's head nodded so hard that he feared it would be shaken off.

"Stop! Stop!" cried the Donkey in his dream, and then he suddenly awakened. He heard a hammering, but it was not on his back. It was outside the case in which he was packed, and he soon noticed that some one was knocking off the boards that formed the cover.

With a wrench and a squeak one of the cover boards was raised, letting in a flood of light. The Nodding Donkey blinked his eyes, coming out of the darkness into the glare of the light. Then he felt himself being lifted up and set on a shelf. At the same time he heard a pleasant voice saying:

"Here is the case of new toys, Daughters. And see, one of the very newest is a Nodding Donkey! I'm sure he will please some little boy or girl!"

The Nodding Donkey looked around him. He was on a shelf in the jolliest toy store he had ever imagined. It was almost as nice as the workshop of Santa Claus. Standing in front of the shelf was a white-haired old man and two ladies, one on either side of him. The three were looking at the Nodding Donkey, who bowed his head at them as if saying:

"How do you do? I am very glad to meet you!"

Chapter Four: The China Cat

T he Nodding Donkey stood straight and stiff on his four legs, with his shiny, new coat of varnish—the one he had received in the workshop of Santa Claus at the North Pole. The Donkey wished he might move about and talk with some of the other toys he saw all around him, but he dared not, as the old gentleman and the two ladies were standing in front of him and looking straight at the toy. All the Donkey dared do was to nod his head, for, being made on purpose to do that, it was perfectly proper for him to do so, just as the Jumping Jack jumped, or some of the funny Clowns banged together their brass cymbals.

"Isn't he the dearest Donkey you ever saw, Angelina?" said one of the ladies to the other.

"He certainly is, Geraldine," was the answer. "But something seems to be the matter with his head. It is loose!"

"Tut! Tut! Nonsense! It is made that way, just the same as the moving head of the Fuzzy Bear," said the old gentleman, whose name was Horatio Mugg. At first the Nodding Donkey had taken this old gentleman for a relative of Santa Claus, for he had the same white hair and whiskers and wore almost the same sort of glasses. But a second look showed the Nodding Donkey that this was not any relation of St. Nicholas. Besides, this toy store was not at all like the workshop of Santa Claus.

The Nodding Donkey was at last on Earth in a toy store, and there, it was hoped, some one would see him and buy him for some boy or girl for Christmas.

The toy store was kept by Mr. Horatio Mugg and his two daughters, one being named Angelina and the other Geraldine.

Mr. Horatio Mugg was the jolliest toy-store man you can imagine! Since his own two daughters had grown up he seemed to think he must look after all the other children in his neighborhood. He was always glad to see the boys and girls in his store. He liked to have them look at the toys, and sometimes he showed them how steam engines or flying machines worked.

Of course there were many dolls, big and little—Sawdust Dolls, Bisque Dolls, Wooden Dolls, some very handsomely dressed, with silk or satin dresses and white stockings and white kid shoes. And some had the cutest hats, and some even had gloves, think of that!

And then the animals—Lions and Tigers, and a Striped Zebra, and funny Monkeys and Goats, Dogs, Spotted Cows and many kinds of Rocking Horses. And even funny little Mice, that ran all around the floor when they were wound up.

And then the other toys—trains of cars, fire engines, building blocks, and oh! so many, many things! It was truly a wonderful place, was that store. It was a place where you could spend an hour or two and the time would fly so fast you would scarcely know where it had gone to.

Mr. Mugg knew all about toys, which kind were the best for boys, which the girls liked the best, and he knew which to put in his window so the children would stop and press their noses flat against the glass to look and see the playthings.

"Yes, the Nodding Donkey will be a fine toy for Christmas," said Mr. Mugg, looking over the tops of his glasses at the new arrival. "This last box of playthings I received are the best we ever had. Santa Claus and his men certainly are preparing a fine Christmas this year."

"I think I shall dust off the Donkey," said Geraldine. "He will be much shinier then, and look better."

"And I must dust the China Cat," said her sister Angelina. "She is so white that the least speck shows on her. Real white cats are very fussy about keeping themselves clean, so I do not see why a white China Cat should not be treated the same way. You dust the Nodding Donkey, Geraldine, and I'll dust the Cat."

"That China Cat seems to act as if she wanted to speak to me," thought the Donkey. "Perhaps, after the store is closed to-night, as the workshop of Santa Claus is closed, I may speak to her."

Up and down and to and fro the head of the Nodding Donkey moved as Geraldine Mugg dusted him. Then she set him back on the shelf, as her sister did the China Cat.

"Come here, Daughters, and see this set of Soldiers," called Mr. Mugg, who was unpacking more toys from the box. "They are the nicest we ever had."

"Oh, what fine red coats they wear!" said Angelina.

"And how their guns shine!" exclaimed Geraldine. "Our store will look lovely when we get all the toys placed in it."

"I think the store looks very well as it is," thought the Nodding Donkey to himself, as he stood straight and stiff on his shelf, his coat of varnish glistening in the light. "I never saw such a wonderful place."

And, indeed, the toy store of Mr. Horatio Mugg was a place of delight for all boys and girls. I could not begin to tell you all the things that were in it. Mr. Mugg kept only toys. All the different sorts that were ever made were there gathered together, ready for the Christmas trade.

And as the Nodding Donkey, standing beside the white China Cat, looked on and listened, he saw boys and girls, with their fathers or mothers, coming in to look at the toys. Some were ordered to be put away until Christmas should come. Others were taken at once, to be mailed perhaps to some far-off city.

As the Nodding Donkey watched he saw a little boy with blue eyes and golden hair come in and point to a Jack in the Box.

"Please, Mother, will you tell Santa Claus to bring me that for Christmas?" begged the little boy.

"Yes, I will do that," his mother promised. "And now, Sister, what would you like?" the lady asked.

The Nodding Donkey looked down and saw a little girl, with dark hair and brown eyes standing beside the little boy. This girl pointed to a large doll, and, to his surprise, the Donkey saw that it was the same one he had spoken to in the packing case.

"You may put that Doll aside for my little girl for Christmas, Mr. Mugg," said the lady.

"Very well, Madam, it shall be done," replied the toy man, and he lifted the Cloth Doll down off the shelf.

"Oh, dear! she is going away, and I shall never see her again," thought the Nodding Donkey. "That is the only sad part of life for us toys. We make friends, but we never know how long we may keep them. We are so often separated."

Mr. Mugg put the doll down under the counter, where no other little girl might see her and want her. Then the toy man reached up and gently touched the head of the Donkey, so that it nodded harder than ever.

"Here is a new toy that just came in," said Mr. Mugg. "It is one of the latest. It is called a Nodding Donkey, and once you start his head going it will move for hours."

"Oh, it is nice!" said the lady. "Would you rather have that than your Jack in the Box, Robert?" she asked the little boy.

The boy stood first on one foot and then on the other. He looked first at the Jack in the Box and then at the Donkey.

"They are both nice," he said; "but I think I would rather have the Jack. I'll have the Donkey next Christmas."

The Jack in the Box was set aside with the Cloth Doll, and then the lady and the little boy and girl passed on. But all that day there were many other boys and girls who came into the store to look at the toys. Some only came to look, while others, as before, bought the things they wanted, or had them set aside for Christmas.

After a while it began to grow dark in the store, just as it had grown dark in the workshop of Santa Claus.

"Now I will soon be able to move about and talk to the other toys," thought the Nodding Donkey. But this was not to be—just yet.

"Turn on the lights, Angelina," called Mr. Mugg to his daughter, and soon the store was glowing brightly.

"Hum! It seems they work at night here, as well as by day," thought the Nodding Donkey. "It was not so at North Pole Land. But it is very jolly, and I like it."

During the evening, when the lights were glowing, many other customers came in, but there were not so many boys and girls.

The Nodding Donkey had been taken down more than once and made to do his trick of shaking his head, but, so far, no one had bought him. And though the China Cat had also been looked at and admired, no one had bought her.

At last Mr. Mugg stretched his arms, yawned as though he might be very sleepy, and said:

"Turn out the lights, Angelina! It is time to close the shop and go to bed."

Soon the toy shop was in darkness, all except one light that was kept burning all night. The place became very still and quiet, the only noise being made by a little mouse, who came out to get some crumbs dropped by Mr. Mugg, who had eaten his lunch in the store.

"Ahem!" suddenly said the Nodding Donkey. "Do you mind if I speak to you?" he asked the China Cat, who stood near him on the shelf.

"Not at all," was the kind answer. "I was just going to ask how you came here."

"I came direct from the workshop of Santa Claus at the North Pole," answered the Nodding Donkey. "And I suppose, just as we toys could do there, that we are allowed to move about and talk while here."

"Oh, yes," answered the China Cat. "We can make believe we are alive as long as no one sees us. But tell me, how is everything at the North Pole? It is some time since I was there, as I was made early in the season."

"Well, Santa Claus is as happy and jolly as ever," said the Nodding Donkey, "and his men are just as busy. We had a dreadful accident though, coming down to Earth!"

"You did?" mewed the China Cat. "Tell me about it," and she moved her tail from one side to the other.

Before the Nodding Donkey could speak in answer to this request, a voice suddenly asked:

"I say, Nodding Donkey, do you kick?"

"Kick? Of course not," the Nodding Donkey answered. "Why do you ask such a question? Who are you, anyhow?" and he looked all around.

"Hush! Don't get him started," whispered the China Cat. "It's the Policeman with his club, and if he begins to tickle you he'll never stop. Oh, here he comes now! Here comes the Policeman!"

Chapter Five: The Lame Boy

When the China Cat said: "Here comes the Policeman!" the Nodding Donkey, who did not know just what a policeman was, was quite curious to see who was coming. So he walked to the edge of the shelf and bent his head as far down as he could in order to see.

"Be careful! You might fall!" mewed the China Cat.

"Ha! If he falls, then I'll pick him up! That's what I'm here for, to help in case of accident. I could ring for the ambulance!" suddenly came in the same voice that had asked if the Nodding Donkey kicked.

"On second thought perhaps it will be just as well to have an accident. It will give us something to talk about," the voice went on. "Go ahead, Nodding Donkey. Fall off the shelf. I'll pick you up and send you to the toy hospital in the toy ambulance with the clanging bell."

"Indeed I am not going to fall!" brayed the Donkey. "Who is he, anyhow?" he whispered to the China Cat.

"That's the Policeman I was telling you about," was the answer. "Here he comes now!"

And suddenly the Policeman's voice went on, saying:

"Come now! Move along! Don't block up the sidewalk! Move on! Don't loiter here!"

The Nodding Donkey looked to one side and there he saw a toy Policeman, dressed just as a real one would be, with blue coat, brass buttons, a white helmet and a club that swung on the end of a leather string. The Policeman walked]along, for he could do that when a spring inside him was wound up. And as he walked he swung his club to and fro, and said, just like a real policeman:

"Come now, move along! Don't block up the sidewalk." Then he added, in a different tone: "There is no accident now, but if that Nodding Donkey would only fall off the shelf we might have one."

"Indeed, and I'm not going to fall off the shelf just for fun!" brayed the Donkey.

"Oh, aren't you? Then we must make fun in some other way," said the toy Policeman. "How are you feeling?" and with that he jumped up on the shelf beside the Donkey and tickled him in the ribs with the club.

"Oh, don't do—ha! ha!—Don't—ha! ha!—do that!" laughed the Donkey. "You make me feel so funny I may fall!"

"Well, if you do, I'll pick you up," said the Policeman, and he twisted his club around on the Donkey's ribs in such a funny way that the nodding creature laughed "ha! ha!" and "ho! ho!"

"I thought I'd stir things up and make them rather lively!" said the Policeman, with a jolly grin on his red face. "How are you feeling?" he asked, turning to the China Cat.

"I feel quite good enough without having you tickle me," she answered, as she got up to move away.

"Oh, you'll feel ever so much better after I tickle you!" cried the Policeman, and he reached out his club toward the Cat. But he was not quick enough. She slipped behind a Jack in the Box, where the Policeman could not see her.

"Well, I guess I'll tickle you again," said the toy with the club, as he turned back toward the Nodding Donkey.

"Oh, no, don't, please!" begged the long-eared chap. "I've had quite enough. When you tickle me I laugh, and when I laugh my head nods harder than it ought to, and maybe it might nod off."

"Oh, I wouldn't want that to happen!" exclaimed the Policeman. "That would be too bad an accident. I guess I'll walk down the shelf and see if there's a fire anywhere," he went on, and away he stalked, swinging his club from side to side.

"Oh, I hope there isn't a fire here," said the Nodding Donkey, as the China Cat came out from behind the Jack's box. "I am not used to being hot. I came from the cold North Pole."

"No, there isn't any fire. If there were you would soon see the toy Fireman and the Fire Engine starting out," replied the China Cat. "I don't like fires myself, and I detest the water they squirt on them. We cats don't like water, you know."

"So I have heard," said the Nodding Donkey.

"Dear me! there's a speck of dirt on my]tail," suddenly mewed the China Cat, and she leaned over, and with her red tongue washed her tail clean.

Meanwhile the Policeman walked on down the counter, as though it were a street, and he swung his club and said: "Move on now! Don't crowd the sidewalk! Everybody must keep moving!"

"Isn't he funny?" asked the Nodding Donkey.

"He is when he doesn't tickle you," said the China Cat, as she looked in a Doll's mirror to see if she had any more specks of dirt on her white coat. But she was nice and clean, was the China Cat.

Then the toys in the store of Horatio Mugg began to have lots of fun. They told stories, sang songs, made up riddles for one another to guess and played tag and hide-and-go-seek. They were allowed to do all this because it was night and no one was watching them. But as soon as daylight came and Mr. Mugg or Miss Angelina or Miss Geraldine or any of the customers came into the store, the toys must be very still and quiet.

"Is this the only store you were ever in?" asked the Donkey of the Cat, as they sat near each other after a lively game of tag.

"No, I was in one other," was the answer. "It was a store in which there lived a Sawdust Doll, a Lamb on Wheels, a Monkey on a Stick and many other playthings."

"Why did you leave?" asked the Donkey. "Was it because there were no other cats there for you to mew to?"

"No, it was not that," was the answer.

"Then why did you leave?" asked the Nodding Donkey.

"Well, one Christmas I was bought by a gentleman who sent me to a lady," was the answer. "She was a lady who was always changing things that came to her from the store. She would buy a thing one day and change it, or send it back, the next.

"And when I came to her as a Christmas present, she happened to have a little China Dog. I guess she thought the dog might bark at me. Anyhow, she sent me back to the store, only she sent me here instead of to the store where the Calico Clown and the other toys lived, and the mistake was never found out. Mr. Mugg and his daughters took me in, and I have been here ever since."

"Do you ever see your friend, the Monkey on a Stick, or hear from the Sawdust Doll?" asked the Donkey.

"Once in a while," was the answer. "Sometimes, when the grown folk buy toys for children they pick out the wrong ones, and the toys are brought back or exchanged. These toys that come back tell us of the houses where they have spent a few days.

"Once a Jumping Jack who was brought back in this way told about being in a house where the Sawdust Doll lived, and where there was also a White Rocking Horse I used to know."

"I should like to meet the White Rocking Horse," said the Nodding Donkey. "He might be a distant relation of mine."

"Perhaps," agreed the China Cat. "But now I think it is time we got back on our shelves. I see daylight beginning to peep in the window, and it would never do for Mr. Mugg or Miss Angelina or Miss Geraldine to see us moving about."

"I suppose not," said the Nodding Donkey, somewhat sadly.

"Move along, everybody! Move back to your places! Daylight is coming!" called the Policeman, as he walked past swinging his club.

And, a little later, when all the toys were back on the shelves, the sun rose, and in came Mr. Mugg to open the store for the day.

All that day people came and went in the toy store, some coming to look, and others to buy. Some of the toys were taken away, and the Nodding Donkey wondered when it would be his turn. But, though he was often taken up, shown and admired, no one purchased him.

"I know what I will do, so that Donkey will be sold!" said Mr. Mugg in the afternoon.

"What?" asked Miss Angelina.

"I will put him in the show window," answered her father.

"Oh, let me decorate the show window!" begged Miss Geraldine. "I'll make up a scene with a Christmas tree, and put the Nodding Donkey under it."

"Very well," agreed Mr. Mugg. "I will leave the show window to you, Geraldine. Make it look as pretty as you can."

And Miss Geraldine did. She got a little Christmas tree and set it up in a box. Then she put some tiny electric lights on it, and also some toys. Other toys were put under the tree, and one of these was the Nodding Donkey.

"Oh, now I can see things!" said the Donkey to himself, as he found he could look right out into the street. It was a scene he had never observed before. All his life had been spent in the workshop of Santa Claus or in the toy store. He was most delighted to look out into the street.

It was snowing, and crowds were hurrying to and fro, doing their Christmas shopping. After the show window in the store of Mr. Horatio Mugg had been newly decorated by Miss Geraldine, many boys and girls and grown folk, too, stopped to peer in. They looked at the Nodding Donkey, at the Jumping Jacks, at the Dolls, the toy Fire Engines, at the Soldiers and at the Policeman.

Toward evening, when the lights had just been set aglow, the Nodding Donkey saw, coming toward the window, a little lame boy. He had to walk on crutches, and with him was a lady who had hold of his arm.

"Oh, Mother, look at the new toys!" cried the lame boy. "And see that Donkey! Why, he's shaking his head at me! Look, he's making his head go up and down! I guess he thinks I asked you if you'd buy him for me, and he's saying 'yes'; isn't he, Mother?"

"Perhaps," answered the lady. "Would you like that Nodding Donkey for Christmas, Joe?"

"Oh, I just would!" cried the lame boy. "Let's go in and look at him. Maybe I can hold him in my hands! Oh, I'd just love that Nodding Donkey!"

Chapter Six: A New Home

For a minute or two longer the lame boy and his mother stood in front of the show window of the toy shop of Mr. Horatio Mugg and his two daughters. The lame boy looked at the Nodding Donkey and the Nodding Donkey bobbed his head in such a funny fashion that the lame boy smiled.

"I'm glad I could make him do that," thought the Donkey. "He doesn't look so sad when he smiles. I wonder what is the matter with him that he walks in such a funny way?"

Of course the Nodding Donkey did not know what it meant to be lame. His own wooden legs were straight and stiff, and he did not need crutches, as did the lame boy.

"Be sure it is the Nodding Donkey you want, and not some other toy," said the boy's mother, as they looked at the things in the window.

"Yes, Mother, I'd rather have him than anything else," the boy answered, and into the store they went. Mr. Mugg came out from behind the counter.

"Would you like to look at some toys?" asked the storekeeper.

"My little boy thinks he would like the Nodding Donkey in the window," said the lady, whose name was Mrs. Richmond.

"Ah, yes, that is a very fine toy!" said Mr. Mugg, with a smile for the lame boy. "It is one of the very latest from the shop of Santa Claus. Geraldine, please show the boy the Nodding Donkey," Mr. Mugg called, and as Joe, the lame boy, walked along with Miss Geraldine, Mr. Mugg said to Mrs. Richmond:

"I am very sorry to see that your boy has to go on crutches."

"Yes, his father and I feel very sad about it," Joe's mother answered. "We have already had the doctors do almost everything they can to cure him, but now we fear he must have another and worse operation. I dread it, and that is why I would get him almost anything to make him happy. He seemed very pleased with the Nodding Donkey."

"I'm sure Joe will like that toy," said Mr. Mugg.

And when Joe had the wooden animal in his hands, and saw how much faster the head nodded at him, the lame boy smiled and said:

"Oh, this is the nicest toy I ever had!"

"I am glad you like it," said the storekeeper. "Geraldine, please wrap up the Nodding Donkey for Joe."

All this while the Nodding Donkey had said nothing, of course, and he had done nothing, except to shake his head. He took one last look around the toy store as he was being wrapped up in paper by Miss Geraldine. The Nodding Donkey saw the Jack in the Box and the China Cat peering at him.

"I wish I might say good-by to them," thought the four-legged toy, "but I suppose it isn't allowed. I shall be lonesome without them."

The China Cat wished she might wave her paw, or even the tip of her tail, at her friend, the Nodding Donkey, and the Jack in the Box did seem to nod a farewell, but perhaps that was because he was on a spring, and could move so easily. As for the China Cat, she had to keep straight and stiff.

With the Nodding Donkey safely wrapped in paper under his arm, Joe left the store of Mr. Mugg with his mother. Joe limped along on his crutches, and he had to go slowly. But he was smiling happily, and for the first day in a long time he forgot about his lameness.

And when his mother saw her son smiling, she, too, smiled. But she was worried about another operation that Joe must go through. The doctor had said that one of his legs had grown so crooked that the only way to fix it was to break it, and let it grow together again, straight.

But now, with his Nodding Donkey, Joe thought nothing about operations, or his crutches, or about being lame. All his mind was on the Nodding Donkey, and he even tore a little hole in the paper so he could look through and make sure his toy was all right.

His mother saw him tearing this hole as they sat in the street car riding home, and as she looked down at him sitting beside her she smiled and asked:

"Aren't you afraid your Nodding Donkey will take cold?"

"Oh, no, Mother," Joe answered. "It is nice and warm in this car. But I'll hold my hand over the hole if you want me to, and that will keep out the wind when we walk along the street."

Soon Joe and his mother left the car, to walk toward their home, which was not far from the corner. The weather was getting colder now, and even inside the wrapping paper the Nodding Donkey could feel it, though the lame boy did hold his hand over the hole.

"I wonder what sort of place I am coming into?" thought the Nodding Donkey, as he felt himself being carried inside a house. Wrapped up as he was, of course he could see nothing. But he could feel that the house was warm, for being out in the cold air was almost like the time he had been tossed from the sleigh of Santa Claus into the snowdrift.

"Now I'll have some fun!" cried Joe, as he took the paper off his toy. "Will you please get me my Noah's Ark, Mother? I'll take the animals and have a circus."

Joe sat down to a table and placed the Nodding Donkey in front of him. Up and down and sidewise bobbed the loose head of the toy. And, as he nodded, the Donkey had a chance to look about him. His new home was quite different from the gay toy store he had been taken from. Here was only a plain house, though it was neat and clean and pretty.

"I think I shall like it here," said the Donkey to himself. "I believe Joe will be good and kind to me. I am going to be lonesome at first, but that cannot be helped."

However, the Nodding Donkey was not lonesome now, for Joe's mother set on the table in front of the boy a rather battered old Noah's Ark. From this Joe took out an elephant, a tiger, a lion, a camel and many other animals. They were not as large or as fine as the Nodding Donkey, and they looked at him in a rather queer way, did these animals from the Noah's Ark. Of course they did not dare say or do anything as long as Joe was looking at them.

"Now I will pretend that this table is the circus ring," said Joe, talking to himself, as he often did. "I will put the Nodding Donkey in the middle and all the other animals around him. Then I'll be the Ringmaster and make believe they are doing tricks."

So Joe put the Nodding Donkey in the very center of the table, where the new toy bobbed his head up and down and sidewise, just as he had done in the store of Mr. Mugg and in the workshop of Santa Claus.

"Now comes the Tiger," said Joe, going on with his circus play, and he set that striped animal down near the Donkey. "And then the Lion. I hope they don't bite my new Donkey."

185

But the Noah's Ark animals were very good and kind, and they did not so much as open their mouths at the Nodding Donkey. Joe played away and had lots of fun at his pretend circus, while his mother got the supper ready. Once when she came into the room where the lame boy sat at the table, Mrs. Richmond said:

"I just saw some friends of yours going past, Joe."

"Who were they?" asked Joe.

"Arnold and Sidney," was the answer. "Arnold had his Bold Tin Soldier, and Sidney was carrying his Calico Clown."

"Oh, I want to see them!" cried Joe. "They have such fun with their toys, and I want them to come in and see mine."

"I'm afraid it is too late—they have gone on home," answered Mrs. Richmond, but Joe took his crutches, which stood near his chair, and hobbled into the front room, where he could look out in the street to see the boys of whom his mother had spoken.

The Nodding Donkey was left on the table with the other animals from the Noah's Ark. As Mrs. Richmond, as well as Joe, was out of the room, and there was no one to look at them, the animals could do as they pleased.

"How do you do?" politely asked the Lion. "We are glad you have come to live here, Mr. Nodding Donkey. But where is the Noah's Ark that you belong in? It must be very large."

"I did not come out of a Noah's Ark," the Donkey answered, with a friendly nod of his head. "I came first from the workshop of Santa Claus, at the North Pole, and just now I came from a toy store."

"Yes, we, too, were in each of those places, years ago," said the Tiger. "But we have belonged to the little lame boy for a long while. He is very good to us, and you will like it here."

"I heard the boy's mother speak of a Bold Tin Soldier and a Calico Clown," said the Donkey. "Do they belong here?"

"No; they are toys that belong to boys who sometimes come to play with Joe," answered the Elephant. "Then we have jolly times! You ought to see that Calico Clown! He is so funny! And you ought to hear him tell about the time in the toy store when his trousers caught fire!"

"That never happened in the toy store where I was—not in Mr. Mugg's store," said the Donkey.

"No, that was another store," said the Elephant. "You'll like the Calico Clown, I know you will, and the Bold Tin Soldier, too. Arnold and Sidney will bring them over some day."

"Now that I think of it, I believe I have heard those toys spoken of in the workshop of Santa Claus," said the Donkey. "The China Cat also mentioned them. Yes, I should like to see them. But we had better stop talking. I think I hear Joe or his mother coming back."

There was a noise at the door, but it was not made by the lame boy or his mother. They were both at the front window, looking down the street at Arnold and Sidney, who were going home, one with his Bold Tin Soldier and the other with his Calico Clown.

And then, all of a sudden, something covered with fur and with a big, bushy tail, like a dustbrush, jumped up on the table and sprang at the Nodding Donkey.

Chapter Seven: The Flood

"**L**ook out there!" roared the Noah's Ark Lion. "Here! What are you going to do?" snarled the Noah's Ark Tiger.

Of course neither of these animals made very much noise, being quite small, but they did the best they could.

"Come over by me, Mr. Nodding Donkey, if you are afraid!" called the Elephant through his trunk. He was the largest animal in the Noah's Ark, but even he was not as big as the Donkey. As for that nodding toy, he reared back on his hind legs when he saw the strange animal, covered with fur and with the big tail like a dustbrush, jump on the table. The toy animals could move and talk among themselves now, as long as no human being was in the room.

The furry animal stood on the table in the midst of the toys. He sat up on his hind legs and seemed to be eating something that he held in his forepaws.

"Are you a cat?" asked the Noah's Ark Camel, sort of making his two humps shiver.

"No, I'm not a cat," was the answer. "I am a Chattering Squirrel, and I am eating a nut. I live in a hollow tree just outside this house, and, seeing a window open and all you toys on the table, I jumped in to see what fun you were having."

"Oh, that's all right," said the Nodding Donkey politely. "We are glad to see you. But even I was scared, at first. We were just talking among ourselves while the lame boy is away. He was playing circus with us."

"I know the lame boy," said the Chattering Squirrel. "He is very kind to me. He puts nuts out for me to eat. I am eating one now.

"We are Glad to See You," said the Nodding Donkey.

Will you have a nibble?" and the squirrel held out the nut to the Nodding Donkey.

"No, thank you; I don't eat nuts," returned the new toy.

"I eat other things, too," went on the Squirrel. "I take them right out of the lame boy's hand, and I never nip him, for I like him and he likes me. I am sorry he is lame."

"So am I," said the Nodding Donkey. "I felt sorry for him when he looked in the store window of Mr. Mugg's shop, and I nodded to him so that he smiled. But hush! Here he comes now!"

And this time it was the lame boy and his mother coming back into the room where the Nodding Donkey and the Noah's Ark toys had been left on the table. Instantly each toy became stark and stiff and no longer moved or spoke. But the Chattering Squirrel, not being a toy, could do as he pleased. So he frisked his tail and nibbled the nut.

"Oh, Mother! See! There is Frisky, my tame Squirrel!" cried Joe. "He must have come in through the window to see my Nodding Donkey. Hello, Frisky!" cried the lame boy, and then when he put down his hand the Chattering Squirrel scrambled across the table and let Joe rub his soft fur.

"I guess he is looking for something to eat," said Mrs. Richmond, with a smile. "He wants his supper, as you want yours, Joe, and as your father will, as soon as he gets home. You had better put away your toys now—your Nodding Donkey and the Noah's Ark animals—and get ready for supper. I think there are a few more nuts left which you may give Frisky."

"Oh, he'll love those, Mother!" cried Joe. And when he had put away his toys he brought out some more nuts for the Squirrel, who liked them very much.

The Nodding Donkey was put up on the mantel shelf in the dining room, but the Noah's Ark toys, being older, were set aside in a closet.

"I want Daddy to see my Donkey as soon as he comes in," said Joe, and he waited for his father. Soon Mr. Richmond's step was heard in the hall, and Joe hobbled on his crutches to meet him. Frisky, the Chattering Squirrel, had skipped out of the open window in the kitchen as soon as he had eaten the nuts Joe gave him.

"How is my boy to-night?" asked Mr. Richmond, as he hugged Joe.

"Oh, I'm fine!" was the answer. "And look what Mother bought me!"

Joe pointed to the Nodding Donkey on the mantel.

"Well, he is a fine fellow!" exclaimed Mr. Richmond. "Where did he come from?"

"From the toy shop," Joe answered, and then, even though supper was almost ready, he had to show his father how the Donkey nodded his head.

"He surely is a jolly chap!" cried Daddy Richmond, when he had taken up the Donkey and looked him all over. "And now how are your legs?" he asked Joe.

"They hurt some; but I don't mind them so much when I have my Donkey," was the answer.

After supper Joe again played with his toy, and, noticing that their son was not listening, Mr. and Mrs. Richmond talked about him in low voices.

"He doesn't really seem to be much better," said the father sadly.

"No," agreed the mother. "I am afraid we shall have to let the doctor break that one leg and set it over again. That may make our boy well."

"I hope so," said Mr. Richmond, and both he and his wife were sad as they thought of the lame one.

But Joe was happier than he had been in some time, for he had his Nodding Donkey to play with. When the time came to go to bed, Joe put the Donkey away in the closet with the Noah's Ark, his toy train of cars, the ball he tossed when his legs did not pain him too much, and his other playthings.

"Well, how do you like it here?" asked the toy Fireman of the toy train, when the house was all quiet and still and the toys were allowed to do as they pleased.

"I think I shall like it very much," was the Donkey's answer.

"I would give you a ride on this toy train," said the Engineer in the cab across from the Fireman, "but you are too large to get in any of the cars."

"But we aren't!" cried the Tiger. "Come on, Mr. Lion, let's go for a ride while we have the chance!"

"All right!" agreed the Lion from the Noah's Ark.

So then, in the closet where they had been put away for the night, the small animals rode up and down the floor in the toy train. The Fireman made believe piles of coal under the boiler, and the Engineer turned on the steam and made the cars go. The Fireman rang the bell, and the Engineer tooted the whistle.

The Nodding Donkey, being rather large, could not fit in the train, but the other toys were just right, and they had a fine time.

"Perhaps if you climbed up on top of the cars I might give you a ride," said the Engineer after he had taken all the Noah's Ark animals on short trips around the closet floor.

"Oh, thank you; but I might fall off and get my head out of order so it would not nod," answered the Donkey. "I think I'll just keep quiet this evening."

"Perhaps you could tell us a story," suggested the Camel. "Tell us the latest news from North Pole Land, where Santa Claus lives. It is a long time since we were there."

"Yes, I could do that," agreed the Nodding Donkey. "And I'll tell you how we ran into a snow bank."

So the Nodding Donkey did this, telling the Noah's Ark animals the same story that I have told you, thus far, in this book. The night passed very happily for the toys in the closet.

When morning came the toys had to become quiet, for it was not allowed for them to be heard talking or to be seen at their make believe fun.

Then began many happy days for the Nodding Donkey. Joe, the lame boy, made a little stable for his new toy, building it out of pieces of wood. He put some straw from the chicken coop in it, so the Donkey would have a soft bed on which to sleep.

Joe played all sorts of games with his new toy. Sometimes it would be a circus game, and again the lame boy would tie little bundles of wood on his Donkey's back, making believe they were gold and diamonds which the animal was carrying down out of pretend mines.

One day Arnold and Sidney, two boys who lived not very far from the home of Joe, came over with their playthings. Arnold brought his Bold Tin Soldier and his company and Sidney his Calico Clown. The three boys looked at the Nodding Donkey and admired him very much, and Joe had fun playing with the Soldier and the Clown.

After a while Mrs. Richmond called to Joe and his chums:

"Come out into the kitchen, boys, and I'll give you some bread and jam," and you can easily believe the boys did not take long to hurry out, Joe stumping along on his crutches.

Meanwhile the Donkey, the Clown, and the Soldier and his men, being left by themselves in the other room, had a chance to talk.

"I am so glad to meet you," brayed the Donkey. "I have heard so much about you."

"Did you hear how once I burned my trousers?" asked the Calico Clown.

"I heard it mentioned," the Donkey said; "but I should like to hear more about it."

"I'll tell you," offered the funny chap. So he related that tale, just as it is told in another of these books.

"Well, that was quite an adventure," said the Donkey, when all had been told. "I suppose you have had adventures, too?" he went on, looking at the Bold Tin Soldier.

"Oh, a few," was the answer.

"Tell them about the time, in the toy shop, when you drew your sword and frightened away the rat that was coming after the Sawdust Doll and the Candy Rabbit," suggested the Clown.

"All right, I will," said the Soldier, and he did. You may read, if you like, about the Candy Rabbit and the Sawdust Doll in the books written especially about those toys.

So the Nodding Donkey listened to the stories told by the Soldier and the Clown, and he was just wishing he might have adventures such as they had had, when back into the room came Joe and his friends. They had finished eating the bread and jam. Then the boys played again with their toys until it was time for Arnold and Sidney to go home.

And now I must tell you of a wonderful adventure that befell the Nodding Donkey about a week after he had come to live with the lame boy, and how he saved Joe's home from being flooded with water.

Joe had been playing with his Nodding Donkey all day, but toward evening the little lame boy's legs pained him so that he had to be put to bed in a hurry. And in such a hurry that he forgot all about the Nodding Donkey and left him on the floor in the kitchen, under the sink, which Joe had pretended was a cave of gold.

"I wonder if I am to stay here all night! It is growing bitterly cold, too!" thought the Donkey, as Joe's father and mother took their boy up to bed. "They must have forgotten me."

And that is just what had happened. After Joe had gone to sleep his father and mother sat in the dining room talking about him.

"I think we shall have to have the doctor come and see Joe tomorrow," said Mr. Richmond. "His legs seem to be getting worse."

"Yes," answered Mrs. Richmond. "Something must be done."

They were both very sad, and sat there silent for some time.

Meanwhile, out in the kitchen, at the sink, something was happening. Suddenly a water pipe burst. It did not make any noise, but the water began trickling down over the floor in a flood. Right where the Nodding Donkey stood, in the pretend cave, the water poured. It rose around the legs of the Donkey, and he felt himself being lifted up and carried across the kitchen toward the dining room door.

The burst pipe had caused a flood, and the Nodding Donkey was right in it!

Chapter Eight: A Broken Leg

Had Mr. and Mrs. Richmond not been in the next room, the Nodding Donkey might have kicked up his heels and have jumped out of the stream of water that was running from the burst pipe of the sink across the floor. But knowing people were so close at hand, where they might catch sight of him, the Donkey dared not move.

All he could do was to float along with the stream of water, which was now getting higher and higher and larger and larger. The water felt cold on the legs of the Donkey, for this was now winter, and the water was like ice. So the Nodding Donkey shivered and shook in the cold water of the flood, and wondered what would happen.

Out in the dining room, next the kitchen, sat Joe's father and mother. They were silent and sad, thinking of their lame boy.

They were thinking so much about him, and what the doctors would have to do to him to make him well and strong, that neither of them paid any heed to the running water. If they had not been thinking so much about Joe they might have heard the hissing sound.

But suddenly Mrs. Richmond, who was looking at the floor, gave a start, and half arose from her chair.

"Look!" she cried to her husband. "There is Joe's Nodding Donkey!"

"Why!" exclaimed Mr. Richmond, "it is floating along on a stream of water! The frost has made a pipe burst in the kitchen and the water is spurting out! Quick! We must shut off the running water!"

It did not take Joe's father long to shut off the water from the burst pipe. That was all that could be done then, as no plumber could be had. Mrs. Richmond lifted the Donkey up off the floor and out of the water, drying him on a towel. And you may well believe that the Donkey was very glad to be warm and dry again. He was afraid his varnish coat would be spoiled, but I am glad to say it was not.

"It's a lucky thing we sat here talking, and that I saw the Donkey come floating in," said Mrs. Richmond, when the water had been mopped up. "If I had not, the whole house might have been flooded by morning."

"Yes," agreed her husband. "Joe's Nodding Donkey did us a good turn. He saved a lot of damage. The water in the kitchen will not do much harm, but if it had flooded the rest of the house it would."

Then the Donkey was put away in the closet where he belonged, together with the animals from the Noah's Ark.

"How cold and shivery you are, Mr. Donkey," said the Noah's Ark Lamb, when the Donkey had been placed on the closet shelf, after the flood.

"I guess you'd be cold and shivery, too, if you had been through such an adventure as just happened to me!" answered the Donkey.

"Oh, tell us about it!" begged the Lion. "We have been quite dull here all evening, wondering where you were."

So the Donkey told his story of the burst pipe, and after that the animals went to sleep.

Joe was quite surprised when, the next morning, he was told what had happened. And when the plumber came to fix the broken pipe Joe showed the man the Nodding Donkey who had first given warning of the flood.

"He is a fine toy!" said the plumber.

After this Joe's Nodding Donkey had many adventures in his new home. I wish I had room to tell you all of them, but I can only mention a few.

The weather grew colder and colder, and some days many snowflakes fell. The Donkey, looking out of the window, saw them, and he thought of Santa Claus and North Pole Land.

Joe was not as lively as he had been that day he went to Mr. Mugg's store and bought the toy. There were days when Joe never took the Nodding Donkey off the shelf at all. The wooden toy just had to stay there, while Joe lay on a couch near the window and looked out.

"This is too bad!" thought the Donkey. "Joe ought to run about and play like Arnold and Sidney. They have lots of fun in the snow, and they take out the Calico Clown and the Bold Tin Soldier, too. I wish Joe would take me out. I don't mind the cold of the snow as much as I minded the cold water."

But Joe seemed to have forgotten about his Nodding Donkey. The toy stood on a shelf over the couch where the lame boy lay. Once in a while Joe would ask his mother to hand him down the Donkey, but more often the lame boy would lie with his eyes closed, doing nothing.

Then, one day, a sad accident happened. Mrs. Richmond was upstairs, getting Joe's bed ready for him. Though it was not yet night, he said he felt so tired he thought he would go to bed. On the shelf over his head was the Nodding Donkey.

Suddenly, in through a kitchen window that had been left open came Frisky, the Chattering Squirrel. Over the floor scampered the lively little chap, and he gave a sort of whistle at Joe.

"Oh, hello, Frisky!" said the lame boy, opening his eyes. "I'm glad you came in!"

Of course Frisky could not say so in boy language, but he, too, was glad to see Joe.

"Come here, Frisky!" called Joe, and he held out his hand.

"I guess he has some nuts for me," thought the squirrel, and he was right. In one pocket Joe had some nuts, and now he held these out to his little live pet.

Frisky took a nut in his paw, which was almost like a hand, and then, as squirrels often do, he looked for a high place on which he might perch himself to eat. Frisky saw the shelf over Joe's couch, the same shelf on which stood the Nodding Donkey.

"I'll go up there to eat the nut," said Frisky to himself.

Up he scrambled, but he was such a lively little chap that in swinging his tail from side to side he brushed it against the Nodding Donkey.

With a crash that toy fell to the floor near Joe's couch!

"Oh, Frisky! Look what you did!" cried Joe. But the squirrel was so busy eating the nut that he paid no attention to the Donkey.

Joe picked up his plaything. One of the Donkey's varnished legs was dangling by a few splinters.

"Oh! Oh, dear!" cried Joe. "My Donkey's leg is broken! Now he will have to go on crutches as I do! Mother! Come quick!" cried Joe. "Something terrible has happened to my Nodding Donkey!"

Chapter Nine: A Lonesome Donkey

"**W**hat is the matter, Joe? What has happened?" asked Mrs. Richmond, hurrying downstairs, leaving her son's bed half made.

Mrs. Richmond, hurrying into the room where she had left Joe lying on the couch, saw him sitting up and holding his Nodding Donkey in his hands.

"Oh, look, Mother!" and Joe's voice sounded as if he might be going to cry. "Look what Frisky did to my Donkey! Knocked him off the shelf, and his left hind leg is broken."

"That is too bad," said Mrs. Richmond, but her face showed that she was glad it was not Joe who was hurt. "Yes, the Donkey's leg is broken," she went on, as she took the toy from her son. "Frisky, you are a bad squirrel to break Joe's Donkey!" and she shook her finger at the chattering little animal, who, perched on the shelf, was eating the nut the boy had given him.

"Oh, Mother! Frisky didn't mean to do it," said Joe. "It wasn't his fault. I guess the Nodding Donkey was too close to the edge of the shelf. But now his leg is broken, and I guess he'll have to go on crutches, the same as I do; won't he, Mother?"

The Nodding Donkey did not hear any of this. The pain in his leg was so great that he had fainted, though Joe and his mother did not know this. But the Donkey really had fainted.

"No, Joe," said Mrs. Richmond, after a while, "your Donkey will not have to go on crutches, and I hope the day will soon come when you can lay them aside."

"What do you mean, Mother?" Joe asked eagerly. "Do you think I will ever get better?"

"We hope so," she answered softly. "In a few days you are going to a nice place, called a hospital, where you will go to sleep in a little white bed. Then the doctors will come and, when you wake up again, your legs may be nice and straight so, after a while, you can walk on them again without leaning on crutches."

"Oh, won't I be glad when that happens!" cried Joe, with shining eyes. "But what about my Nodding Donkey, Mother? Can I take him to the hospital and have him fixed, too, so he will not need crutches?"

"Well, we shall see about that," Mrs. Richmond said. "I'll tie his leg up now with a rag, and when your father comes home he may know how to fix it. I never heard of a donkey on crutches."

"I didn't either!" laughed Joe. He felt a little happier now, because he hoped he might be made well and strong again, and because he hoped his father could fix the broken leg of the Nodding Donkey.

Mrs. Richmond got a piece of cloth, and, straightening out the Donkey's leg as best she could, she tied it up. Then she put the toy far back on the shelf, laying it down on its side so it would not fall off again, or topple over.

Frisky scampered out of the window, back to his home in the hollow tree at the end of the yard. Frisky never knew what damage he had done. He was too eager to eat the nut Joe had given him.

"Now lie quietly here, Joe," his mother said. "I will soon have your bed ready for you, and then you can go to sleep."

"I don't want to go until Daddy comes home, so he can fix my Donkey," said the boy, and his mother allowed him to remain up until Mr. Richmond came from the office.

"Oh, ho! So the Donkey has a broken leg, has he?" asked Mr. Richmond in his usual jolly voice, when he came in where Joe was lying on the couch. "Well, I think I can have him fixed."

"How?" asked the little lame boy.

"I'll take him back to the same toy store where you bought him," answered his father. "Mr. Mugg knows how to mend all sorts of toys."

By this time the Donkey had gotten over the fainting fit, as his leg did not hurt him so much after Mrs. Richmond had tied the rag around it. And now the Donkey heard what was said.

"Take me back to the toy store, will they?" thought the Donkey to himself. "Well, I shall be glad to have my leg mended, and also to see the China Cat and some of my other friends. But I want to come back to Joe. I like him, and I like it here. Besides, I am near the Calico Clown and the Bold Tin Soldier. Yes, I shall want to come back when my leg is mended."

Mr. Richmond, still leaving on the Donkey's leg the rag Mrs. Richmond had wound around it, put the toy back on the shelf. Then he carried Joe up to bed.

"When will the doctors operate on our boy, to make him better?" asked Mrs. Richmond of her husband, when Joe was asleep.

"In about a week," was his answer. "I stopped at the hospital to-day, and made all the plans. Joe is to go there a week from today."

"Will his Nodding Donkey be mended by that time?" asked Mrs. Richmond. "I think Joe would like to take it to the hospital with him."

"I'll try to get Mr. Mugg to finish it so Joe may have it," said Mr. Richmond. "Poor boy! He has had a hard time in life, but if this operation is a success he will be much happier."

All night long the Nodding Donkey lay on the shelf, his broken leg wrapped in the cloth. He did not nod now, for, lying down as he was, his head could not shake and wabble. Besides, the toy felt too sad and was in too much pain to nod, even if he had stood on his feet. But of course he couldn't stand up with a broken leg. Indeed not!

In the closet, where they were kept, the animals from Noah's Ark talked among themselves that night.

"Where is the Nodding Donkey?" asked the Lion. "Why is he not here with us?"

"I hope he hasn't become too proud, because he is a new, shiny toy and we are old and battered," said the Tiger sadly.

"Nonsense!" rumbled the Elephant. "The Nodding Donkey is not that kind of toy. He would be here if he could. Some accident has happened, you may depend on it."

"Well, I'm glad my train didn't run over him," said the Engineer of the toy locomotive.

"It was some kind of accident, I'm sure," insisted the Elephant. "I heard Joe cry out, and his mother came running downstairs."

And it was an accident, as you know. All night the Nodding Donkey lay on the shelf in the dining room. He had no other toys to talk to, and perhaps it was just as well, for he did not feel like talking with his broken leg hurting him as it did.

Early the next morning Mr. Richmond was on his way to the office, taking the Nodding Donkey with him.

"Let me see him once more before you take him to the toy shop to be fixed!" begged Joe, who had been told what was to be done with his plaything.

Joe's father put the Nodding Donkey into his son's hands.

"Poor fellow!" murmured Joe, gently touching the broken leg. "You are a cripple like me, now. I hope they make you well again."

Then, with another kind pat, Joe gave the Donkey back to his father, and, a little later, Mr. Richmond walked into Mr. Mugg's store with the toy. "Hum! Yes, that is a bad break, but I think I can fix it," said the jolly old gentleman.

"Let me see," begged Miss Angelina, peering over her father's shoulder, with a dustbrush under her arm. She had been dusting the toys ready for the day's business.

"The leg isn't broken all the way off," said Miss Geraldine, who was washing the face of a China Doll, that, somehow or other, had fallen in the dust.

"Yes, that is a good thing," observed Mr. Mugg. "I can glue the parts together and the Donkey will be as strong as ever. Leave it here, Mr. Richmond. I'll fix it."

"And may I have it back this week?" asked the other. "My boy is going to the hospital to have his legs made strong, if possible, and I think he would like to take the Donkey with him."

"You may have it day after tomorrow," promised the toy man.

The Nodding Donkey was still in such pain from his broken leg that he did not pay much attention to the other toys in the store. But Mr. Mugg lost no time in getting to work on the broken toy.

"Heat me the pot of glue, Geraldine," he called to his daughter, "and get me some paint and varnish. When I mend the broken leg I'll paint over the splintered place, so it will not show."

The Nodding Donkey was taken to a work bench. Mr. Mugg, wearing a long apron and a cap, just like the workmen in the shop of Santa Claus, sat down to begin.

With tiny pieces of wood, put in the broken leg to make it as strong as the others that were not broken, with hot, sticky glue, and with strands of silk thread, Mr. Mugg worked on the Nodding Donkey. The toy felt like braying out as loudly as he could when he felt the hot]glue on his leg, but he was not permitted to do this, since Mr. Mugg was looking at him. So he had to keep silent, and in the end he felt much better.

"There, I think you will do now," said Mr. Mugg, as he tightly bound some bandages on the Donkey's leg. "When it gets dry I will paint it over and it will look as good as new."

The mended Donkey was set aside on a shelf by himself, and not among the toys that were for sale. All day and all night long he remained there. He was feeling too upset and in too much pain to be lonesome. All he wished for was to be better.

In the morning he was almost himself again. Mr. Mugg came, and, finding the glue hard and dry, took off the bandages. Then with his knife he scraped away little hard pieces of glue that had dried on the outside, and the toy man also cut away some splinters of new wood that stuck out.

"Now to paint your leg, and you will be finished," said Mr. Mugg.

The smell of the paint and varnish, as it was put on him, made the Nodding Donkey think of when he had first come to life in the workshop of Santa Claus. He was feeling quite young and happy again.

"There you are!" cried Mr. Mugg, as he once more set the Donkey on the shelf for the paint and varnish to dry. And this time the Donkey was allowed to be among the other toys, though he was not for sale.

That night in the store, when all was quiet and still, the Nodding Donkey shook his head and spoke to the China Cat, who was not far away.

"Well, you see I am back here again," said the Nodding Donkey.

"Have you come to stay?" asked the China Cat. "You can't imagine how surprised I was when I saw you brought in! But what has happened?"

Then the Donkey told of his accident, and how he had been mended.

"Your leg looks all right now," said the China Cat, glancing at it in the light of the one lamp Mr. Mugg left burning when he closed his store.

"Yes, I am feeling quite myself again," said the Donkey. "But I am not here to stay. I must go back to Joe, the lame boy."

"At least we shall have a chance to talk over old times for a little while," said the China Cat. "I came near being sold yesterday. A lady was going to buy me for her baby to cut his teeth on. Just fancy!"

"I don't believe you would have liked that," said the Donkey.

"No, indeed!" mewed the China Cat. Then she and the Donkey and the other toys talked for some hours, and told stories. On account of his paint not being dry the Donkey did not walk around, jump or kick as he had used to do.

In the morning the toys had to stop their fun-making, for Mr. Mugg and his daughters came to open the store for the day. And in the afternoon Mr. Richmond called to get the mended toy.

And you can imagine how glad Joe was to get his Donkey back again.

"I'll never let Frisky break any more of your legs," said Joe, as he hugged the Donkey to him. "I'll take you to bed with me tonight."

But though Joe was allowed to take his Donkey to bed with him, it was thought best not to send the toy to the hospital with the little boy, when he went early the next week.

"Good-by, Nodding Donkey!" called Joe to his toy, as he was driven away; and when Mrs. Richmond put the mended Donkey away on the closet shelf, there were tears in her eyes.

The Nodding Donkey knew that something was wrong, but he did not understand all that was happening. He had seen Joe taken away, and he saw himself put in the closet with the Noah's Ark animals.

"What is the matter?" asked the Lion. "Is Joe tired of playing with you, as he grew tired of us?"

"I hope not," said the Nodding Donkey sadly.

But as that day passed, and the next, the Nodding Donkey grew very lonesome for Joe, for he had learned to love the little lame boy.

Chapter Ten: Joe Can Run

About a week after Joe had been taken to the hospital, where he had been put in a little white bed, with a rosy-cheeked nurse to look after him, there came a knock on the door of the house where Joe lived, and where the Nodding Donkey also had his home.

"Is Joe here?" asked a little girl named Mirabell, who carried in her arms a toy Lamb on Wheels.

"Joe? No, dear, he isn't here. He is in the hospital having his lame legs fixed," answered Mrs. Richmond. "Didn't you hear about his going away?"

"No," answered Mirabell, "I didn't. But Sidney said Joe had a Nodding Donkey, and I brought my Lamb on Wheels to see the Donkey."

"That is very kind of you," said Mrs. Richmond. "Come in. We are quite worried about Joe, and we hope he will get well and strong so he can run about. But it will be some time yet before he comes from the hospital."

Mirabell entered the house with her Lamb on Wheels. The little girl looked sad when she heard about Joe, but a smile came over her face when she saw the Nodding Donkey, which Joe's mother brought from the closet.

"Oh, what a lovely Donkey!" cried Mirabell. "See, Lamb!" and she held up her toy. "Meet Mr. Nodding Donkey!"

The Donkey nodded his head, but the Lamb could not do that. However, she looked kindly at the nodding toy.

While Mirabell was playing with her Lamb and the Donkey there came another knock on the door of Joe's house.

"It is Herbert with his Monkey on a Stick," said Mrs. Richmond. "Come in," she added, as she opened the door.

"Is Joe back yet?" asked Herbert, after he had said "hello" to Mirabell and put his Monkey toy on the table.

"No, Joe is still in the hospital," answered the lame boy's mother. "He will be home in about three weeks, we hope. Here is his Nodding Donkey toy."

"Oh, that's fine!" cried Herbert. "Arnold told me about it, and I wanted to see it. My mother told me about Joe going to the hospital, and I came to see how he was."

"It is very kind of you," said Joe's mother. "Now I'll leave you children to play with your toys awhile, until I call up the hospital on the telephone and see how Joe is to-day. I have not had a chance to visit him yet."

Herbert and Mirabell had fun playing together, and with the Lamb on Wheels, the Monkey on a Stick, and the Nodding Donkey. After a while the children were given some bread and jam by Mrs. Richmond, who called them into another room to eat it.

"I heard from the hospital that Joe is much better to-day," said Mrs. Richmond, as she spread more bread and butter for her little visitors.

While they were left in the room by themselves, the toys spoke to one another.

"You are a new one, aren't you?" asked the Lamb of the Donkey.

"Yes," was the answer. "Joe got me only a little while before he was taken to the hospital, wherever that is. I guess I was in the hospital myself, when I had my broken leg mended."

"Oh, tell us about it!" begged the Monkey, as he climbed to the top of his stick and slid down again.

So the Donkey told how Frisky had knocked him off the shelf, breaking his leg.

"And Joe had something the matter with his legs, too, so that's why he had to go to the hospital," added the Donkey, as he finished his story. "I do hope he comes back soon, for I am lonesome without him."

The toys spent a happy half hour together, and then when Mirabell and Herbert came back into the room, having finished their bread and jam, the Donkey, the Lamb, and the Monkey had to become quiet.

"We'll come over again, when Joe gets home," said Mirabell, as she and Herbert left.

"And we'll get the other boys and girls and give him a toy party," added the owner of the Monkey.

"Oh, that will be lovely!" said Mrs. Richmond.

The Nodding Donkey was put back in the closet, where he told the Noah's Ark animals all about the visit of the Monkey and Lamb.

"I have heard of those toys," said tElephant. "They know the Sawdust Doll, the White Rocking Horse, the Candy Rabbit, and the Bold Tin Soldier."

211

"My, what a lot of jolly toys there are!" said the Donkey. And then he grew silent, thinking of poor little Joe in the hospital.

Joe did not have an easy time. He was very ill and in great pain, but the kind doctors and nurses looked well after him, and his father and mother went to see him almost every day. One afternoon, when Joe had been in the hospital for what seemed to him a whole year, his father and the doctor came into the room. There was also a nurse, and she began to put on Joe the clothes he wore in the street.

"What is going to happen?" asked the boy.

"I am going to take you home, and give your mother a joyful surprise," said his father.

"Oh, how glad I am!" cried Joe. "And then I can see my Nodding Donkey, can't I? Is he all right, Daddy?"

"As right and as fine as ever," answered Mr. Richmond.

Joe could hardly sit still during the ride home. He got out of the automobile and went through the snow up to the front door. His father opened it, and Joe saw his mother standing at the end of the hall.

For a moment Mrs. Richmond could hardly believe what she saw.

"Joe! Joe, my little boy!" she cried. "Oh, you have come home again! Are you all right? Are your legs better? Can you walk?"

"Can I walk, Mother!" cried Joe, in a happy voice. "Of course I can! I can walk without my crutches, and I can run! I can run! See!"

And with that Joe ran down the hall and into his mother's arms.

Oh, what a joyful happy time there was! Joe's legs were straight and strong again, and he did not need his crutches any more.

"And now where is my Nodding Donkey?" he asked. "I want to see him!"

"I'll get him for you," offered his mother, and when the toy was set on the table near Joe, it nodded its head to welcome him home.

"Oh, my dear Donkey! how I missed you while I was in the hospital," said Joe.

"And I missed you, too," thought the Donkey.

Two or three days after this, when Joe had gotten used to being at home again, there came a knock at the door. Outside happy voices were talking and laughing.

When Joe opened the door there stood Dorothy with her Sawdust Doll, Dick with his White Rocking Horse, Arnold with his Bold Tin Soldier, Mirabell with her Lamb, Madeline, who had a Candy Rabbit, Herbert, who carried a Monkey on a Stick, and Sidney with the Calico Clown.

"Surprise on Joe! Surprise on Joe!" cried the children. "We have come to make a Toy Party for you and your Nodding Donkey!"

"Oh, how glad I am!" Joe laughed. "Look at my legs!" he went on. "They are straight now, and I don't have to go on crutches. And my Nodding Donkey, who had a broken leg, is well, too! He doesn't have to go on crutches, either!"

"Hurray!" cried Dick, and all the other boys and girls said: "Hurray! Hurray! Hurray!"

Then the Toy Party began, and the children and the toys had so much fun that it would take three books just to tell about half of it. Joe and his Nodding Donkey were the guests of honor, and all the others tried to make them feel happy. And Joe was happy! One look at his smiling face told that.

As for the Nodding Donkey, you could tell by the way he moved his head that never, in all his life, had he had such a good time.

When Mrs. Richmond called the children to the dining room to eat, the toys were left by themselves in a playroom.

"Ladies and Gentlemen," said the Calico Clown in his jolly voice, "we have all met together, after a long time of being apart. We have all had good times together, and now I hope you will all agree with me when I say that we are glad to welcome the Nodding Donkey among us."

"Yes, he is very welcome," said the Sawdust Doll. "We are glad he has come to live in this part of the world."

"I am glad of it myself," said the Nodding Donkey. "I never knew, while I was in the workshop of Santa Claus, that so many things could happen down here. Yes, I am very happy that I came. There is only one thing I wish."

"What is that?" asked the Monkey.

"I wish the China Cat were here," said the Donkey. "She lives in Mr. Mugg's store, and I'm sure you would all like her, she is so clean and white."

"Three cheers for the China Cat!" called the Bold Tin Soldier, waving his sword.

And the toys cheered among themselves.

"Tell me more about this China Cat," begged the Candy Rabbit to the Donkey. "Is she anything like me?"

The Nodding Donkey is Welcomed by the Calico Clown.

The Nodding Donkey was just going to tell about the China Cat when Joe and the other children came trooping back into the room, having finished their lunch.

"Now let's play circus!" cried Joe. "We have a lot of toys and animals now. Let's play circus."

And so they did. But as there is a story to tell about the China Cat, and as I have no room in this book, I will make up another, and it will be all about the Nodding Donkey's friend, the white China Cat, and how she had many adventures, but managed to keep herself clean.

As for Joe and his friends, they had a very Merry Christmas and a Happy New Year, and the Nodding Donkey lived for a long while after that, happy and contented, and he never even had so much as a pain in the broken leg that Mr. Mugg had mended so nicely.

ENGLAND

Old Father Christmas

J.H. Ewing
ILLUSTRATIONS GORDON BROWNE

T he custom of Christmas-trees came from Germany. I can
remember when they were first introduced into England,
and what wonderful things we thought them. Now, every
village school has its tree, and the scholars openly discuss whether
the presents have been 'good,' or 'mean,' as compared with other
trees in former years. The first one that I ever saw I believed to
have come from Good Father Christmas himself; but little boys
have grown too wise now to be taken in for their own amusement.
They are not excited by secret and mysterious preparations in the
back drawing-room; they hardly confess to the thrill—which I feel
to this day—when the folding doors are thrown open, and amid the
blaze of tapers, mamma, like a Fate, advances with her scissors to
give everyone what falls to his lot.

"Well, young people, when I was eight years old I had not seen a Christmas-tree, and the first picture of one I ever saw was the picture of that held by Old Father Christmas in my godmother's picture-book.

"'What are those things on the tree?' I asked.

"'Candles,' said my father.

"'No, father, not the candles; the other things?'

"'Those are toys, my son.'

"'Are they ever taken off?'

"'Yes, they are taken off, and given to the children who stand around the tree.'

"Patty and I grasped each other by the hand, and with one voice murmured, 'How kind of Old Father Christmas!'

"By and by I asked, 'How old is Father Christmas?'

"My father laughed, and said, 'One thousand eight hundred and thirty years, child,' which was then the year of our Lord, and thus one thousand eight hundred and thirty years since the first great Christmas Day.

"'He looks very old,' whispered Patty.

"And I, who was, for my age, what Kitty called 'Bible-learned,' said thoughtfully, and with some puzzledness of mind, 'Then he's older than Methuselah.'

"But my father had left the room, and did not hear my difficulty.

"November and December went by, and still the picture-book kept all its charm for Patty and me; and we pondered on and loved Old Father Christmas as children can love and realize a fancy friend. To those who remember the fancies of their childhood I need say no more.

"Christmas week came, Christmas Eve came. My father and mother were mysteriously and unaccountably busy in the parlour (we had only one parlour), and Patty and I were not allowed to go in. We went into the kitchen, but even here was no place of rest for us. Kitty was 'all over the place,' as she phrased it, and cakes, mince pies, and puddings were with her. As she justly observed, 'There was no place there for children and books to sit with their toes in the fire, when a body wanted to be at the oven all along. The cat was enough for her temper,' she added.

"As to puss, who obstinately refused to take a hint which drove her out into the Christmas frost, she returned again and again with soft steps, and a stupidity that was, I think, affected, to the warm hearth, only to fly at intervals, like a football, before Kitty's hasty slipper.

"We had more sense, or less courage. We bowed to Kitty's behests, and went to the back door.

"Patty and I were hardy children, and accustomed to 'run out' in all weathers, without much extra wrapping up. We put Kitty's shawl over our two heads, and went outside. I rather hoped to see something of Dick, for it was holiday time; but no Dick passed. He was busy helping his father to bore holes in the carved seats of the church, which were to hold sprigs of holly for the morrow—that was the idea of church decoration in my young days. You have improved on your elders there, young people, and I am candid enough to allow it. Still, the sprigs of red and green were better than nothing, and, like your lovely wreaths and pious devices, they made one feel as if the old black wood were bursting into life and

219

leaf again for very Christmas joy; and, if only one knelt carefully, they did not scratch his nose.

"Well, Dick was busy, and not to be seen. We ran across the little yard and looked over the wall at the end to see if we could see anything or anybody. From this point there was a pleasant meadow field sloping prettily away to a little hill about three quarters of a mile distant; which, catching some fine breezes from the moors beyond, was held to be a place of cure for whooping-cough, or kincough, as it was vulgarly called. Up to the top of this Kitty had dragged me, and carried Patty, when we were recovering from the complaint, as I well remember. It was the only 'change of air' we could afford, and I dare say it did as well as if we had gone into badly drained lodgings at the seaside.

"This hill was now covered with snow and stood off against the gray sky. The white fields looked vast and dreary in the dusk. The only gay things to be seen were the berries on the holly hedge, in the little lane—which, running by the end of our back-yard, led up to the Hall—and the fat robin, that was staring at me. I was looking at the robin, when Patty, who had been peering out of her corner of Kitty's shawl, gave a great jump that dragged the shawl from our heads, and cried:

"'Look!'

"I looked. An old man was coming along the lane. His hair and beard were as white as cotton-wool. He had a face like the sort of apple that keeps well in winter; his coat was old and brown. There was snow about him in patches, and he carried a small fir-tree.

"The same conviction seized upon us both. With one breath, we exclaimed, 'It's Old Father Christmas!'

"I know now that it was only an old man of the place, with whom we did not happen to be acquainted and that he was taking a little fir-tree up to the Hall, to be made into a Christmas-tree. He was a very good-humoured old fellow, and rather deaf, for which he made up by smiling and nodding his head a good deal, and saying, 'aye, aye, to be sure!' at likely intervals.

"As he passed us and met our earnest gaze, he smiled and nodded so earnestly that I was bold enough to cry, 'Good-evening, Father Christmas!'

"'Same to you!' said he, in a high-pitched voice.

"'Then you are Father Christmas?' said Patty.

"'And a happy New Year,' was Father Christmas's reply, which rather put me out. But he smiled in such a satisfactory manner that Patty went on, 'You're very old, aren't you?'

"'So I be, miss, so I be,' said Father Christmas, nodding.

"'Father says you're eighteen hundred and thirty years old,' I muttered.

"'Aye, aye, to be sure,' said Father Christmas. 'I'm a long age.'

"A very long age, thought I, and I added, 'You're nearly twice as old as Methuselah, you know,' thinking that this might have struck him.

"'Aye, aye,' said Father Christmas; but he did not seem to think anything of it. After a pause he held up the tree, and cried, 'D'ye know what this is, little miss?'

"'A Christmas-tree,' said Patty.

"And the old man smiled and nodded.

"I leant over the wall, and shouted, 'But there are no candles.'

"'By and by,' said Father Christmas, nodding as before. 'When it's dark they'll all be lighted up. That'll be a fine sight!'

"'Toys, too, there'll be, won't there?' said Patty.

"Father Christmas nodded his head. 'And sweeties,' he added, expressively.

"I could feel Patty trembling, and my own heart beat fast. The thought which agitated us both was this: 'Was Father Christmas bringing the tree to us?' But very anxiety, and some modesty also, kept us from asking outright.

"Only when the old man shouldered his tree, and prepared to move on, I cried in despair, 'Oh, are you going?'

"'I'm coming back by and by,' said he.

"'How soon?' cried Patty.

"'About four o'clock,' said the old man smiling. 'I'm only going up yonder.'

"And, nodding and smiling as he went, he passed away down the lane.

"'Up yonder!' This puzzled us. Father Christmas had pointed, but so indefinitely that he might have been pointing to the sky, or the fields, or the little wood at the end of the Squire's grounds. I thought the latter, and suggested to Patty that perhaps he had some place underground like Aladdin's cave, where he got the candles, and all the pretty things for the tree. This idea pleased us both, and we amused ourselves by wondering what Old Father Christmas would choose for us from his stores in that wonderful hole where he dressed his Christmas-trees.

"'I wonder, Patty,' said I, 'why there's no picture of Father Christmas's dog in the book.' For at the old man's heels in the lane there crept a little brown and white spaniel looking very dirty in the snow.

"'Perhaps it's a new dog that he's got to take care of his cave,' said Patty.

"When we went indoors we examined the picture afresh by the dim light from the passage window, but there was no dog there.

"My father passed us at this moment, and patted my head. 'Father,' said I, 'I don't know, but I do think Old Father Christmas is going to bring us a Christmas-tree to-night.'

"'Who's been telling you that?' said my father. But he passed on before I could explain that we had seen Father Christmas himself, and had had his word for it that he would return at four o'clock, and that the candles on his tree would be lighted as soon as it was dark.

"We hovered on the outskirts of the rooms till four o'clock came. We sat on the stairs and watched the big clock, which I was just learning to read; and Patty made herself giddy with constantly looking up and counting the four strokes, toward which the hour hand slowly moved. We put our noses into the kitchen now and then, to smell the cakes and get warm, and anon we hung about the parlour door, and were most unjustly accused of trying to peep. What did we care what our mother was doing in the parlour?—we, who had seen Old Father Christmas himself, and were expecting him back again every moment!

"At last the church clock struck. The sounds boomed heavily through the frost, and Patty thought there were four of them. Then, after due choking and whirring, our own clock struck, and we counted the strokes quite clearly—one! two! three! four! Then we got Kitty's shawl once more, and stole out into the back-yard. We ran to our old place, and peeped, but could see nothing.

"'We'd better get up on to the wall,' I said; and with some difficulty and distress from rubbing her bare knees against the cold stone, and getting the snow up her sleeves, Patty got on to the coping of the little wall. I was just struggling after her, when something warm and something cold coming suddenly against the bare calves of my legs made me shriek with fright. I came down 'with a run' and bruised my knees, my elbows, and my chin; and the snow that hadn't gone up Patty's sleeves went down my neck. Then I found that the cold thing was a dog's nose and the warm thing was his tongue; and Patty cried from her post of observation, 'It's Father Christmas's dog and he's licking your legs.'

"It really was the dirty little brown and white spaniel, and he persisted in licking me, and jumping on me, and making curious little noises, that must have meant something if one had known his language. I was rather harassed at the moment. My legs were sore, I was a little afraid of the dog, and Patty was very much afraid of sitting on the wall without me.

"'You won't fall,' I said to her. 'Get down, will you?' I said to the dog.

"'Humpty Dumpty fell off a wall,' said Patty.

"'Bow! wow!' said the dog.

"I pulled Patty down, and the dog tried to pull me down; but when my little sister was on her feet, to my relief, he transferred his attentions to her. When he had jumped at her, and licked her several times, he turned around and ran away.

"'He's gone,' said I; 'I'm so glad.'

"But even as I spoke he was back again, crouching at Patty's feet, and glaring at her with eyes the colour of his ears.

"Now, Patty was very fond of animals, and when the dog looked at her she looked at the dog, and then she said to me, 'He wants us to go with him.'

"On which (as if he understood our language, though we were ignorant of his) the spaniel sprang away, and went off as hard as he could; and Patty and I went after him, a dim hope crossing my mind—'Perhaps Father Christmas has sent him for us.'

"The idea was rather favoured by the fact he led us up the lane. Only a little way; then he stopped by something lying in the ditch— and once more we cried in the same breath, 'It's Old Father Christmas!'

"Returning from the Hall, the old man had slipped upon a bit of ice, and lay stunned in the snow.

"Patty began to cry. 'I think he's dead!' she sobbed.

"'He is so very old, I don't wonder,' I murmured; 'but perhaps he's not. I'll fetch father.'

"My father and Kitty were soon on the spot. Kitty was as strong as a man; and they carried Father Christmas between them into the kitchen. There he quickly revived.

"I must do Kitty the justice to say that she did not utter a word of complaint at the disturbance of her labours; and that she drew the old man's chair close up to the oven with her own hand. She was so much affected by the behaviour of his dog that she admitted him even to the hearth; on which puss, being acute enough to see how matters stood, lay down with her back so close to the spaniel's that Kitty could not expel one without kicking both.

"For our parts, we felt sadly anxious about the tree; otherwise we could have wished for no better treat than to sit at Kitty's round table taking tea with Father Christmas. Our usual fare of thick bread and treacle was to-night exchanged for a delicious variety of cakes, which were none the worse to us for being 'tasters and wasters'—that is, little bits of dough, or shortbread, put in to try the state of the oven, and certain cakes that had got broken or burnt in the baking.

"Well, there we sat, helping Old Father Christmas to tea and cake, and wondering in our hearts what could have become of the tree.

"Patty and I felt a delicacy in asking Old Father Christmas about the tree. It was not until we had had tea three times round, with tasters and wasters to match, that Patty said very gently: 'It's quite dark now.' And then she heaved a deep sigh.

"Burning anxiety overcame me. I leaned toward Father Christmas, and shouted—I had found out that it was needful to shout——

"'I suppose the candles are on the tree now?'

"'Just about putting of 'em on,' said Father Christmas.

"'And the presents, too?' said Patty.

"'Aye, aye, to be sure,' said Father Christmas, and he smiled delightfully.

"I was thinking what further questions I might venture upon, when he pushed his cup toward Patty saying, 'Since you are so pressing, miss, I'll take another dish.'

"And Kitty, swooping on us from the oven, cried, 'Make yourself at home, sir; there's more where these came from. Make a long arm, Miss Patty, and hand them cakes.'

"So we had to devote ourselves to the duties of the table; and Patty, holding the lid with one hand and pouring with the other, supplied Father Christmas's wants with a heavy heart.

"At last he was satisfied. I said grace, during which he stood, and, indeed, he stood for some time afterward with his eyes shut—I fancy under the impression that I was still speaking. He had just said a fervent 'amen,' and reseated himself, when my father put his head into the kitchen, and made this remarkable statement:

"'Old Father Christmas has sent a tree to the young people.'

"Patty and I uttered a cry of delight, and we forthwith danced round the old man, saying, 'How nice! Oh, how kind of you!' which I think must have bewildered him, but he only smiled and nodded.

"'Come along,' said my father. 'Come, children. Come, Reuben. Come, Kitty.'

"And he went into the parlour, and we all followed him.

"My godmother's picture of a Christmas-tree was very pretty; and the flames of the candles were so naturally done in red and yellow that I always wondered that they did not shine at night. But the picture was nothing to the reality. We had been sitting almost in the dark, for, as Kitty said, 'Firelight was quite enough to burn at meal-times.' And when the parlour door was thrown open, and the tree, with lighted tapers on all the branches, burst upon our view, the blaze was dazzling, and threw such a glory round the little gifts, and the bags of coloured muslin, with acid drops and pink rose drops and comfits inside, as I shall never forget. We all got something; and Patty and I, at any rate, believed that the things came from the stores of Old Father Christmas. We were not undeceived even by his gratefully accepting a bundle of old clothes which had been hastily put together to form his present.

"We were all very happy; even Kitty, I think, though she kept her sleeves rolled up, and seemed rather to grudge enjoying herself (a weak point in some energetic characters). She went back to her oven before the lights were out and the angel on the top of the tree taken down. She locked up her present (a little work-box) at once. She often showed it off afterward, but it was kept in the same bit of tissue paper till she died. Our presents certainly did not last so long!

"The old man died about a week afterward, so we never made his acquaintance as a common personage. When he was buried, his little dog came to us. I suppose he remembered the hospitality he had received. Patty adopted him, and he was very faithful. Puss always looked on him with favour. I hoped during our rambles together in the following summer that he would lead us at last to the cave where Christmas-trees are dressed. But he never did.

"Our parents often spoke of his late master as 'old Reuben,' but children are not easily disabused of a favourite fancy, and in Patty's thoughts and in mine the old man was long gratefully remembered as Old Father Christmas."

ENGLAND

Boreas Bluster's Christmas Present

MRS. W.J. HAYS
ILLUSTRATIONS FLORENCE STORER

Chapter One

It had been a hard, cold, cruel winter, and one that just suited old Frozen Nose, the Storm King, whose palace of ice was on the north shore of the Polar Sea. He had ordered Rain, Hail, and Snow, his slaves, to accompany Lord Boreas Bluster on an invasion of the temperate zone, and when they had done his bidding he harnessed up his four-in-hand team of polar bears and went as far south as he dared, just to see how well they had obeyed him. How he roared with laughter when he found nearly all vegetation killed, and the earth wrapped in a white mantle as thick as his own bear-

229

skins piled six feet deep! There was no nonsense about that sort of work.

"Catch any pert, saucy little flowers sticking up their heads through such a blanket!" said Frozen Nose to himself. "No, no; I've fixed 'em for a few years, anyhow. They're dead as door-nails, and Spring with all her airs and graces will never bring them to life again. Ugh! how I hate 'em and all sweet smells! Wish I might never have anything but whale-oil on my hair and handkerchiefs for the rest of my life!"

"There's no fear but what you will, and stale at that," said the ugliest of his children, young Chilblain, giving his father's big toe a tweak as he passed, and grinning when he heard Frozen Nose grumble out,

"There's the gout again, I do believe!"

But Boreas Bluster, coming in just then, saw what was going on, and gave Chilblain a whack that sent him spinning out of the room.

To tell the truth, Boreas was not as hardhearted as he looked. He was the most honest and straightforward of all Frozen Nose's friends. To be sure, he had to obey stern commands, and do many things that required a show of fierceness, but in the course of his travels he often yielded to a kind impulse, and restrained his fury when to indulge it would have pleased old Frozen Nose mightily.

This very day he had met with a strange adventure, which had been the occasion of a hasty return to the palace, and had so stirred his heart that the whack he gave young Chilblain was but the safety-valve to his feelings—a sort of letting off of steam which otherwise might have exploded and burst every block of ice in the realm.

In the many furious storms which had occurred of late Boreas had seen the destruction of numerous forests, and had even assisted in laying waste the country. But one night an avalanche had buried a hamlet from which only one living soul had escaped, and that was a young child—a mere sprig of a girl, with hair like the flax and eyes like its flowers, a little, timid, crying child—whom B.B. had actually taken in his arms and carried all the way out of the woods, over the mountains, and finally into Frozen Nose's own palace by the Polar Sea.

Never had such a thing happened before. Never had the tones of a child's voice pierced his dull ears, and made that big sledge-hammer of a heart positively ache with its throbs. It was a new and even a dangerous feeling; for though he made young Chilblain's impertinence the pretext of an outburst, he might just as readily have given a cuff to the hoary-headed Prime-minister, Sir Solomon Snow-Ball—and then there would have been a revolution. But happily for the peace of the Polar Sea palace, B.B. was satisfied with Chilblain's howl of rage, and in another moment had sunk down into his favorite arm-chair of twisted walrus tusks, and was lost in thought.

It was a curious scene, these three old men half asleep in their bear-skins, smoking long pipes of smouldering sea-weed. No fire danced on the hearth, no lamp shed its lustre, but the moon's pale beams gleamed on the glittering walls and lit the ice-crystals with its silver rays. B.B.'s thoughts seemed to be of a troublesome nature, for he sighed heavily, almost creating a whirlwind, and at last, looking cautiously at his companions, and seeing they were asleep, he rose and went softly from the room. In the hall was a huge pile of furs, among which B.B. gently pushed until he found the object of his search, which, lifting carefully, he bound about him with thongs of reindeer hide. Then pulling on his immense snow-shoes, and drawing his cap closely about his ears, he went out into the night.

B.B. was aware that it would be impossible for him to keep his little Flax-Flower any longer in Frozen Nose's dominions; indeed, he had only hidden her in the hall until he could decide what course to pursue, for he knew only too well that Chilblain, in seeking revenge, would be sure to discover his secret, and do all he could to injure him. Personally he had little to fear, but the punishment for mortals entering Frozen Nose's realm was death, and Flax-Flower was mortal.

With the speed for which he was so celebrated, Boreas slid over the ground in a southerly direction, never stopping until he had come upon what seemed to be a river which led down to a dark forest of pine-trees.

He was now at least three thousand miles from the Storm King's palace, and could afford to rest. Wiping his brow, and panting still with his recent efforts, Boreas drew a corner of the bundle of furs away from the face of Flax-Flower, and looked at the sleeping child. As he did so a thrill of tenderness made him long to kiss her, but he knew that his rough caress would chill her with fear. So, softly wrapping her up again, he plunged into the pine forest. Stopping again when in the middle of it, he gave a shrill whistle, which was responded to by one fainter and farther away, and presently a dwarf in the garb of an Esquimau emerged from the dusky gloom, and bending low, said,

"What will you, my master?"

"I would see thy lord, the good St. Nicholas—the Storm King's enemy. Is he at home?"

"He is at home, but he is no man's enemy. What message shall I bear him?'

"Tell him that Boreas, of the Frozen Noses, awaits him." The dwarf vanished, and returned.

"My lord bids thee enter, but entreats thee to be gentle, and remember the manners of his court."

"That was a needless charge, considering my errand. Never has my mood been more peaceful. But it strikes me as passing strange thus to dictate terms to one of my station," responded Boreas, proudly.

"Pardon," answered the dwarf, "but we are no sticklers for ceremony, and recognize no rank save goodness. Follow me if it be thy wish to enter."

Pushing aside the heavy boughs on which the snow lay in icy masses that rattled and clashed like bolts and bars, he uncovered a low-arched opening into what seemed a vast snow-bank. Through this tunnel he and Boreas made their way to a broad court, which was as airy as a soap-bubble, round in shape, with pillars and dome of glass, through which streamed rays of light softer than sunshine and brighter than moonbeams.

From this court a broad, low stairway led to another apartment, which was as free from any show or splendor as the kitchen of a farm-house, and, indeed, in its suggestion of homely comfort and hospitality it was not unlike that cheery place. A Saxon motto, meaning "Welcome to those who hunger," was carved in the wooden frame of the fireplace. The floor was sanded, the tables and chairs were of oak, blackened by age, as were also the timbers of the ceiling, and cut and carved with curious devices.

On a big settle by the fire sat an old man, whose twinkling eyes could but just see through the shaggy and snowy brows which overhung them, and whose white beard fell in a flowing mass upon his breast. What could be seen of his face bore a kind expression.

"Ho, ho, old Bluster!" he cried, in a clear and merry voice, drawing up and around him the sheepskin mantle which was beside him, "What new freak is this of yours to enter our peaceful dwelling?

Methought you were so sworn to do the Storm King's bidding that no power other than his rough sway could compel your presence. Come you on your own account or on his? Be it either, you are free to partake of our bounty. Ho, there, Merrythought! heave on more logs and heat the poker, that we may thrust it fizzing into our tankards: 'tis always bitter cold when Boreas is abroad."

The dwarf skipped quickly to his task, assisted by a dozen others, and Boreas, unstrapping his bundle, drew little Flax-Flower, still sleeping, from the furs.

"Mine is a strange errand, good Claus—so strange, that I hardly know myself to be myself. Rough and stormy as I am ever, a child's misery has made me once gentle. You know my mad career, my furious passions, and that they indeed are the strength of the Storm King's realm. Too well I knew that I should be but the sport of mocking derision if I appealed to his mercy in behalf of this suffering child. Mercy, did I say? He knows none. Death alone could have met this little creature, whose cries have aroused within me the deepest feelings I have ever known. To be honest, I have not always been the fierce being I appear. Many and many a time, unknown to you, I have followed you on your errands of love and pity, and watched with admiration the course you have pursued. This has induced me now to come and ask your favor for my treasure. Wake, little Flax-Flower, wake!" he continued, gently kissing the child's eyes, who, so stirred, rubbed her sleepy lids with rosy little fists, and looked around in astonishment.

"Ha!" said the good St. Nicholas; "This is indeed a strange story for you to tell, friend Bluster. Ho, there, Merrythought! send for Mrs. Christmas, my house-keeper. The child may be frightened at our grim faces. But what a pretty little dear it is!" said Claus, in the kindest tones, putting out his big fat hand to caress her. To Boreas's surprise Flax-Flower did not shrink from his salute, but with a bright smile bounded into the old man's arms and kissed him.

Turning away with a pang of jealousy, Boreas muttered, "She wouldn't kiss me; but no matter. That settles it. She's in the right place, and I'll leave her. Farewell, Claus; I'm off. No, no; I've no time for eating and drinking. Frozen Nose will be thundering at my absence already. There's a storm brewing even now; I feel it in my bones." So saying, he tramped noisily out of the apartment, nearly knocking over a fleshy dame in ruffled cap and whitest apron, whose rosy cheeks were like winter apples, and who bore in her hands a huge mince-pie in which was stuck a sprig of mistletoe.

Chapter Two

"**C**ome mother, cease thy spinning, and look at the lovely tree that Olaf has brought thee; it stands as straight as himself in the best room. Surely thou wilt deck it to please him."

"Ah, Fritz! how can I?" said the forester's wife, rising from her wheel, with a sad but sweet smile, in obedience to her husbands wishes.

"But there is surely no reason for longer indulging thy grief. Our child is too happy in heaven to wish her return to earth, and whatever the good God sends of pleasure or innocent mirth we should take with thankfulness. Look at the tree; it is the very image of Olaf's own strong youth. Make it pretty to-night, and he will be glad. A good friend is he for two lonely beings like us to possess."

"You are right, Fritz," said the wife, wiping a tear from her eyes. "For Olaf's sake I will dress the tree and bake a cake." So saying, she tidied up her best parlor, and took from a brass-bound chest the gay ribbons and trinkets which had not been used since the Christmas eve her little one last spent on earth.

Very lonely and sad would these two people have been but for Olaf, the son of their nearest neighbor. It was he whose clear ringing voice might be heard in the forest when returning from his work, and Fritz said that it made labor light but to hear him. It was he, too, who, when Fritz had been lamed by the fall of a tree, had borne him home on his strong young shoulders; so it was no wonder that the good wife was grateful to him. Often at evening he made their fireside bright with his songs and merry stories, and now it was but just that they should shake off their sorrow for his sake; so the good wife drew out her spotless board, and kneaded spice-cakes, and spread her best damask, and set out the fine china.

"Ah, if I had my little one!" murmured the good woman. "but God knows best," she quickly added, as she remembered many blessings.

"Here comes Olaf!" shouted Fritz from below. "Come quickly, lest he think thee tardy."

"Yes, yes, I come. I see him," was her reply. "but what is that he carries—something he has picked up on the way?"

"A Christmas gift for thee," was the merry answer from Olaf's ringing voice, as he laid a strange bundle in her arms.

Chapter Three

L ittle Flax-Flower had been with St. Nicholas a whole long week. In that time she had been in every nook and corner of his dwelling. She had seen all his elves and dwarfs at work manufacturing every known toy to be found in the world. She had watched the dolls' dress-makers; she had ridden the toy horses; she had blown the brass bugles and beaten the drums until Mrs. Christmas had to put cotton in her ears.

Now all this was very delightful, and made Santa Claus laugh long and loud. He would not have cared if she had brought the house down on his ears, so long as she had a bright smile and a kiss for him. But when Boreas Bluster stopped to see how his young ward was getting on, he shook his head gravely and told Mrs. Christmas he feared she was spoiling Flax-Flower. But Mrs. Christmas laughed just in the same manner that Santa Claus had done, and declared that the child must have all she wanted.

Unfortunately, Flax-Flower went into the kitchen one day, and finding all the cooks busily making sugar-plums, helped herself so largely to taffy that she was made very ill; she ate, besides, quite a menagerie of lemon-candy elephants, camels, and kangaroos, which disagreed with themselves and with her; so that her head ached, and she had to be put to bed, with a hot-water bottle and a mustard draught for companions. This happened just as Boreas had stopped in to inquire about his pet, and he shook his head gravely when Mrs. Christmas related the incident. But Santa Claus only laughed till the air seemed full of merriment.

"Ah, my dear Claus, I see you have too easy and gentle a nature to deal with wilful little mortals in an every-day way; besides, you have to think of so many that it unfits you for the care of a single one," said Boreas, in his least gruff manner. "I shall have to find another home for Flax-Flower."

"Well," replied St. Nicholas, "I confess I can refuse nothing to a good child. Children to me are all like so many empty stockings—made to be filled. But I have had some doubts about keeping Flax-Flower. Mrs. Christmas and I are afraid it will make the others jealous; it is that, and not the stuffing down lollipops, that makes me think you are right. Now her feast-day comes soon—I mean Mrs. Christmas's day," said Santa Claus, with a nod—"And if you will just give my sleigh a lift, I think I can tuck in Flaxie and carry her to some people I know—some people who will appreciate her and be kind to her; yes, and even cross in a wholesome way, seeing that's what you approve of."

Here Santa pretended to be very gruff himself, but Boreas saw through it. He knew that St. Nicholas, on the whole, believed that Flaxie would be better off without so much amusement and without so many temptations to do nothing but play all day long, and this was the way the matter ended.

Just before Christmas day Santa Claus's sleigh was brought out into the beautiful court I have described; eight lively young reindeer were harnessed to it, and thousands of toys were packed in it; furs were wrapped around Flaxie, who was now quite well, and Mrs. Christmas herself made up a box of delicacies for her to eat on the way.

"Think of us often, dear child," she whispered, "And give my love to everybody."

Then the dwarfs gave the sleigh a push from behind, the bells of the harness rang out a merry peal, the reindeer pranced, Santa Claus snapped his whip, and away they flew, with Boreas behind them on his snow-shoes.

"Now, Flaxie," said Santa Claus, after they had skimmed over the snow with lightning speed for hours, "before you go to sleep, as I see you are doing, I want to speak to you. I want you always to remember this visit to my house with pleasure, and tell all the children you may meet how much I love them, how much it pleases me to know that they are good, and how it really distresses me when they are not; tell them, too, that as long as Mrs. Christmas lives we will do all we can for their happiness, and all we ask in return is a grateful spirit. Do you think you can remember all this? Well, as you say you can, tell them also to hang up an extra stocking, whenever there is room by the chimney, for some little waif that hasn't a stocking to hang up for himself. Now go to sleep as soon as you please, and may your dreams be sweet!"

Cuddled down in the comfortable furs, Flaxie knew nothing more till she found herself awake and in the arms of a tall young fellow whose name was Olaf, and who carried her into the brightest, nicest little parlor, and set her down in front of a fine Christmas-tree, saying,

"There, Mistress Kindheart, see what Christmas has brought you. I found her in the forest, and a great bearded giant told me to bring her to you."

"Oh, Olaf, it is my little Lena come back, I do believe!" cried the woman, while tears of joy ran down her face.

"Nay, mother, nay," said her husband; "but she shall take our lost one's place. Come, little one, tell us who thou art and from whence thou art come."

Then Flaxie told the story of her visit to St. Nicholas, while Olaf, Fritz, and his wife listened in amazement.

Much as Flax-Flower had enjoyed all she had seen and done, it was delightful to be again with people of her own flesh and blood, and learn to say the sweet word "Mother."

That Christmas was a merry one, but no merrier than the many which came after, for Flax-Flower became a dutiful daughter to the kind people who gave her a home. She and Olaf were like sister and brother to each other, and they were known throughout all the country-side for their kindness to the poor and unfortunate, especially at Christmas-time.

Frozen Nose still reigns in his palace on the Polar Sea, and it is mainly owing to him and his wicked son Chilblain that nothing more is known of that still unexplored region; but Boreas Bluster spends much of his time with good St. Nicholas and Mrs. Christmas. He tires of the severity of his life, and likes a snug corner where he can relate the story of his finding Flax-Flower, whom he still loves very tenderly. Often on an evening he ventures down to take a peep at her in her happy home, and little does she suspect that the cooling breeze at the close of a warm day is Boreas's gift of thoughtful kindness.

Babouscka

ADELAIDE SKEEL

ILLUSTRATIONS THE WERNER COMPANY 1899

I f you were a Russian child you would not watch to see Santa Klaus come down the chimney; but you would stand by the windows to catch a peep at poor Babouscka as she hurries by.

Who is Babouscka? Is she Santa Klaus' wife? No, indeed. She is only a poor little crooked wrinkled old woman, who comes at Christmas time into everybody's house, who peeps into every cradle, turns back every coverlid, drops a tear on the baby's white pillow, and goes away very sorrowful.

And not only at Christmas time, but through all the cold winter, and especially in March, when the wind blows loud, and whistles and howls and dies away like a sigh, the Russian children hear the rustling step of the Babouscka. She is always in a hurry. One hears her running fast along the crowded streets and over the quiet country fields. She seems to be out of breath and tired, yet she hurries on.

Whom is she trying to overtake?

She scarcely looks at the little children as they press their rosy faces against the window pane and whisper to each other, "Is the Babouscka looking for us?"

No, she will not stop; only on Christmas eve will she come up-stairs into the nursery and give each little one a present. You must not think she leaves handsome gifts such as Santa Klaus brings for you. She does not bring bicycles to the boys or French dolls to the girls. She does not come in a gay little sleigh drawn by reindeer, but hobbling along on foot, and she leans on a crutch. She has her old apron filled with candy and cheap toys, and the children all love her dearly. They watch to see her come, and when one hears a rustling, he cries, "Lo! the Babouscka!" then all others look, but one must turn one's head very quickly or she vanishes. I never saw her myself.

Best of all, she loves little babies, and often, when the tired mothers sleep, she bends over their cradles, puts her brown, wrinkled face close down to the pillow and looks very sharply. What is she looking for? Ah, that you can't guess unless you know her sad story.

Long, long ago, a great many yesterdays ago, the Babouscka, who was even then an old woman, was busy sweeping her little hut. She lived in the coldest corner of cold Russia, and she lived alone in a lonely place where four wide roads met.

These roads were at this time white with snow, for it was winter time. In the summer, when the fields were full of flowers and the air full of sunshine and singing birds, Babouscka's home did not seem so very quiet; but in the winter, with only the snow-flakes

and the shy snow-birds and the loud wind for company, the little old woman felt very cheerless. But she was a busy old woman, and as it was already twilight, and her home but half swept, she felt in a great hurry to finish her work before bed-time. You must know the Babouscka was poor and could not afford to do her work by candle-light. Presently, down the widest and the lonesomest of the white roads, there appeared a long train of people coming.

They were walking slowly, and seemed to be asking each other questions as to which way they should take. As the procession came nearer, and finally stopped outside the little hut, Babouscka was frightened at the splendor. There were Three Kings, with crowns on their heads, and the jewels on the Kings' breastplates sparkled like sunlight. Their heavy fur cloaks were white with the falling snow-flakes, and the queer humpy camels on which they rode looked white as milk in the snow-storm. The harness on the camels was decorated with gold, and plates of silver adorned the saddles. The saddlecloths were of the richest Eastern stuffs, and all the servants had the dark eyes and hair of an Eastern people.

The servants carried heavy loads on their backs, and each of the Three Kings carried a present. One carried a beautiful transparent jar, and in the fading light Babouscka could see in it a golden liquid which she knew from its color must be myrrh. Another had in his hand a richly woven bag, and it seemed to be heavy, as indeed it was, for it was full of gold. The third had a stone vase in his hand, and from the rich perfume which filled the snowy air, one could guess the vase to have been filled with incense.

Babouscka was terribly frightened, so she hid herself in her hut, and let the servants knock a long time at her door before she dared open it and answer their questions as to the road they should take to a far-away town. You know she had never studied a geography lesson in her life, was old and stupid and scared. She knew the way across the fields to the nearest village, but she knew nothing else of all the wide world full of cities. The servants scolded, but the Three Kings spoke kindly to her, and asked her to accompany them on their journey that she might show them the way as far as she knew it. They told her, in words so simple that she could not fail to understand, that they had seen a Star in the sky and were following it to a little town where a young Child lay. The snow was in the sky now, and the Star was lost out of sight.

"Who is the Child?" asked the old woman.

"He is a King, and we go to worship him," they answered. "These presents of gold, frankincense and myrrh are for Him. When we find Him we will take the crowns off our heads and lay them at His feet. Come with us, Babouscka!"

What do you suppose? Shouldn't you have thought the poor little woman would have been glad to leave her desolate home on the plains to accompany these Kings on their journey?

But the foolish woman shook her head. No, the night was dark and cheerless, and her little home was warm and cosy. She looked up into the sky, and the Star was nowhere to be seen. Besides, she wanted to put her hut in order—perhaps she would be ready to go to-morrow. But the Three Kings could not wait; so when to-morrow's sun rose they were far ahead on their journey. It seemed like a dream to poor Babouscka, for even the tracks of the camels' feet were covered by the deep white snow. Everything was the same as usual; and to make sure that the night's visitors had not been a fancy, she found her old broom hanging on a peg behind the door, where she had put it when the servants knocked.

Now that the sun was shining, and she remembered the glitter of the gold and the smell of the sweet gums and myrrh, she wished she had gone with the travellers. And she thought a great deal about the little Baby the Three Kings had gone to worship. She had no children of her own—nobody loved her—ah, if she had only gone! The more she brooded on the thought, the more miserable she grew, till the very sight of her home became hateful to her.

It is a dreadful feeling to realize that one has lost a chance of happiness. There is a feeling called remorse that can gnaw like a sharp little tooth. Babouscka felt this little tooth cut into her heart every time she remembered the visit of the Three Kings.

After a while the thought of the Little Child became her first thought at waking and her last at night. One day she shut the door of her house forever, and set out on a long journey. She had no hope of overtaking the Three Kings, but she longed to find the Child, that she too might love and worship Him. She asked every one she met, and some people thought her crazy, but others gave her kind answers. Have you perhaps guessed that the young Child whom the Three Kings sought was our Lord himself?

People told Babouscka how He was born in a manger, and many other things which you children have learned long ago. These answers puzzled the old dame mightily. She had but one idea in her ignorant head. The Three Kings had gone to seek a Baby. She would, if not too late, seek Him too.

She forgot, I am sure, how many long years had gone by. She looked in vain for the Christ-child in His manger-cradle. She spent all her little savings in toys and candy so as to make friends with little children, that they might not run away when she came hobbling into their nurseries.

Now you know for whom she is sadly seeking when she pushes back the bed-curtains and bends down over each baby's pillow. Sometimes, when the old grandmother sits nodding by the fire, and the bigger children sleep in their beds, old Babouscka comes hobbling into the room, and whispers softly, "Is the young Child here?"

Ah, no; she has come too late, too late. But the little children know her and love her. Two thousand years ago she lost the chance of finding Him. Crooked, wrinkled, old, sick and sorry, she yet lives on, looking into each baby's face—always disappointed, always seeking. Will she find Him at last?

A Night with Santa Claus

Anna R. Annan

Illustrations Mary Cowles Clark

N ot very long ago, and not far from here, lived a little boy named Bobby Morgan. Now I must tell at once how Bobby looked, else how will you know him if you meet him in the street? Blue-eyed was Rob, and fair-haired, and pug-nosed—just the sweetest trifle, his mother said.

Well, the day before Christmas, Rob thought it would be a fine thing to run down Main Street and see what was going on. After dinner his mother put on his fur cap and bright scarf, and filled his pockets with crackers and cookies. She told him to be very polite to Santa Claus if he should happen to meet him.

Off he trotted, merry as a cricket, with now a skip and now a slide. At every corner he held his breath, half expecting to run into Santa himself. Nothing of the sort happened, however, and he soon found himself before the gay windows of a toy shop.

There he saw a spring hobby-horse, as large as a Shetland pony, all saddled and bridled, too,—lacking nothing but a rider. Rob pressed his nose against the glass, and tried to imagine the feelings of a boy in that saddle. He must have stood there all day, had not a ragged little fellow pulled his coat. "Wouldn't you just like that popgun?" he piped.

"Catch me looking at popguns!" said Rob shortly. But when he saw how tattered the boy's jacket was he said more softly, "P'r'raps you'd like a cooky."

"Try me wunst!" said the shrill little voice.

There was a queer lump in Rob's throat as he emptied one pocket of its cakes and thrust them into the dirty, eager hands. Then he marched down the street without so much as glancing at that glorious steed again.

Brighter and brighter grew the windows, more and more full of toys. At last our boy stood, with open eyes and mouth, before a great store lighted from top to bottom, for it was growing dark. Rob came near taking off his cap and saying, "How do you do, sir?"

To whom, you ask. Why, to an image of Santa Claus, the size of life, holding a Christmas tree filled with wonderful fruit.

Soon a happy thought struck Rob. "Surely this must be Santa Claus's own store, where he comes to fill his basket with toys! What if I were to hide there and wait for him?"

As I said, he was a brave little chap, and he walked straight into the store with the stream of big people. Everybody was busy. No one had time to look at our mite of a Rob. He tried in vain to find a quiet corner, till he caught sight of some winding stairs that led up to the next story. He crept up, scarcely daring to breathe.

What a fairyland! Toys everywhere! Oceans of toys! Nothing but toys, excepting one happy little boy. Think of fifty great rocking-horses in a pile; of whole flocks of woolly sheep and curly dogs with the real bark in them; stacks of drums; regiments of soldiers armed to the teeth; companies of firemen drawing their hose carts; no end of wheelbarrows and velocipedes!

Rob screwed his knuckles into his eyes, as a gentle hint that they had better not play him any tricks, and then stared with might and main.

Suddenly Rob thought he heard a footstep on the stairs. Fearing to be caught, he hid behind a baby-wagon. No one came, however, and as he felt rather hungry, he took out the remaining cakes and had a fine supper.

Why didn't Santa Claus come?

Rob was really getting sleepy. He stretched out his tired legs, and, turning one of the woolly sheep on its side, pillowed his curly head upon it. It was so nice to lie there, looking up at the ceiling hung with toys, and with the faint hum of voices in his ears. The blue eyes grew more and more heavy. Rob was fast asleep.

Midnight! The bells rang loud and clear, as if they had great news to tell the world. What noise is that besides the bells? And look, oh, look! Who is that striding up the room with a great basket on his back? He has stolen his coat from a polar bear, and his cap, too, I declare! His boots are of red leather and reach to his knees. His coat and cap are trimmed with wreaths of holly, bright with scarlet berries.

Good sir, let us see your face—why! that is the best part of him,—so round, and so ruddy, such twinkling eyes, and such a merry look about those dimples! But see his long white beard; can he be old?

Oh, very, very old. Over nineteen hundred years. Is that not a long life, little ones? But he has a young heart, this dear old man, and a kind one. Can you guess his name? "Hurrah for Santa Claus!" Right—the very one.

He put his basket down near Robby, and with his back turned to him shook the snow from his fur coat. Some of the flakes fell on Rob's face and roused him from his sleep. Opening his eyes, he saw the white figure, but did not stir nor cry out, lest the vision should vanish.

But bless his big heart! He had no idea of vanishing till his night's work was done. He took a large book from his pocket, opened]to the first page, and looked at it very closely.

"Tommy Turner," was written at the top, and just below was a little map—yes, there was Tommy's heart mapped out like a country. Part of the land was marked good, part of it bad. Here and there were little flags to point out places where battles had been fought during the year. Some of them were black and some white; wherever a good feeling had won the fight there was a white one.

"Tommy Turner," said Santa Claus aloud, "six white flags, three black ones. That leaves only three presents for Tommy; but we must see what can be done for him."

So he bustled among the toys, and soon had a ball, a horse, and a Noah's ark tied up in a parcel, which he tossed into the basket.

Name after name was read off, some of them belonging to Rob's playmates, and you may be sure that the little boy listened with his heart in his mouth.

"Robby Morgan!" said Santa Claus.

In his excitement that small lad nearly upset the cart, but Santa did not notice it.

"One, two, three, four, five, six, seven" — Rob's breath came very short—"whites!"

He almost clapped his hands.

"One, two, three, blacks! Now I wonder what that little chap would like—here's a drum, a box of tools, a knife, a menagerie. If he hadn't run away from school that day and then told a lie about it I'd give him a rocking-horse."

Rob groaned in anguish of spirit.

"But, bless him! he's a fine little fellow, and perhaps he will do better next year if I give him the horse."

That was too much for our boy. With a "Hurrah!" he jumped up and turned a somersault right at Santa Claus's feet.

"Stars and stripes!" cried Santa. "What's this?"

"Come along, I'll show you the one!" cried Rob.

Santa Claus allowed himself to be led off to the pile of horses. You may believe that Rob's sharp eyes soon picked out the one with the longest tail and the thickest mane.

"Well, he beats all the boys that ever I saw! What shall I do with the little spy?"

"Oh, dear Santa Claus," cried Robby, hugging the red boots, "do just take me along with you. I'll stick tight when you slide down the chimney."

"Yes, I guess you will stick tight—in the chimney, my little man."

"I mean to your back," half sobbed Rob.

Santa Claus can't bear to see little folks in trouble, so he took the boy into his arms, and asked where he wanted to go.

"To Tommy Turner's, and, oh, you know, that boy in the awful old jacket that likes popguns," was the breathless reply.

Of course he knew him, for he knows every boy and girl in Christendom; so a popgun was added to the medley of toys. Santa Claus then strapped Rob and the basket on his back. He next crept through an open window to a ladder he had placed there, down which he ran as nimbly as a squirrel. The reindeer before the sledge were in a hurry to be off, and tinkled their silver bells right merrily. An instant more and they were snugly tucked up in the white robes; an instant more and they were flying like the wind over the snow.

Ah! Tommy's home. Santa Claus sprang out, placed the light ladder against the house, and before Rob could wink a good fair wink they were on the roof, making for the chimney. Whether it swallowed him, or he swallowed it, is still a puzzle to Robby.

Tommy lay sleeping in his little bed and dreaming of a merry Christmas. His rosy mouth was puckered into something between a whistle and a smile. Rob longed to give him a friendly punch, but Santa Claus shook his head. They filled his stocking and hurried away, for empty little stockings the world over were waiting for that generous hand.

On they sped again, never stopping until they came to a wretched little hovel. A black pipe instead of a chimney was sticking through the roof.

Rob thought, "Now I guess he'll have to give it up." But no, he softly pushed the door open and stepped in.

On a ragged cot lay the urchin to whom Robby had given the cookies. One of them, half eaten, was still clutched in his hand. Santa Claus gently opened the other little fist and put the popgun into it.

"Give him my drum," whispered Rob, and Santa Claus, without a word, placed it near the rumpled head.

How swiftly they flew under the bright stars! How sweetly rang the bells!

When Santa Claus reined up at Robby's door he found his little comrade fast asleep. He laid him tenderly in his crib, and drew off a stocking, which he filled with the smaller toys. The rocking-horse he placed close to the crib, that Rob might mount him on Christmas morning.

A kiss, and he was gone.

P.S.—Rob's mother says it was all a dream, but he declares that "It's true as Fourth of July!" I prefer to take his word for it.

Piccola

KATE DOUGLAS WIGGIN & NORA A. SMITH
ILLUSTRATIONS HOUGHTON MIFFLIN COMPANY 1890

P iccola lived in Italy, where the oranges grow, and where all the year the sun shines warm and bright. I suppose you think Piccola a very strange name for a little girl; but in her country it was not strange at all, and her mother thought it the sweetest name a little girl ever had.

Piccola had no kind father, no big brother or sister, and no sweet baby to play with and to love. She and her mother lived all alone in an old stone house that looked on a dark, narrow street. They were very poor, and the mother was away from home almost every day, washing clothes and scrubbing floors, and working hard to earn money for her little girl and herself. So you see Piccola was alone a great deal of the time; and if she had not been a very happy, contented little child, I hardly know what she would have done. She had no playthings except a heap of stones in the back yard that she used for building houses, and a very old, very ragged doll that her mother had found in the street one day.

But there was a small round hole in the stone wall at the back of her yard, and her greatest pleasure was to look through that into her neighbor's garden. When she stood on a stone, and put her eyes close to the hole, she could see the green grass in the garden, smell the sweet flowers, and even hear the water plashing into the fountain. She had never seen anyone walking in the garden, for it belonged to an old gentleman who did not care about grass and flowers.

One day in the autumn her mother told her that the old gentleman had gone away, and had rented his house to a family of little American children, who had come with their sick mother to spend the winter in Italy. After this, Piccola was never lonely, for all day long the children ran and played and danced and sang in the garden. It was several weeks before they saw her at all, and I am not sure they would ever have done so but that one day the kitten ran away, and in chasing her they came close to the wall, and saw Piccola's black eyes looking through the hole in the stones. They were a little frightened at first, and did not speak to her; but the next day she was there again, and Rose, the oldest girl, went up to the wall and talked to her a little while. When the children found that she had no one to play with and was very lonely, they talked to her every day, and often brought her fruits and candies, and passed them through the hole in the wall.

One day they even pushed the kitten through; but the hole was hardly large enough for her, and she mewed and scratched, and was very much frightened. After that the little boy said he should ask his father if the hole might not be made larger, and then Piccola could come in and play with them. The father had found out that

Piccola's mother was a good woman, and that the little girl herself was sweet and kind, so that he was very glad to have some of the stones broken away, and an opening made for Piccola to come in.

How excited she was, and how glad the children were when she first stepped into the garden! She wore her best dress, a long bright-colored woolen skirt and a white waist. Round her neck was a string of beads, and on her feet were little wooden shoes. It would seem very strange to us—would it not?—to wear wooden shoes; but Piccola and her mother had never worn anything else, and never had any money to buy stockings. Piccola almost always ran about barefooted, like the kittens and the chickens and the little ducks. What a good time they had that day, and how glad Piccola's mother was that her little girl could have such a pleasant, safe place to play in, while she was away at work!

By and by December came, and the little Americans began to talk about Christmas. One day, when Piccola's curly head and bright eyes came peeping through the hole in the wall, they ran to her and helped her in; and as they did so, they all asked her at once what she thought she would have for a Christmas present. "A Christmas present!" said Piccola. "Why, what is that?"

All the children looked surprised at this, and Rose said, rather gravely, "Dear Piccola, don't you know what Christmas is?"

Oh, yes, Piccola knew it was the happy day when the baby Christ was born, and she had been to church on that day, and heard the beautiful singing, and had seen a picture of the Babe lying in the manger, with cattle and sheep sleeping round about. Oh, yes, she knew all that very well, but what was a Christmas present?

Then the children began to laugh, and to answer her all together. There was such a clatter of tongues that she could hear only a few words now and then, such as "chimney," "Santa Claus," "stockings," "reindeer," "Christmas Eve," "candies and toys." Piccola put her hands over her ears, and said, "Oh, I can't understand one word. You tell me, Rose."

Then Rose told her all about jolly old Santa Claus, with his red cheeks and white beard and fur coat, and about his reindeer and sleigh full of toys. "Every Christmas Eve," said Rose, "he comes down the chimney, and fills the stockings of all the good children; so, Piccola, you hang up your stocking, and who knows what a beautiful Christmas present you will find when morning comes!"

Of course Piccola thought this was a delightful plan, and was very pleased to hear about it. Then all the children told her of every Christmas Eve they could remember, and of the presents they had had; so that she went home thinking of nothing but dolls, and hoops, and balls, and ribbons, and marbles, and wagons, and kites. She told her mother about Santa Claus, and her mother seemed to think that perhaps he did not know there was any little girl in that house, and very likely he would not come at all. But Piccola felt very sure Santa Claus would remember her, for her little friends had promised to send a letter up the chimney to remind him.

Christmas Eve came at last. Piccola's mother hurried home from her work; they had their little supper of soup and bread, and soon it was bedtime,—time to get ready for Santa Claus. But oh! Piccola remembered then for the first time that the children had told her she must hang up her stocking, and she hadn't any, and neither had her mother.

How sad, how sad it was! Now Santa Claus would come, and perhaps be angry because he couldn't find any place to put the present. The poor little girl stood by the fireplace; and the big tears began to run down her cheeks. Just then her mother called to her, "Hurry, Piccola; come to bed." What should she do? But she stopped crying, and tried to think; and in a moment she remembered her wooden shoes, and ran off to get one of them. She put it close to the chimney, and said to herself, "Surely Santa Claus will know what it's there for. He will know I haven't any stockings, so I gave him the shoe instead."

Then she went off happily to her bed, and was asleep almost as soon as she had nestled close to her mother's side. The sun had only just begun to shine, next morning, when Piccola awoke. With one jump she was out on the floor and running toward the chimney. The wooden shoe was lying where she had left it, but you could never, never guess what was in it.

Piccola had not meant to wake her mother, but this surprise was more than any little girl could bear and yet be quiet; so she danced to the bed with the shoe in her hand, calling, "Mother, mother! look, look! see the present Santa Claus brought me!"

Her mother raised her head and looked into the shoe. "Why, Piccola," she said, "a little chimney swallow nestling in your shoe? What a good Santa Claus to bring you a bird!"

"Good Santa Claus, dear Santa Claus!" cried Piccola; and she kissed her mother and kissed the bird and kissed the shoe, and even threw kisses up the chimney, she was so happy.

When the birdling was taken out of the shoe, they found that he did not try to fly, only to hop about the room; and as they looked closer, they could see that one of his wings was hurt a little. But the mother bound it up carefully, so that it did not seem to pain him, and he was so gentle that he took a drink of water from a cup, and even ate crumbs and seeds from Piccola's hand. She was a proud little girl when she took her Christmas present to show the children in the garden. They had had a great many gifts,—dolls that could say "mamma," bright picture-books, trains of cars, toy pianos; but not one of their playthings was alive, like Piccola's birdling. They were as pleased as she, and Rose hunted about the house till she found a large wicker cage that belonged to a blackbird she once had. She gave the cage to Piccola, and the swallow seemed to make himself quite at home in it at once, and sat on the perch winking his bright eyes at the children. Rose had saved a bag of candies for Piccola, and when she went home at last, with the cage and her dear swallow safely inside it, I am sure there was not a happier little girl in the whole country of Italy.

Father Christmas at Home

Mrs. M.H. Spielmann

Illustrations Arthur Rackham

Twilight

It was afternoon on a cold December day. Eva, all alone in the schoolroom, sat down on the hearthrug and looked thoughtfully into the fire. She was, however, not quite alone, for her tiny Yorkshire terrier sprang on her lap, and after turning round and round, pawing at her frock as though to make a comfortable hollow, settled cosily down.

"Dot," she said, smoothing the hair back from its eyes, "I'm very miserable. Tomorrow is Christmas Eve, and every one is happy except me. I'm in trouble again. Somehow, I'm always in trouble—I've spoilt my velvet frock washing your feet—and you didn't want them washed, did you?" The Honourable Dot—to give it its full title—looked desirous of forgetting the incident, then licked her hand as a reply seemed expected.

"Perhaps if I had some brothers and sisters they'd get into mischief sometimes, and it wouldn't always be me." Dot paid no heed to her grammar, was bored, and sighed heavily.

"I really didn't mean it when I said, 'I gloried in being naughty.' Don't snore, Honourable! There'll be complaints from next door."

It was curious, but Eva was having remorse, brought on by all the talk of Peace and Goodwill which was in the air. "I've tried things before," she muttered; "but I know what I'll do this time," she exclaimed, "I'll give a cot to a hospital!"

The little dog growled a protest as she suddenly got up from the floor. Eva counted the money in her money-box. "I've five shillings all but three farthings. I'm sure that is nothing like enough!" she mused. "It must cost at least a million sterling pounds!" Tears came into her eyes, but they flowed down on to a smile, as she thought of some one who always managed to do kind deeds and who might help her. Father Christmas! Eva thought of asking no less a person than Father Christmas himself to advise her. But how to find him and get a nice quiet chat with him was the difficulty. That he would come to her on Christmas Eve she had no doubt, as he never forgot her; but she had only managed to be awake and see him once, a long time ago, and then she but got a glimpse of him, for he rushed out of her room as though in a terrible hurry.

Dot's little mistress slept badly that night; she was racking her brain as to how she could manage to remain awake so as to see Father Christmas when he came, and then how she could coax him to stay for a talk—for she knew quite well how busy he must be when he was on his rounds.

The following afternoon, during a general rummage that was going on to find tiny candles and coloured glass balls that were over from last year's Christmas tree, Eva picked up a scrap of printed paper, which had come out of an old cracker. She took it upstairs to her favourite spot on the hearthrug, and read it aloud to Dot:—

"Father Christmas sends this note
From out his mansion by the moat,
To all who live on land and sea,
To honour Christmas Day with glee—
Inviting them to pass his way,
With glee to honour Christmas Day."

Eva flushed with excitement. "Why, it's a message from him!" she cried. "It's some kind of invitation!" and she gave Dot such a squeeze of delight that the little creature squeaked shrilly, scurried off, and laid low under the table. She thought and puzzled and pondered over the lines she had just read. At last she grasped their meaning. "Of course! How simple, after all!" she concluded. "He lives at some moated house, and I must go to him, not wait for him to come to me. He always comes down the chimney—that's the way I must go up!"

Eva didn't hesitate a moment. The opportunity had come for which she longed. She ran downstairs into the large, old-fashioned hall, which was overheated as usual, by the hot-air pipes, for the huge chimney-place was too much of a curiosity ever to be used. Here, she felt sure, was the starting-point of her adventure.

Luckily no one was about. It was windy when she looked up the great chimney, so she took her long, fair hair, and made it into a loose plait in order to keep it from blowing about her face. Then she prepared to start and secure the first footing.

Eva had never been up a chimney before, and when she began climbing she was quite surprised to find how nice and clean it was, with steps, and all white tiles. She toiled up, and up, and could see blue sky and fleeting white clouds above. After a time she stopped to rest in a little recess in the chimney side. When she started climbing again, the blue sky faded away, twilight came on, and in this very, very long chimney the light became quite dim.

Very soon, however, she felt with a little thrill of pleasure the keen air all around her head and shoulders, and she knew she had come to the top. Fortunately there was a ladder—already placed for Father Christmas to mount—and down that she went, looking below all the time so as not to make a false step. It was a very, very long ladder indeed, and Eva began to think she would have to go on stepping down for ever, when at last she found herself on the ground again—in a country field with hoar frost stiffening the blades of grass, across which she ran straight ahead as hard as ever she could go.

Starlight

O nce only did she halt by the side of a lane to consider what she should do if she couldn't find her destination after all.

Two robins alighted in front of her, hopped about, and fluttered forward; they were so persistent that they interested her and she followed them. They flew along a side path, and Eva ran after them—ran till she arrived eager and breathless at a wooden bridge, and found that she was in a park; that above her was the dark vault of heaven decked out in all its diamonds; that the bridge led across a moat; and that in front of her was a splendid old country mansion brilliantly lighted up, where the robins alighted on a window-sill, and paying no further attention to her, busied themselves with crumbs.

It was a very, very long ladder.

Then Eva advanced, almost in spite of herself, went up the front steps, and standing on tiptoe, lifted the knocker and let it fall. The knocker resounded for a while musically, like a peal of bells; when they ceased, the door opened, and a very ancient man confronted her. He was tall and thin and bent, and was dressed in draperies, with bare legs, and he had a funny little curl in the middle of his bald forehead.

"Is Father Christmas at home, please?" faltered Eva.

"Yes, little Madam," came the reply. "Do you want to see him? Really? But you will be astonished—I warn you. Aren't you frightened?"

"Not a bit," replied Eva.

"Brave little girl!" said the very ancient man. "Come in!" and he ushered her into an old oak-panelled room. It had a delicious sense of comfort, and a delight about it which, for the moment, she didn't try to define. Her attention was attracted by catching sight of what she thought was her own reflection in the large mirror against the wall—it was a little girl who came in at the same time, and was of exactly her own height. As she looked closer she saw that the other child was uglier than herself, unkind in expression, slovenly in appearance, and tried to hide herself, rather, in the dark corner where she remained. And Eva, in the novel surroundings, soon forgot all about her.

At the far end was a great log fire, and near it a huge arm-chair, in which sat a stout, healthy, red-faced old gentleman warmly wrapped in a crimson dressing-gown; he was leaning back, thinking or dozing. Eva advanced with soft steps. She was full of eagerness and excitement, for she recognised the white-bearded, handsome old face at once from the many coloured portraits she had seen. It was Father Christmas himself! Eva never knew what impelled her to do it, but when she got close to him she simply threw her arms around his neck and kissed him.

"Bless my soul!" exclaimed Father Christmas, starting; and catching her up, he seated her on his knee. He recognised her at once. "How you've grown since last year, Eva!" and he looked at her with beaming eyes. "I suppose you know you're trespassing? and the penalty is forty crackers or a kiss!" And he chuckled and laughed so merrily that she felt quite comfortable, finding trespassing a very pleasant occupation, and wasn't a bit alarmed at the penalty.

"And what brings me this honour?" he continued.

"Good evening, Father Christmas," spoke up Eva quite boldly. "I'm afraid I disturbed you."

"I suppose you know you're trespassing?"

"Oh yes, you've disturbed me all right," he replied briskly, "but I was only resting a little after my labours before going on my rounds tonight."

"What labours?"

"Toys. Toys and sweets. I've been making toys and things all the year through, and have only just got them finished in time. I love making crackers, too; I spend all my evenings writing mottoes for them."

"I found your invitation, Mr. Christmas."

"Bless me! did you now? Ah!" He stroked his beard thoughtfully for a moment and remained silent. Eva looked about her in amazement.

"Those are all secrets!" he observed after a time. Father Christmas included with a sweep of the arm the toys which were everywhere about—hanging from the ceiling, lying about on the tables and sofas, standing as ornaments on the mantelpiece, filling the shelves of the bookcases, peeping from behind the glass cabinets—toys wherever one looked.

He arose, and taking her by the hand, led her round to enjoy the pretty sight; and paying no attention whatever to the sullen little girl in the corner, he asked Eva if she would like to see around his domain. "Oh yes, yes," she cried. She quite appreciated the special honour that was being done her.

"They'll be coming in here soon to pack," he added. "I'm going to leave all these secrets myself at their destinations."

There was a tremendous bustle going on at the rear of the premises, where a whole army of packers, carriers, postmen, and porters were hurrying about letting down toys from the loft, packing them, labelling them to places far and wide; loading them on huge vans which came rumbling in and out of the courtyard with cracking of whips, and parting shouts of "Good luck!"

Superintending the arrangements, walking to and fro, was the very ancient man. He was so alert, and always on the spot where wanted, yet Eva was thinking his age must at least be two hundred, when Father Christmas said kindly: "My dear, this is my father—he is known as Father Time, and you have known him without having really met him face to face before."

"I didn't recognise him, and I didn't know he was your father, sir," she whispered.

"Why, yes. Don't you know that my full name is Christmas Time?"

"Of course it is," she exclaimed with a laugh.

The next visit was through a covered way to the printing works—where the mottoes and "directions" for toys and Father Christmas's visiting cards were printed. These cards were all different in design, and each was a beautiful picture stamped with his name, and his own motto, "Peace and Goodwill."

Behind was the sweet factory, with its tempting packets and muslin stockings of all sizes full of sugar-plums. But, as Father Time appeared, Father Christmas whispered that he feared they must not linger, and led the way up a spiral staircase in order to enable Eva to have a peep into the toy-loft, where men were letting the toys down into the busy yard below. How she would have loved to stay longer in each delightful place, but without a murmur she followed her guide below and back to the oak-panelled room. It looked so bare and different without the toys—much like any ordinary room.

"And now, my dear," he said, "you must excuse me for a short time, as I must go upstairs and get ready."

"Please, ought I to be going?" she asked politely.

"No, no. Not yet." And he went away, up the grand staircase, to his bedroom. There he took from the drawer his scarlet fur-lined cloak and hood with wide swansdown trimming, which had been put away in lavender, chose his thickest top-boots, and humming a song, proceeded to array himself for the long, cold journey in store for him that night.

Meanwhile, the moment he left his little visitor downstairs, the strange-looking child approached her.

"What's your name?" asked Eva pleasantly.

"Eva," came the surly reply.

"Why, that's my name!"

"Of course. I know you, I know you through and through—good and bad—and I wish I didn't."

"You're a horrid story-teller," said Eva angrily.

"Supposing I am! It's easier to tell stories than to tell the truth. Saves a lot of trouble. Besides, it's nice. You know that as well as I do."

Eva would have liked to deny it, only she felt too scornful. "Saves trouble?" she said to herself. "Makes trouble." But she flushed as she remembered she had once thought that too, but only for a moment; and she was ashamed of it now. She was ruffled and uncomfortable at the proximity of this horrid girl, who now said slyly: "Look over there in that cupboard, there's a doll that has been forgotten. I want it, and I'm going to take it and hide it under my pinafore."

"You mayn't—you mustn't!" cried Eva. "It would be stealing."

"I don't care. Father Christmas won't know."

"Yes, he will. I shall tell him!"

"Then I'll say it was given to me."

"You horrid girl! You dreadful story-teller!"

"Don't be silly. What does it matter telling stories and stealing, so long as you're not found out?"

"It's just as bad if you're not found out. But you are bound to be found out," cried Eva, in horror and disgust as she saw her approach the coveted treasure. "I tell you, wicked people are always found out; they never escape unpunished."

"I want it, and I'm going to have it."

"You mustn't. Come away—you shan't!" shouted Eva, running after her; and she seized her by both wrists. "Come away! Oh, do come away!"

"You fool! leave me alone. Get away!" and with a scoffing laugh the girl shook herself free, sprang on a sofa, opened the cupboard, and stretched out her hand.

Without a word Eva threw herself upon her, slammed-to the glass door, and in the struggle they fell together on the floor. There was a crash of broken glass, and through the noise Eva heard the voice of her opponent saying faintly: "Let me go! You have won!"

When she got up, carefully shaking the bits of glass from her frock, and looked round, the horrid little girl had disappeared. The next moment her host stood in the doorway with a curious smile on his face.

"I'm going now," he said; "will you come?"

"Oh, please, Father Christmas," exclaimed Eva ruefully, as she looked at the glass on the floor, "do wait! I want to explain something—I——"

"I can't keep my father waiting," he answered gently. She followed him to the front door. There in the frosty night a beautiful sledge was in waiting, hung with baskets and sacks overflowing with toys and sweets. Father Christmas took his seat and beckoned to Eva. To her joy he lifted her on to his lap and wrapped his great coat about her. Father Time, who was on the box, shook the reins, and the two reindeer, impatient to be off, sped rapidly away amid the jangling of bells, carrying the travellers over the bridge, through the park, past holly and fir trees all powdered with glistening frost, out over the country into the bright, crisp night.

Moonlight

T here was Eva with Father Christmas, all snug amongst his soft furs, on his rounds.

"Why do you take some toys yourself," she asked, "and send others away in the great carts?"

"Those in the carts are for my export and wholesale trade—shops, and so on; these Itake are for my special favourites. You're on my list, my dear, you know." Eva's heart was full of tenderness and pride, but tears were in her eyes as she said, peering appealingly into his kind face — "May I whisper something?"

He bent his head—and she whispered.

"Bless my soul!" was all Father Christmas replied, but he looked very pleased and jolly.

"And I should like to pay for it," continued Eva; "I've got five shillings all but three farthings."

"Never mind about that, my dear."

"But I'm sure I ought," she replied dubiously. "Dear Father Christmas, you are always doing kindnesses; could you tell me how to do something like giving a cot to a hospital, or a free library, or something? That's what I really came to ask you about, only I forgot it until now. I'm so often in trouble, and I've so often tried to do some good, but it doesn't come off somehow," and she sighed.

"What you ask me is a secret," he answered. "Some people are quick to find it out for themselves. Some people never find it out. But I will tell it to you, dear, because I know that by to-morrow you will be on the high road to guessing it. It is this: You need not give things. You needn't try to be good. Try only not to be troublesome.

If you are sweet, and gentle, and kind, you give happiness—not only do you give it, but you can then only find happiness yourself." Somehow, it didn't sound a bit like a sermon; it was more like being told the delightfully easy answer to a difficult sum. Eva nestled closer to her dear old friend as she listened—it was all so peaceful, reassuring, and soothing.

The two reindeer ... sped rapidly away

The moon was shining down on the sledge and its strange occupants, and Eva was just going to ask if he could tell her who the other little girl was, and all about her, when she felt her arms were being disengaged from where they clung about him, and she found herself gently deposited on firm ground, and alone.

The Honourable Dot barked with delight because it was Christmas Eve, and it was going with its little mistress to dine downstairs; and very joyful and succulent the event proved to be. Not long after, when it was fast asleep in its basket, Eva was sitting up in bed waiting anxiously to receive the visit of her recent host. Father Christmas had done her so much good, and she wanted to tell him so, as she had had no opportunity of doing before.

She was dropping asleep in that attitude, when she heard a slight noise. Immediately she started up, and clutching tightly at a rapidly retreating figure, she laughed aloud to find she had succeeded in catching Father Christmas, who, mildly yielding to her entreaties, sat down by her side.

"I have wakened you," he said regretfully.

"Oh no, I was waiting for you." And she told him about the happy time she had spent with him, and thanked him nicely. "What a dreadful little girl that other Eva was!" she concluded. "Who was she?"

"Ah," said Father Christmas very quickly, "she is what you might be were you to give way to bad feelings. I wish you a Merry Christmas and a Happy New Year, my dear!" and without explaining further he kissed her and rapidly withdrew on his business.

Daylight

Outside the un-curtained window the sun was shining. Snow had been falling softly, and was piled high on the sill. And over the hushed landscape from the far distance the Christmas bells were ringing. Eva joyfully hugged a large doll, which she had found asleep on her pillow.

It was only later, when she thought over past events in detail, that it appeared to her, though she had not paid attention to it at the time, that Father Christmas seemed ill at ease when he was her visitor—perhaps it was because he was in a hurry. Somehow he was different from the stout, merry-faced old gentleman she had been to see; he had strangely shrunk to nearly as thin as her own father, and as pale, comparatively, which she thought very odd!

And when she looked up into that wonderful and mysterious old chimney again, she saw that it was all dark and black, and as uninviting as any ordinary dirty old chimney; so that it was quite hopeless for her ever to venture up it again to find old Father Christmas "At Home."

The Animals' Christmas Tree

JOHN P. PETERS

ILLUSTRATIONS MARY COWLES CLARK

O nce upon a time the animals decided to have a Christmas tree, and this was how it came about: The swifts and the swallows in the chimneys in the country houses, awakened from their sleep by joy and laughter, had stolen down and peeped in upon scenes of happiness, the center of which was always an evergreen tree covered with wonderful fruit, bright balls of many colours, and sparkling threads of gold and silver, lying like beautiful frost-work among the green fir needles.

A sweet, fairy-like figure of a Christ Child or an angel rested high among the branches, and underneath the tree were dolls and sleds and skates and drums and toys of every sort, and furs and gloves and tippets, ribbons and handkerchiefs, and all the things that boys and girls need and like; and all about this tree were gathered always little children with faces—oh! so full of wonderment and expectation, changing to radiant, sparkling merriment as toys and candies were taken off the tree or from underneath its boughs and distributed among them.

The swifts and swallows told their feathered friends all about it, and they told others, both birds and animals, until at last it began to be rumoured through all the animal world that on one day in the year the children of men were made wonderfully happy by means of some sort of festival which they held about a fir tree from the forest. Now, of course, the tame animals and the house animals, the dogs and the cats and the mice, knew something more about this festival. But then, they did not exchange visits with the wild animals, because they felt themselves above them.

They were always trying to be like men and women, you know, putting on airs and pretending to know everything; but, after all, they were animals and could not help making friendships now and then with the wild creatures, especially when the men and women were not there. And when they were asked about the Christmas tree, they told still more wonderful stories than the swifts and the swallows from the chimneys had told, for some of them had taken part in these festivals, and some had even received presents from the tree, just like the children.

They said that the tree was called a Christmas tree, because that strange fruit and that wonderful frosting came on it only in the Christmas time, and that the Christmas time was the time when men and women and little children, too, were always kind and good and loving, and gave things to one another; and they said, moreover, that on the Christmas tree grew the things which every one wanted, and which would make them happy, and that it was so, because in the Christmas time everyone was trying to make everyone else happy and to think of what other people would like. This they said was what they had seen and heard told about Christmas trees. They did not quite understand why it was so, but they knew that the Christmas tree, when rightly made, brought the

Christmas spirit, and they had heard men say that the Christmas spirit was the great thing, and that that was what made everyone happy.

Well, the long and the short of it was that the animals talked of it in their dens and on their roosts, in the fields, and in the forests, wild beasts and tame alike—the cows and the horses in their stalls, the sheep in their fold, the doves in their cotes and the poultry in the poultry-yard, until all agreed that a Christmas tree would be a grand thing for the wild and tame alike. Like the men, they, too, would have a tree of their very own. But how to do it?

Then the lion called a meeting of all the creatures, wild and tame; for you know the lion is king of beasts and when he calls they all must come. You know, too, that before and during and after these animal congresses there is a royal peace. The lamb can come to the meeting and sit down by the wolf, and the wolf dare not touch him; the dove may perch on the bough between the hawk and the owl and neither will harm him, when the great king of beasts has summoned them all together to take counsel. But you know all about the rules of the animals, for you have read them in books, and you have seen the pictures: how the lion sits on his throne with a crown on one side of his head, and all the other creatures gather about—the elephant, and giraffe, the hippopotamus, the buffalo, wolves and tigers and leopards, foxes and deer, goats and sheep, monkeys and orang-outangs, parrots and robins and turkeys and swans and storks and eagles and frogs and lizards and alligators, and all the rest besides.

Then, when the lion had called the meeting to order, the swifts and the swallows told what they had seen, and a fat little pug-dog, with a ribbon and a silver bell about his neck, wheezed out a story of a Christmas tree that he had seen, and how a silver bell had grown on that tree for him and a whole box of the best sweets he had ever dreamed of while he lay comfortably snoozing on his cushion before the fire. And a Persian cat, with her hair turned the wrong way, mewed out her story of a Christmas tree that she had attended, and told how there was a white mouse made of cream cheese for her creeping about beneath the branches.

Then the monkeys chattered and the elephants trumpeted, the horses neighed, the hyenas laughed, and each in his own way argued for a Christmas tree and told what he would do to help make it.

The elephant would go into the forest, and choose the tree and pull it up. The buffaloes would drag it in. The giraffe would fix the ornaments on the higher limbs, because its neck was long. The monkeys would scramble up where the giraffe could not reach. The squirrels could run out on the slender twigs and help the monkeys. The birds would fly about and get the golden threads and put them on the tree with their beaks. The fire-flies would hide themselves among the branches and sparkle like diamonds, and the glow-worms promised to help the fire-flies by playing candles, if someone would lift them up and put them on the branches. The parrots and paroquets and other birds of gay plumage would give feathers to hang among the branches, and the humming-birds promised to flutter in and out among the twigs, and the sheep to give white wool to lie like snow among the boughs.

Then the parrots screeched and the peacocks screamed with delight, and you and I never could have told whether anybody voted aye or nay; but the lion knew; and the owl, for he was clerk, set it down in the minutes, as the lion bade him, that all the birds and beasts would do their part. So each planned what he could do. Even the little beetle, who makes great balls of earth, thought that if he could only once see one of those gay balls that grow on the children's Christmas tree, he might make some for the animals' tree. Different birds and beasts told of the oranges and apples and holly-berries and who knows what they could get and hang upon the tree. You see the animals came from many places, and then, too, they could send the carrier pigeons to go and bring fruit and berries, and who knows what besides, from oh, so far away, because the carrier pigeons can fly through the air no one knows how fast or how far.

Well, I cannot tell you everything that each one was going to do, but if you will go and get your Noah's ark and take the animals out one by one, then you surely will think it out for yourself, for you have all the animals there.

And so they arranged how they would ornament the tree, and the next thing was to decide what presents should be hung on the tree or put beneath its boughs, for each one must have his present. Well, after much discussion in roars, and bellows, crows and croaks, lows and screams and bleats, and baas and grunts, and all the other sounds of birds and beast language, it was voted that each might choose the present he wished hung on the tree. The clerkly owl should call their names one by one, and each might declare his choice. So they began.

The parrots and the macaws thought that they would like oranges and bananas and such things, which would look so pretty on the tree, too; and so they were arranged for. The robins and the cedar birds chose cherries; the the partridges, partridge berries, the squirrels, the red and grey and black, nuts and apples and pears. The monkeys said the popcorn strings would do for them, and the cats and dogs, remembering the Christmas gift which the pug-dog and Persian cat had told about, asked for tiny mice made of cream cheese or chocolate. By and by it came the pig's turn to tell his choice. "Grunt, grunt!" said the pig, "I want a nice pail of swill hung on the very lowest bough of all."

"Ugh!" said the black leopard, so sleek and so clean.

"Faugh!" said the gazelle, with his dainty sense of smell.

"Neigh!" said the horse, so daintily groomed.

"What!" roared the lion, "what's that you want?"

"A pail of swill," grunted the pig. "Each one has chosen what he wants, and I have a right to choose what I want."

"But," roared the lion, "each one has chosen something beautiful to make the tree a joy to all."

"Grunt, grunt," said the pig. "The parrots and macaws are going to have oranges and bananas, and the robins and the cedar birds red cherries, the partridges, their berries, the squirrels, nuts and apples and pears, the dog and the cat, their cream and chocolate mice. They all have what they want to eat. Grunt, grunt," said he; "I will have what I want to eat, too, and what I want is a pail of swill."

Now, you see it had been voted, as I told you, that each should have what he wanted hung on the tree for him, and so the lion could not help himself. If the pig chose swill, swill he must have, and angrily he had to roar: "If the pig wants swill, a pail of swill he must have, hung on the lowest bough of the tree!"

Then the wolf's wicked eyes gleamed, for his turn was next, and he said: "If the pig has swill because he wants swill to eat, I must have what I want to eat, and I want a tender lamb, six months old." And at that all the lambs and the sheep bleated and baaed.

"Ha, ha!" barked the fox; "then I want a turkey!" And the turkeys gobbled in fear.

"And I," said the tiger, "want a yearling calf." And the cows and the calves lowed in horror.

"And I," said the owl, the clerk, "I want a plump dove."

"And I," said the hawk, "will take a rabbit."

"And I," said the leopard, "want a deer or a gazelle."

Then all was fear and uproar. The hares and rabbits scuttled into the grass; the gazelles and the deer bounded away; the sheep and the cattle crowded close together; the small birds rose in the air in flocks; and the Christmas tree was like to have come to grief and ended, not in Christmas joy, but in fear and hatred and terror.

Then a little lamb stepped out and bleated: "Ah! king lion, it would be very sad if all the animals should lose their Christmas tree, for the very thought of that tree has brought us closer together, and here we were, wild and tame, fierce and timid, met together as friends; and oh! king lion, rather than there should not be a tree, they may take me and hang me on it. Let them not take the turkeys and gazelles and the calves and the rabbits and all the rest that they have chosen. Let the tigers and leopards, and wolves and foxes and eagles, and hawks and owls and all their kind be content that their Christmas present shall be a lamb; and so we may come together again and have our happy Christmas tree, and each have what he wishes."

"But," said the lion, "what will you have? If you give yourself, then you will have no Christmas present."

"Yes," said the lamb, "I, too, shall have what I want, for I shall have brought them all together again, and made each one happy."

Then a dove fluttered down from a tree and landed on the ground beside the lamb, and very timidly and softly she cooed: "Take me, too, king lion, as the present for the owls and the hawks, and the weasels and minks, because for them a lamb is too big. I am the best present for them. Take me, king lion!"

Then the lion roared: "See what the lamb and the dove have done! My food, oh, tigers and leopards and wolves and eagles and all your kind, is like your food; but I would rather eat nothing from our Christmas tree than take this lamb or dove for my present."

Then all the beasts kept still, because the lion roared so loud and angrily, and the birds that were flying away settled on the branches of the trees, and the gazelles stopped their running and turned their heads to listen, and the rabbits peeped out through the grass and brush where they had hid. Then the lion turned to the pig, and roared:

"See this lamb and this dove! Are you not ashamed for what you have done? You have spoiled all our happiness. Will you take back your choice, you pig, or do you wish to ruin our Christmas tree?"

"Grunt, grunt," said the pig, "it is my right. I want something good. I don't care for your lambs and your doves. I want my swill!"

Then the lion roared again: "Have all chosen?" and all answered, "Yes."

"Then," said the lion, "it is my choice."

And all said: "It is."

"I love fat and tender pigs. I choose a pig for my Christmas gift," roared the lion.

Did you ever hear a pig squeal? Oh, how that pig squealed then! And he got up on his fat little legs and tried to run away, but all the animals gathered around in a ring and the hyenas laughed, and the jackals cried, and the dogs and the wolves and the foxes headed him off and hunted the poor pig back again. Then, when the pig found that he could not run away, he lay down on his back with his feet in the air and squealed with all his might: "Oh, I don't want the swill; oh, I don't want the swill! I take it all back! I don't want anything!"

But at first no one heard him, because all were talking at once in their own way—barking and growling and roaring and chattering; but by and by the lion saw that the pig was squealing something, so he roared for silence, and then they all heard the pig squeal out that he did not want any swill. And the lion roared aloud: "You have heard. Has the owl recorded that the pig will have no swill?"

"Yes," said the owl.

"Then," said the lion, "record that the lion wants no pig."

Then the tiger growled: "And I want no calf," and one by one the leopard and the eagle, the wolf and the fox, the hawk and owl, and all their kind, took back their votes.

And so it came about that the animals did have a Christmas tree after all; but instead of hanging lambs and doves upon the tree, they agreed that they could hang little images of lambs and doves, and other birds and animals, too, perhaps. And by and by the custom spread until the humans came to hang the same little images on their trees, too, and when you see a little figure of a lamb or a dove on the Christmas tree, you may know that it is all because the lamb and the dove, by their unselfishness, saved the animals from strife; for neither thought what he wanted from the tree, but each was ready to give himself for the others, so that they might not fight and kill one another at the Christmas time.

The Christmas Princess

MRS. MOLESWORTH

ILLUSTRATIONS A. BEARDSLEY

I n the olden times there lived a king who was worthy of the
name. He loved his people, and his people loved him in return.
His kingdom must have been large; at least it appears to be
beyond doubt that it extended a good way in different directions,
for it was called the Kingdom of the Four Orts, which, of course, as
everybody knows, means that he had possessions north, south,
east, and west.

It was not so large, however, but that he was able to manage it well for himself—that is to say, with certain help which I will tell you of. A year never passed without his visiting every part of his dominions and inquiring for himself into the affairs of his subjects. Perhaps—who can say?—the world was not so big in those days; doubtless, however that may have been, there were not so many folk living on it.

Many things were different in those times: many things existed which nowadays would be thought strange and incredible. Human beings knew much more than they do now about the other dwellers on the earth. For instance, it was no uncommon case to find learned men who were able to converse with animals quite as well as with each other. Fairies, of course, were often visible to mortal eyes, and it was considered quite natural that they should interfere for good—sometimes, perhaps, for evil; as to that I cannot say—in human affairs. And good King Brave-Heart was especially favored in this way. For the help which, as I said, was his in governing his people was that of four very wise counselors indeed—the four fairies of the North and the South, the East and the West.

These sisters were very beautiful as well as very wise. Though older than the world itself, they always looked young. They were very much attached to each other, though they seldom met, and it must be confessed that sometimes on such occasions there were stormy scenes, though they made it up afterward. And the advice they gave was always to be relied upon.

Now, King Brave-Heart was married. His wife was young and charming, and devotedly fond of him. But she was of a rather jealous and exacting disposition, and she had been much spoilt in her youth at her own home. She was sweet and loving, however, which makes up for a good deal, and always ready to take part in any scheme for the good of their people, provided it did not separate her from her husband. They had no children, though they had been married for some years; but at last there came the hope of an heir, and the Queen's delight was unbounded—nor was the King's joy less than hers.

It was late autumn, or almost winter, when a great trouble befell the pretty Queen. The weather had grown suddenly cold, and a few snowflakes even had fallen before their time. But Queen Claribel only clapped her hands at the sight, for with the winter she hoped the baby would come, and she welcomed the signs of its approach on this account. The King, however, looked grave, and when the next morning the ground was all white, the trees and the bushes covered with silvery foliage, he looked graver still.

"Something is amiss," he said. "The Fairy of the North must be on her way, and it is not yet time for her visit."

And that very afternoon the snow fell again, more heavily than before, and the frost-wind whistled down the chimneys and burst open the doors and windows, and all the palace servants went hurrying and scurrying about to make great fires and hang up thick curtains and get everything in order for the cold season, which they had not expected so soon.

"It will not last," said the King, quietly. "In a few days there will be milder weather again." But, nevertheless, he still looked grave. And early the next morning, as he was sitting with the Queen, who was beginning to feel a little frightened at the continuance of the storm, the double doors of her boudoir suddenly flew open, an icy blast filled the room, and a tall, white-shrouded figure stood before them.

"I have come to fetch you, Brave-Heart," she said abruptly. "You are wanted, sorely wanted, in my part of the world. The people are starving: the season has been a poor one, and there has been bad faith. Some few powerful men have bought up the grain, which was already scarce, and refuse to let the poor folk have it. Nothing will save their lives or prevent sad suffering but your own immediate presence. Are you ready? You must have seen I was coming."

She threw off her mantle as she spoke and sank on to a couch. Strong as she was, she seemed tired with the rate at which she had traveled, and the warm air of the room was oppressive to her. Her clear, beautiful features looked harassed; her gray eyes full of anxiety. For the moment she took no notice of the Queen.

"Are you ready?" she repeated.

"Yes, I am ready!" said Brave-Heart, as he rose to his feet.

But the Queen threw herself upon him, with bitter crying and reproaches. Would he leave her, and at such a time, a prey to all kinds of terrible anxiety? Then she turned to the fairy and upbraided her in unmeasured language. But the spirit of the North glanced at her with calm pity.

"Poor child!" she said, "I had almost forgotten you. The sights I have seen of late have been so terrible that they absorb me. Take courage, Claribel! Show yourself a queen. Think of the suffering mothers and their little ones whom your husband hastens to aid. All will be well with you, believe me. But you, too, must be brave and unselfish."

It was no use. All she said but made the Queen more indignant. She would scarcely bid her husband farewell: she turned her back to the fairy with undignified petulance.

"Foolish child," said the Northern spirit. "She will learn better some day."

Then she gave all her attention to the matter she had come about, explaining to the King as they journeyed exactly the measures he must take and the difficulties to be overcome. But though the King had the greatest faith in her advice, and never doubted that it was his duty to obey, his heart was sore, as you can understand.

Things turned out as he had said. The severe weather disappeared again as if by magic, and some weeks of unusually mild days followed. And when the winter did set in for good at last, it was with no great rigor. From time to time news reached the palace of the King's welfare. The tidings were cheering. His presence was effecting all that the fairy had hoped.

So Queen Claribel ought to have been happy. But she was determined not to be. She did nothing but cry and abuse the fairy, declaring that she would never see her dear Brave-Heart again, and that if ever her baby came she was sure it would not live, or that there would be something dreadful the matter with it.

"It is not fair," she kept saying, "it is a shame that I should suffer so."

And even when on Christmas Eve a beautiful little girl was born, as pretty and lively and healthy as could be wished, and even though the next day brought the announcement of the King's immediate return, Claribel still nursed her resentment, though in the end it came to be directed entirely against the fairy. For when she saw Brave-Heart again, his tender affection and his delight in his little daughter made it impossible for her not to "forgive him," as she expressed it, though she could not take any interest in his accounts of his visit to the north and all he had been able to do there.

A great feast was arranged in honor of the christening of the little Princess. All the grand people of the neighborhood were bidden to it, nor, you may be sure, did the good King forget the poorer folk. The four fairies were invited, for it was a matter of course that they should be the baby's godmothers. And though the Queen would gladly have excluded the Northern fairy, she dared not even hint at such a thing. But she resolved in her own mind to do all in her power to show that she was not the welcome fairy.

On such occasions, when human beings were honored by the presence of fairy visitors, these distinguished guests were naturally given precedence of all others, otherwise very certainly they would never have come again. Even among fairies themselves there are ranks and formalities, and the Queen well knew that the first place was due to the Northern spirit.

But she gave instructions that this rule should be departed from, and the Snow fairy, as she was sometimes called, found herself placed at the King's left hand, separated from him by her sister of the West, instead of next to him on the right, which seat, on the contrary, was occupied by the fairy of the South. She glanced round her calmly, but took no notice; and the King, imagining that by her own choice perhaps, she had chosen the unusual position, made no remark. And the feast progressed with the accustomed splendor and rejoicing.

But at the end, when the moment arrived at which the four godmothers were expected to state their gifts to the baby, the Queen's spite could be no longer concealed.

"I request," she exclaimed, "that for reasons well known to herself, to the King, and to myself, the Northern fairy's gift may be the last in order instead of the first."

The King started and grew pale. The beautiful, soft-voiced fairy of the South, in her glowing golden draperies, would fain have held back, for her affection for her sterner sister was largely mingled with awe. But the Snow fairy signed to her imperiously to speak.

"I bestow upon the Princess Sweet-Heart," she said, half tremblingly, "the gift of great beauty."

"And I," said the spirit of the East, who came next, her red robes falling majestically around her, her dark hair lying smoothly in its thick masses on her broad, low forehead, "I give her great powers of intellect and intelligence."

"And I," said the Western fairy, with a bright, breezy flutter of her sea-green garments, "health—perfect health and strength of body, as my gift to the pretty child."

"And you," said the Queen bitterly, "you, cold-hearted fairy, who have done your best to kill me with misery, who came between my husband and me, making him neglect me as he never would have done but for your influence—what will you give my child? Will you do something to make amends for the suffering you caused? I would rather my pretty baby were dead than that she lived to endure what I have of late endured."

"Life and death are not mine to bestow or to withhold," said the Northern spirit calmly, as she drew her white garments more closely round her with a majestic air. "So your rash words, foolish woman, fortunately for you all, cannot touch the child. But something—much—I can do, and I will. She shall not know the suffering you dread for her with so cowardly a fear. She shall be what you choose to fancy I am. And instead of the name you have given her, she shall be known for what she is—Princess Ice-Heart." She turned to go, but the King on one hand, her three sisters on the other, started forward to detain her.

"Have pity!" exclaimed the former.

"Sister, bethink you," said the latter; the Western fairy adding beseechingly, the tears springing in her blue eyes, which so quickly changed from bright to sad, "Say something to soften this hard fate. Undo it you cannot, I know. Or, at least, allow me to mitigate it if I can."

The Snow fairy stopped; in truth, she was far from hard-hearted or remorseless, and already she was beginning to feel half sorry for what she had done.

"What would you propose?" she said coldly.

The fairy of the West threw back her auburn hair with a gesture of impatience.

"I would I knew!" she said. "'Tis a hard knot you have tied, my sister. For that which would mend the evil wrought seems to me impossible while the evil exists—the cure and the cessation of the disease are one. How could the heart of ice be melted till tender feelings warm it, and how can tender feelings find entrance into a feelingless heart? Alas! alas! I can but predict what sounds like a mockery of your trouble," she went on, turning to the King, though indeed by this time she might have included the Queen in her sympathy, for Claribel stood, horrified at the result of her mad resentment, as pale as Brave-Heart himself. "Hearken!" and her expressive face, over which sunshine and showers were wont to chase each other as on an April day—for such, as all know, is the nature of the changeful, lovable spirit of the West—for once grew still and statue-like, while her blue eyes pierced far into the distance. "The day on which the Princess of the Icy Heart shall shed a tear, that heart shall melt—but then only."

The Northern fairy murmured something under her breath, but what the words were no one heard, for it was not many that dared stand near to her, so terribly cold was her presence. The graceful spirit of the South fluttered her golden locks, and with a little sigh drew her radiant mantle round her, and kissed her hand in farewell, while the thoughtful-eyed, mysterious Eastern fairy linked her arm in that of her Western sister, and whispered that the solution of the problem should have her most earnest study. And the green-robed spirit tried to smile through her tears in farewell as she suffered herself to be led away.

So the four strange guests departed; but their absence was not followed by the usual outburst of unconstrained festivity. On the contrary, a sense of sorrow and dread hung over all who remained, and before long everyone not immediately connected with the palace respectfully but silently withdrew, leaving the King and Queen to their mysterious sorrow.

Claribel flew to the baby's cradle. The little Princess was sleeping soundly; she looked rosy and content—a picture of health. Her mother called eagerly to the King. "She seems just as usual," she exclaimed. "Perhaps—oh! perhaps after all I have done no harm."

For, strange to say, her resentment against the Northern fairy had died away. She now felt nothing but shame and regret for her own wild temper. "Perhaps," she went on, "it was but to try me, to teach me a lesson, that the Snow fairy uttered those terrible words."

Brave-Heart pitied his wife deeply, but he shook his head.

"I dare not comfort you with any such hopes," he said, "my poor Claribel. The fairy is true—true as steel—if you could but have trusted her! Had you seen her, as I have done—full of tenderest pity for suffering—you could never have so maligned her."

Claribel did not answer, but her tears dropped on the baby's face. The little Princess seemed annoyed by them. She put up her tiny hand and, with a fretful expression, brushed them off.

And that very evening the certainty came.

The head nurse sent for the Queen while she was undressing the child, and the mother hastened to the nursery. The attendants were standing round in the greatest anxiety, for, though the baby looked quite well otherwise, there was the strangest coldness over her left side, in the region of the heart. The skin looked perfectly colorless, and the soft cambric and still softer flannel of the finest which had covered the spot were stiff, as if they had been exposed to a winter night's frost.

"Alas!" exclaimed Claribel, but that was all. It was no use sending for doctors—no use doing anything. Her own delicate hand when she laid it on the baby's heart was, as it were, blistered with cold. The next morning she found it covered with chilblains. But the baby did not mind. She flourished amazingly, heart or no heart. She was perfectly healthy, ate well, slept well, and soon gave signs of unusual intelligence. She was seldom put out, but when angry she expressed her feelings by loud roars and screams, though with never a tear!

At first this did not seem strange, as no infant sheds tears during the earliest weeks of its life. But when she grew to six months old, then to a year, then to two and three, and was near her fourth birthday without ever crying, it became plain that the prediction was indeed to be fulfilled.

And the name "Ice-Heart" clung to her. In spite of all her royal parents' commands to the contrary, "Princess Ice-Heart" she was called far and near. It seemed as if people could not help it. "Sweet-Heart we cannot name her, for sweet she is not," was murmured by all who came in contact with her.

And it was true. Sweet she certainly was not. She was beautiful and healthy and intelligent, but she had no feeling. In some ways she gave little trouble. Her temper, though occasionally violent, was, as a rule, placid; she seemed contented in almost all circumstances. When her good old nurse died, she remarked coolly that she hoped her new attendant would dress her hair more becomingly; when King Brave-Heart started on some of his distant journeys she bade him good-bye with a smile, observing that if he never came home again it would be rather amusing, as she would then reign instead of him, and when she saw her mother break into sobs at her unnatural speech she stared at her in blank astonishment.

And so things went on until Ice-Heart reached her seventeenth year. By this time she was, as regarded her outward appearance, as beautiful as the fondest of parents could desire; she was also exceedingly strong and healthy, and the powers of her mind were unusual. Her education had been carefully directed, and she had learnt with ease and interest. She could speak in several languages, her paintings were worthy of admiration, as they were skillful and well executed; she could play with brilliancy on various instruments. She had also been taught to sing, but her voice was metallic and unpleasing. But she could discuss scientific and philosophical subjects with the sages of her father's kingdom like one of themselves.

And besides all this care bestowed upon her training, no stone had been left unturned in hopes of awakening in the unfortunate girl some affection or emotion. Every day the most soul-stirring poetry was read aloud to her by the greatest elocutionists, the most exciting and moving dramas were enacted before her; she was taken to visit the poor of the city in their pitiable homes; she was encouraged to see sad sights from which most soft-hearted maidens would instinctively flee. But all was in vain. She would express interest and ask intelligent questions with calm, unmoved features and dry eyes.

Even music, from which much had been hoped, was powerless to move her to aught but admiration of the performers' skill or curiosity as to the construction of their instruments. There was but one peculiarity about her, which sometimes, though they could not have explained why, seemed to Ice-Heart's unhappy parents to hint at some shadowy hope. The sight of tears was evidently disagreeable to her. More certainly than anything else did the signs of weeping arouse one of her rare fits of anger—so much so that now and then, for days together, the poor Queen dared not come near her child, and tears were to her a frequent relief from her lifelong regrets.

So beautiful and wealthy and accomplished a maiden was naturally not without suitors; and from this direction, too, at first, Queen Claribel trusted fondly that cure might come.

"If she could but fall in love," she said, the first time the idea struck her.

"My poor dear!" replied the King, "to see, you must have eyes; to love, you must have a heart."

"But a heart she has," persisted the mother. "It is only, as it were, asleep—frozen, like the winter stream which bursts forth again into ever fresh life and movement with the awaking spring."

So lovers were invited, and lovers came and were made welcome by the dozen. Lovers of every description—rich and poor, old and young, handsome and ugly—so long as they were of passable birth and fair character, King Brave-Heart was not too particular—in the forlorn hope that among them one fortunate wight might rouse some sentiment in the lovely statue he desired to win. But all in vain. Each prince, or duke, or simple knight, duly instructed in the sad case, did his best: one would try poetry, another his lute, a third sighs and appeals, a fourth, imagining he had made some way, would attempt the bold stroke of telling Ice-Heart that unless she could respond to his adoration he would drown himself.

She only smiled, and begged him to allow her to witness the performance—she had never seen anyone drown. So, one by one, the troupe of aspirants—some in disgust, some in strange fear, some in annoyance—took their departure, preferring a more ordinary spouse than the bewitched though beautiful Princess.

And she saw them go with calmness, though, in one or two cases she had replied to her parents that she had no objection to marry Prince So-and-so, or Count Such-another, if they desired it—it would be rather agreeable to have a husband if he gave her plenty of presents and did all she asked. "Though a sighing and moaning lover, or a man who is always twiddling a fiddle or making verses I could not stand," she would add contemptuously.

So King Brave-Heart thought it best to try no such experiment. And in future no gentleman was allowed to present himself except with the understanding that he alone who should succeed in making Princess Ice-Heart shed a tear would be accepted as her betrothed.

This proclamation diminished at once the number of suitors. Indeed, after one or two candidates had failed, no more appeared— so well did it come to be known that the attempt was hopeless.

And for more than a year Princess Ice-Heart was left to herself— very much, apparently, to her satisfaction.

But all this time the mystic sisters were not idle or forgetful. Several of the aspirants to Ice-Heart's hand had been chosen by them and conveyed to the neighborhood of the palace by their intermediacy from remote lands. And among these, one of the few who had found some slight favor in the maiden's eyes was a special protégé of the Western fairy—the young and spirited Prince Francolin.

He was not one of the sighing or sentimental order of swains; he was full of life and adventure and brightness, and his heart was warm and generous. He admired the beautiful girl, but he pitied her still more, and this pity was the real motive which made him yield to the fairy's proposal that he should try again.

"You pleased the poor child," she said, when she arrived one day at the Prince's home to talk over her new idea. "You made her smile by your liveliness and fun. For I was there when you little knew it. The girl has been overdosed with sentimentality and doleful strains. I believe we have been on a wrong track all this time."

"What do you propose?" said Francolin, gravely, for he could be serious enough when seriousness was called for. "She did not actually dislike me, but that is the most that can be said; and however I may feel for her, however I may admire her beauty and intelligence, nothing would induce me to wed a bride who could not return my affection. Indeed, I could scarcely feel any for such a one."

"Ah no! I agree with you entirely," said the fairy. "But listen—my power is great in some ways. I am well versed in ordinary enchantment, and am most willing to employ my utmost skill for my unfortunate god-daughter."

She then unfolded to him her scheme, and obtained his consent to it.

"Now is your time," she said, in conclusion. "I hear on the best authority that Ice-Heart is feeling rather dull and bored at present. It is some time since she has had the variety of a new suitor, and she will welcome any distraction."

And she proceeded to arrange all the details of her plan.

So it came to pass that very shortly after the conversation I have related there was great excitement in the capital city of the Kingdom of the Four Orts. After an interval of more than a year a new suitor had at length presented himself for the hand of the Princess Ice-Heart. Only the King and Queen received the news with melancholy indifference.

"He may try as the others have done," said Brave-Heart to the messenger announcing the arrival of the stranger at the gates, accompanied by a magnificent retinue; "but it is useless." For the poor King was fast losing all hope of his daughter's case; he was growing aged and care-worn before his time.

"Does he know the terms attached to his acceptance?" inquired the Queen.

Yes, the messenger from the unknown candidate for the hand of the beautiful Ice-Heart had been expressly charged to say that the Prince Jocko—such was the new-comer's name—was fully informed as to all particulars, and prepared to comply with the conditions.

The Princess' parents smiled somewhat bitterly. They had no hope, but still they could not forbid the attempt.

"Prince Jocko?" said the King, "not a very prince-like name. However, it matters little."

A few hours later the royal pair and their daughter, with all their attendants, in great state and ceremony, were awaiting their guest. And soon a blast of trumpets announced his approach. His retinue was indeed magnificent; horsemen in splendid uniforms, followed by a troop of white mules with negro riders in gorgeous attire, then musicians, succeeded by the Prince's immediate attendants, defiled before the great marble steps in front of the palace, at the summit of which the King, with the Queen and Princess, was seated in state.

Ice-Heart clapped her hands.

"'Tis as good as a show," she said, "but where is the Prince?"

As she said the word the cortége halted. A litter, with closely drawn curtains, drew up at the foot of the steps.

"Gracious!" exclaimed the Princess, "I hope he is not a molly-coddle;" but before there was time to say more the curtains of the litter were drawn aside, and in another moment an attendant had lifted out its occupant, who forthwith proceeded to ascend the steps. The parents and their daughter stared at each other and gasped.

Prince Jocko was neither more nor less than a monkey!

But such a monkey as never before had been seen. He was more comical than words can express, and when at last he stood before them, and bowed to the ground, a three-cornered hat in his hand, his sword sticking straight out behind, his tail sweeping the ground, the effect was irresistible. King Brave-Heart turned his head aside. Queen Claribel smothered her face in her handkerchief. Princess Ice-Heart opened her pretty mouth wide and forgot to close it again, while a curious expression stole into her beautiful eyes.

Was it a trick?

No; Prince Jocko proceeded to speak.

He laid his little brown paw on his heart, bowed again, coughed, sneezed, and finally began an oration. If his appearance was too funny, his words and gestures were a hundred times more so. He rolled his eyes, he declaimed, he posed and pirouetted like a miniature dancing-master, and his little cracked voice rose higher and higher as his own fine words and expressions increased in eloquence.

And at last a sound—which never before had been heard, save faintly—made everyone start. The Princess was laughing as if she could no longer contain herself. Clear, ringing, merry laughter, which it did one's heart good to hear. And on she went, laughing ever, till—she flung herself at her mother's feet, the tears rolling down her cheeks.

"Oh, mamma!" she exclaimed, "I never—" and then she went off again.

But Prince Jocko suddenly grew silent. He stepped up to Ice-Heart and, respectfully raising her hand to his lips, gazed earnestly, beseechingly into her face, his own keen sharp eyes gradually growing larger and deeper in expression, till they assumed the pathetic, wistful look of appeal one often sees in those of a noble dog.

"Ah, Princess!" he murmured.

And Ice-Heart stopped laughing. She pressed her hand to her side.

"Father! mother!" she cried, "help me! help me! Am I dying? What has happened to me?" And, with a strange, long drawn sigh she sank fainting to the ground. There was great excitement in the palace, hurrying to and fro, fetching of doctors, and much alarm. But when the Princess had been carried indoors and laid on a couch, she soon revived. And who can describe the feelings of the King and Queen when she turned to them with a smile such as they had never seen on her face before.

"Dearest father, dearest mother," she said, "how I love you! Those strange warm drops that filled my eyes seem to have brought new life to me," and as the Queen passed her arm round the maiden she felt no chill of cold such as used to thrill her with misery every time she embraced her child.

"Sweet-Heart! my own Sweet-Heart!" she whispered.

And the Princess whispered back, "Yes, call me by that name always."

All was rejoicing when the wonderful news of the miraculous cure spread through the palace and the city. But still the parents' hearts were sore, for was not the King's word pledged that his daughter should marry him who had effected this happy change? And this was no other than Jocko, the monkey!

The Prince had disappeared at the moment that Ice-Heart fainted, and now with his retinue he was encamped outside the walls. All sorts of ideas occurred to the King. "I cannot break my word," he said, "but we might try to persuade the little monster to release me from it."

But the Princess would not hear of this.

"No," she said. "I owe him too deep a debt of gratitude to think of such a thing. And in his eyes I read more than I can put in words. No, dear father! you must summon him at once to be presented to our people as my affianced husband."

So again the cortége of Prince Jocko made its way to the palace, and again the litter, with its closely drawn curtains, drew up at the marble steps. And Sweet-Heart stood, pale, but calm and smiling, to welcome her ridiculous betrothed. But who is this that quickly mounts the stairs with firm and manly tread? Sweet-Heart nearly swooned again.

"Jocko?" she murmured. "Where is Jocko? Why, this is Prince Francolin!"

"Yes, dear child," said a bright voice beside her; and, turning round, Sweet-Heart beheld the Western fairy, who, with her sisters, had suddenly arrived. "Yes, indeed! Francolin, and no other!"

The universal joy may be imagined. Even the grave fairy of the North smiled with pleasure and delight, and, as she kissed her pretty god-daughter, she took the girl's hand and pressed it against her own heart.

"Never misjudge me, Sweet-Heart," she whispered. "Cold as I seem to those who have not courage to approach me closely, my heart, under my icy mantle, is as warm as is now your own."

And so it was. Where can we get a better ending than the time-honored one? Francolin and Sweet-Heart were married, and lived happy ever after, and who knows but what, in the Kingdom of the Four Orts, they are living happily still? If only we knew the way thither, we might see for ourselves if it is so.

The Little Girl and the Winter Whirlwinds

FOLK FAIRY TALE
ILLUSTRATIONS GRETL MANUS

EDITOR'S NOTE: *This tale comes from Bulgaria and is by an unknown source.*

O ne year the wicked Winter Witch decided to stop Spring from coming on time and make Winter the only season on Earth. She hid the Sun behind dark clouds and covered the Earth with heavy snow. So one morning the people from a small mountain village woke up and found their houses buried under the snow up to the roofs. They started digging tunnels from their own to the neighboring houses, and gathered in small groups to decide what they could do.

They finally decided that the best thing to do is to send someone on the highest mountain peak, where the good wizard Father Frost lived in his palace of ice and ask him for help.

But no one was willing to go on such a dangerous trip.

"I am ready to go," an old man said. "But I'm afraid I'm too old and slow to reach the peak on time. If only I was 20 years younger... "

"Don't worry, grandfather, I will go!" his little granddaughter said. She was an orphan, living in his home since her parents died.

"No, not you!" the neighbors pitied her: " You are too young and tender for such a hard job!" "You don't even have a warm coat!", "No hat and scarf!", "Not even woolen mittens!"

"I'm not afraid!" The little girl said – "My feet are strong and I'm as fast as a mountain goat!"

"But you'll freeze up there, with no shelter to hide from frost!"

"I will not." the girl said firmly. "I have a warm little heart, full of love for everyone. It will save me from the frost."

"Go, my child." the old man said. "I know your good heart and I trust it."

The children, who were all her friends, gave her their warmest clothes:

"Here, take my coat." one of them said.

"My mittens are so warm. Put them on!" said another.

"Take my hat!", "My scarf!", "My woolen socks!", "And my boots!"

Soon, the little girl was ready to go. She waved back at her friends and started for the snowy mountain peak a quick pace...

She went further and higher, never thinking about rest. Soon she was able to see the glittering ice on top of the highest peak. All of a sudden, the whirlwinds, woke up from their sleep and noticing the little figure in the snow, became furious:

"Who dares to tresspass our property?"

Let's show her who we are!" They screamed.

"Let's blow at her so hard, until she forgets where she's heading for!"

And they started whirling fiercely around the girl.

But she only huddled into her warm coat, and bravely went on.

The whirlwinds got very tired, and one after the other, fell on the ground gasping for breath.

"What a strong girl!" one of them said. "We are exhausted, and she's not even tired..."

"No human being has ever overmastered us, let alone such a fragile little girl... If we can not manage ourselves, let's call our sisters the Blizzards for help."

So they called for the Blizzards...

Hearing them, the Blizzards became very angry:

"She will pay for that!" They roared and threw themselves after her.

It was a long an uneven struggle, but the girl overcame the Blizzards too, thanks to her strong warm heart, that never let her feel fear, or weariness.

The Blizzards fell on the ground breathing heavily.

"That's-s-s -a -s-s-shame!" one of them hissed. "We are not able to stop her! Let's call our mother for help!""

"Mother, mother!" they all screamed. "Come to help!"

Their mother was the Frosty Winter Witch. She came at once, and said:

"I saw everything. Now listen to me: When you can not defeat someone by force, turn things the other way round. Let's be good to her!"

"What do you mean? To kiss her?" a whirlwind asked ironically.

"Nothing of the sort," the Frosty Winter said: "Let's just try to be polite and kind, so she will never suspect us of any evil thoughts...

So the winds stopped and the blizzards went away.

The Frosty Winter Witch appeared before the girl in like a beautiful young woman in a sparkling white gown, with long white hairs and a crown of icy diamonds.

"Am I dreaming, or is this some good mirracle?... the girl thought. " This beautiful lady has the face of my dear mother, and I can hear her sweet voice singing my lullaby!

Oh, how I want to hear some more! I'll sit here for a while..." she said to herself. "I'm so near to the Palace. No more than an hour walking left...I'll be on time..."

The little girl sat down and closed her eyes. The Frosty Winter Witch grinned in delight:

"Sleep, little girl. And may you sleep forever!"

Then she left the sleeping girl on the snowy hill and flew away to tell her children how she managed to deceive the girl.

The little girl was sleeping, smiling happily. But the colour of her face was changing as time passed. Her pink cheeks became at first red, then blue, then waxy yellow... She was slowly freezing...

Until all of a sudden, something stirred the snow. A squeaking sound was heard, and a tiny head showed up from a hole in the snow. It was a little white mouse. Her shiny black eyes fixed on the sitting figure.

"Someone's in trouble!" squeaked the mouse. And right after that a number of little holes opened in the snow, and a number of mice peeped out of the holes.

They ran to the girl, and started massaging her feet and hands. But mice were so little and their labours so inefficient, that they decided to call their friends the rabbits for help. This time bigger holes opened in the snow, and a number of white rabbits peeped out and ran to the rescue.

From the snow-covered pine trees, a number of squirrels jumped down, and soon the girl was covered with white and brown fur all over. The little animals warmed her up with their own furry bodies. They were extremely happy, to see her cheeks becoming pink again.

Soon the girl opened her eyes...

She thanked her new friends for saving her life, and told them why she was here and where she was going. "We are coming with you!" the animals cheered. "We also suffer very much from this never ending Winter."

Flocking around the girl, the animals accompanied her to the Ice Palace. There, they all knocked at the gate, but no one answered...

"What might have happened to Father Frost?" the animals wondered.

"Let's try to open the door! It's not locked!" They opened the heavy gate and the girl stepped in, followed by her friends.

A glittering icy corridor lead them to a big crystal hall. And there, on a gorgeous throne of carved ice, Father Christmas was fast asleep sitting on his icy throne, dressed in silver embroidered clothes. Two squirrels jumped in his lap and tickled his face with their furry tails.

A mighty sneezing sound made them all freeze with fear. But Father Christmas opened his blue eyes and smiled: "What are you doing here, little friends?"

The girl told him everything.

"You mean, I have slept here, while the wicked Winter Witch was trying to stop Spring from coming? Throughout the whole winter?"

Father Christmas asked astonished. "I gues, she decided to outsmart me and stay on Earth forever.!... But I will not let her!

Thank you little ones for waking me up! Now I'll restore the natural order and give everyone what he deserves."

Then he blew on his silver whistle and in an instant, all his subjects appeared in the big crystal hall. He ordered them to go and find the Frosty Winter Witch and bring her to the palace, so he could lock her down in the cellar until next year. He also told them to clear the skies from clouds, so that the sun can melt the snow.

When the big gates opened again, the sun outside was shining and the soft snow had started to melt. The way back was much easier. The new friends parted, promising to help anytime when needed. Everyone in the village cheered, meeting the brave little girl. They were very happy to pick the first snowdrops and give them to her. Spring was also very happy to hear the songs and see the dances the children had prepared specially for her.

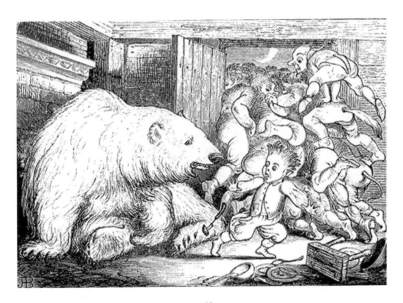

The Cat on the Dovrefell

ASBJØRNSEN & MOE

ILLUSTRATIONS THE KNICKERBOCKER PRESS 1917

O nce on a time there was a man up in Finnmark who had
caught a great white bear, which he was going to take to the
King of Denmark. Now, it so fell out, that he came to the
Dovrefell just about Christmas Eve, and there he turned into a
cottage where a man lived, whose name was Halvor, and asked the
man if he could get house-room there for his bear and himself.

"Heaven never help me, if what I say isn't true!" said the man; "but
we can't give anyone house-room just now, for every Christmas Eve
such a pack of Trolls come down upon us, that we are forced to flit,

and haven't so much as a house over our own heads, to say nothing of lending one to anyone else."

"Oh?" said the man, "if that's all, you can very well lend me your house; my bear can lie under the stove yonder, and I can sleep in the side-room."

Well, he begged so hard, that at last he got leave to stay there; so the people of the house flitted out, and before they went, everything was got ready for the Trolls; the tables were laid, and there was rice porridge, and fish boiled in lye, and sausages, and all else that was good, just as for any other grand feast.

So, when everything was ready, down came the Trolls. Some were great, and some were small; some had long tails, and some had no tails at all; some, too, had long, long noses; and they ate and drank, and tasted everything. Just then one of the little Trolls caught sight of the white bear, who lay under the stove; so he took a piece of sausage and stuck it on a fork, and went and poked it up against the bear's nose, screaming out:

"Pussy, will you have some sausage?"

Then the white bear rose up and growled, and hunted the whole pack of them out of doors, both great and small.

Next year Halvor was out in the wood, on the afternoon of Christmas Eve, cutting wood before the holidays, for he thought the Trolls would come again; and just as he was hard at work, he heard a voice in the wood calling out:

"Halvor! Halvor!"

"Well," said Halvor, "here I am."

"Have you got your big cat with you still?"

"Yes, that I have," said Halvor; "she's lying at home under the stove, and what's more, she has now got seven kittens, far bigger and fiercer than she is herself."

"Oh, then, we'll never come to see you again," bawled out the Troll away in the wood, and he kept his word; for since that time the Trolls have never eaten their Christmas brose with Halvor on the Dovrefell.

UNITED KINGDOM

The Bad Little Goblin's New Year

MARY STEWART

ILLUSTRATIONS ARTHUR RACKHAM

C ome, children dear, let's sit on the floor around the fire, so, and watch those golden flames dancing and leaping. You see that very gay one just springing up the chimney? I know a story about him, a New Year's story. Let's snuggle up closer and look into the fire. You see that piece of coal black wood, there at the end? There was a horrid little goblin once who was as black as that bit of wood. His clothes were all black, his round cap looked like a bit of coal, his pointed shoes were jet black, and his face was dark with dirt and an ugly scowling expression. Altogether he was a horrid looking goblin, and he was just as hateful as he looked. There wasn't a single person who liked him. The birds hated him because he would wait after dark when all the baby birds were cuddled down in the nest, fast asleep. Then he would pop up from under the nest where he had been hiding and cry, "Morning time,

315

wake up!" and all the babies would cry, "Chirp, chirp, Daddy bring us our breakfast!" They opened their bills so wide that it took a long time to shut them and put the excited babies to sleep again. Once Blackie, that was the goblin's name, dropped a bit of twig down into a baby's open bill and the poor bird coughed so hard that he kept the birds in the nests around awake all night. Blackie chuckled with glee and went scurrying off on another prank.

While the mother bunnies were asleep he painted the tiny white flags they wear under their tails with brown mud from the marsh. When morning-time really did come and the mother bunnies woke up and called to their children to follow them, the little bunnies couldn't see any white flags on their mothers' tails to follow, and all got lost in the long grass. It took the whole day to gather them together, and still longer to get those flags clean again.

Blackie jumped for joy. The mother bunnies would have liked to reach him with their sharp claws, but he was too quick for them.

Then Blackie found the holes where the squirrels had hidden their nuts for the winter. It had taken months to gather them, but Blackie waited until they were out hunting again, and he carried all the nuts away and hid them in the roots of an old tree where they would never think of looking!

That wasn't all! Blackie did one last thing so terrible that I don't like to tell you about it. He waited until a robin's nest was full of lovely blue eggs and the father bird was off in search of worms. Then he made such a rustling in the next tree that the mother bird flew off to see what it was, and while she was gone—Blackie danced upon the eggs until they were all broken!

That filled the timid wood creatures with fury. The birds, the rabbits, and the squirrels rushed upon the goblin and drove him before them. The birds pecked him with their beaks, and the squirrels and rabbits hopped after him with their claws outstretched. Away ran Blackie, really frightened at last, faster and faster until he reached the darkest part of the whole forest. There he jumped into a hole in a tree, curling himself up so tightly that his round cap touched his pointed shoes, and while he trembled with fear he heard the birds and bunnies and squirrels go tearing past, thinking that the wicked little goblin was still running ahead of them.

When they had all gone, Blackie peeked out of his hole. Oh, how terribly quiet it was! Not a bird chirped, not a squirrel or a rabbit or a woodchuck lived there. It was so quiet and so dark and so lonely that Blackie began to feel quite forlorn. "I would almost be polite to a tree toad!" he thought, but not even a croak or a buzz or a rustle broke the stillness. The bad little goblin put his head down upon his black knees and went to sleep; there was nothing else to do!

The first sound which woke him up was, "Chop-chop!" He rubbed his eyes and peeked out. He saw woodcutters cutting down trees with their sharp axes. Then he saw them coming toward the tree where he was hiding. Shaking with terror, Blackie curled himself up into a tight ball. Chop-chop-crash! went the tree, and Blackie's head bumped hard against the top of his hole as, still inside it, he felt the tree fall to the ground. That was rather fun, and much excited he peeked out of a crack and watched the men fastening chains around the trees and loading them on wheels. His own tree went, too, and the next thing Blackie heard was saw-saw, as the tree was sawed into logs at a lumber yard. Again he rolled up tight, hoping the knives wouldn't cut him in two, and they didn't! He was still safe in his hole when his log was thrown with others, right down into a dark cellar. It was even drearier there than in the forest and Blackie began to long for some playfellows. "I wouldn't tease them. I'd just play with them nicely," he sighed, and two tears ran down his little black face, washing it almost clean.

Then Blackie heard a strange new sound. It was gayer than a squirrel's chatter, sweeter than a bird's song,—it was a child's laughter! Where did it come from? Blackie stopped crying and listened. It came again and the laughter of other children mingled with it. Blackie peeked out. There was no one in the cellar. He crept out and tiptoed up the stairs, in search of those laughing voices. Hiding in the shadows so that no one could see him, he passed through the kitchen and on into a room full of sunshine and children. He ran in and hid behind a curtain, peeking out curiously.

In the center of the room stood a little golden-haired girl, the one whose laughter he had first heard. But as Blackie watched her with delight he saw her pucker up her face as though she were going to cry. "My dolly, my dear dolly, I can't find her!" she wailed. In a flash all the other boys and girls were searching under chairs and tables for the runaway dolly. They couldn't find her, but Blackie saw a pair of doll's feet poking out from under the sofa. He hopped swiftly across the floor, pulled the doll out by one leg and placed her on a chair beside the little girl.

"Oh, see, my doll's tum back!" she cried, hugging her with joy. "She went for a walk and tame back again!" and taking the doll's two hands in hers she danced with her around the room. The other children danced, too, and their laughter rang out again. "She went for a walk and came back all herself!" they cried.

Blackie thought he had never seen or heard anything so merry, it made him want to dance, also. Poor little black goblin whom the maid, if she had seen him, would have swept out of the room, mistaking him for a bit of coal!

But Blackie took care that no one did see him. Except, perhaps, the children, I don't know whether anyone ever saw him or not. He spent most of the time with them, and somehow they seemed to know that he was there and that he was their friend. Every evening when they had their supper they put a bowl of milk in front of the fire for him, and when they came in to breakfast the bowl was always empty. I don't know how Blackie drank it without being seen, for he still slept in his log in the cellar and was asleep as soon as the children's heads touched their pillows. The children's mother was puzzled over that empty bowl, but she might have guessed there was a friendly goblin in the house by the way lost things were always turning up.

"I can't find my thimble!" the mother would cry. "Come, children, and look for it!" On the floor, under the rug, in the flower pots, and on the tables hunted the children. But hiding behind the curtain Blackie had seen a bit of something gold shining through the tassels of the sofa. Quick as a flash, he pulled it out and placed it on the arm of the mother's chair. "Why, here it is!" she exclaimed. "How did it get there?" The children laughed and winked at each other, as though they understood, but how could they explain about the goblin to mother?

Their father was always looking for his spectacles. Mother, the children, and all the maids would be called in to help search. Before Blackie came they often searched for hours, but he always found them in a twinkling, in a book, perhaps, or under the fender, and would place them right in front of father. "Gracious, look here, there must be some magic around!" he would cry, and the children would jump up and down with glee! They knew all about the magic. They guessed that a little black goblin was also jumping with delight behind the curtain!

One morning,—it was New Year's Day,—Blackie slept longer than usual. He was curled up inside his log, so sound asleep that even the joggling of his home being carried upstairs didn't waken him. Then he was turned upside down, and, opening his eyes, he peeked out of the crack and found that the log was about to be thrown onto the blazing fire! Crash! it went. How very warm it was, and then Blackie heard the children laughing. He poked his head out and saw them all sitting in front of the fire, watching the blaze. All around Blackie red and yellow flames were dancing, so gay, so golden, so happy that Blackie forgot to be frightened. "I want to be gay, too!" he cried. "I want to laugh with the children and dance with the flames." His log caught fire, blazed up and out sprang Blackie,—a little black goblin no longer!

Instead, he was the shiniest, most dancing golden flame that you ever saw! For a few moments he just danced up and down with delight, then, waving and bowing to the children, he cried, "Happy New Year! Happy New Year!" and sprang up the chimney. The children's glad voices echoed after him.

When he reached the top he saw a glorious sight. The sun shining on the snow and ice turned the world into a sparkling Fairy-land, and the sky was as blue as forget-me-nots, or Polly's eyes, or the very bluest thing you have ever seen. Blackie danced with the sunbeams over the glittering ice until he almost ran into a flock of little birds huddled down in the snow, too cold to fly. Their feathers were ruffled and they looked very miserable. "Come play with me!" he cried, dancing around them. He was so gay and so beautiful that they forgot the cold, and flew in circles around him. "Come and join us!" he cried to a group of rabbits who were hunched up upon the snow, half-frozen. They hopped along slowly toward him and then—they, too, forgot the cold while they played games with the golden goblin and the birds, until they were all as merry as the sunbeams. "Happy New Year! Happy New Year!" they called to each other, and to the twinkling flame goblin.

Then Blackie saw some squirrels curled up on the branches of a tree so miserable they couldn't even make-believe scamper. "What is the matter; do you want some nuts?" he cried. "Follow me!" And away he darted to the roots of the tree where, as a naughty little goblin, he had hidden their winter store. The squirrels followed slowly, but when they saw their treasure their eyes sparkled, their teeth chattered with delight, and they scampered back and forth from the tree root to their own holes, their paws full of nuts. They were as gay as Blackie himself. "Happy New Year! Happy New Year!" they cried to their gleaming friend, whom they never dreamed was the bad little goblin they had chased away the autumn before!

So all day and for many days the goblin danced and sang and helped people and birds and the wood creatures. He twinkled as merrily in the sunshine out of doors as he did when he danced in the fire, warming the children and singing them songs.

"It's like Happy New Year every day when the goblin is here!" cried the children, dancing as gayly on the hearth rug as the sprite was dancing within the fire. "There he is now, do you see him? He is dancing and crackling and crying to all of us, 'Happy New Year, Happy New Year!'"

THE END

What to do next?
You can read many more fairy tales on

fairytalez.com

Made in the USA
Las Vegas, NV
15 November 2021